TRU

"I shouldn't say anything," Lord Montacute declared. "But I am being truthful. I find you the most bewitching creature I've ever met, and I desire you with all my heart."

"Please—" Verity began to protest.

"Tell me you don't feel the same," Montacute persisted. "Tell me you feel nothing when I kiss you."

"You're not being fair," Verity whispered.

"You affect me as no other woman ever has," he went on. "And I just want you to admit that I affect you as well."

Verity said nothing, but she did not have to. She closed her eyes as his lips came down on hers, and her senses betrayed her again, her mouth softening helplessly beneath his, her lips parting, her body shivering with pleasure as the tip of his tongue slid slowly against hers, and her own tongue giving him all the answer he needed.

Verity had heard that confession was good for the soul. But surely this kind could not be. . . .

SIGNET REGENCY ROMANCE
Coming in October 1996

June Calvin
My Lord Ghost

Elisabeth Kidd
The Rival Earls

Karen Harbaugh
The Reluctant Cavalier

Barbara Allister
A Love Match

HALLOWEEN MAGIC

by

Sandra Heath

A SIGNET BOOK

SIGNET
Published by the Penguin Group
Penguin Books USA Inc., 375 Hudson Street,
New York, New York 10014, U.S.A.
Penguin Books Ltd, 27 Wrights Lane,
London W8 5TZ, England
Penguin Books Australia Ltd, Ringwood,
Victoria, Australia
Penguin Books Canada Ltd, 10 Alcorn Avenue,
Toronto, Ontario, Canada M4V 3B2
Penguin Books (N.Z.) Ltd, 182-190 Wairau Road,
Auckland 10, New Zealand

Penguin Books Ltd, Registered Offices:
Harmondsworth, Middlesex, England

First published by Signet, an imprint of Dutton Signet,
a division of Penguin Books USA Inc.

First Printing, September, 1996
10 9 8 7 6 5 4 3 2 1

Copyright © Sandra Heath, 1996

All rights reserved

 REGISTERED TRADEMARK—MARCA REGISTRADA

Printed in the United States of America

for Natalie Hunt
with continuing appreciation

Chapter One

It began on Halloween, 1818. There were violent thunderstorms all over England, and at the village of Wychavon, set deep in the woods of a remote Shropshire valley, the weather was so bad that all thought of the traditional bonfire and torchlit procession had to be abandoned. Turnip lanterns flickered at windows, autumn leaves whirled wildly through the rain-soaked darkness, and the wind moaned like a lost soul in the eaves as the children sat around cozy hearths, listening to fearsome tales of witches, ghosts, and demons.

But a real witch came to Wychavon that night. Elderly Admiral Villiers had been shocked when he looked out of the manor house window and by a flash of lightning saw a mysterious young woman cowering naked in the garden. He immediately sent the servants out to bring her safely inside. She was beautiful, frightened, and had lost her memory—or so she claimed—and when she tearfully begged him to protect her, the gallant old man didn't hesitate to consent.

The last of his line, and a confirmed bachelor all his life, he fell immediately and hopelessly in love. He called her Judith, which had been his mother's name, and two months later, on Christmas Eve, to everyone's astonishment, he made her his wife. Two months after that, on St. Valentine's Day, 1819, he was drowned when his horse threw him into a mill pool, and Judith inherited everything the Villiers family owned.

But his death was no accident, and the tears she wept were as false as everything else about her, for she was really Meg Ashton, a vengeful Tudor sorceress who had returned on the two hundredth anniversary of her death to punish the descendants of those who had sent her to the stake. The judge of her trial had been a Villiers, and that was why she had used her black arts upon the unfortunate admiral. Now, on May Eve, 1819, six months to the day since her reappearance in Wychavon, she turned her attention to her next victim.

Nicholas, Lord Montacute, was the last of his line too, and his country seat was at Wychavon Castle, just outside the village. She intended him to suffer exactly the same fate as the admiral, because his ancestor had not only supplied the evidence that had convicted her, but had destroyed a stone circle dedicated to her terrible mistress, Hecate, goddess of witchcraft and darkness.

As the church clock struck twelve, and May Eve commenced, Judith slipped barefoot into the night. Her long chestnut hair was loose, and beneath her flowing velvet cloak the only thing she wore was the red garter of Hecate. She carried five new black candles, and a silver censer in which Lord Montacute's stolen desk seal rested on a bed of magic herbs.

Mist obscured everything as she made her way over the village green, which was divided in two by the river that had carved the valley. Willows fringed the banks, and a ford and stepping stones were the only means of crossing from one side to the other. Because it was May Eve, a maypole stood in readiness for the following days' celebrations. Its ribbons were motionless in the damp night air, and its garlanded top was lost beyond the haze.

Suddenly she tripped on a length of yellow embroidery thread caught tightly around a clump of reeds near the stepping stones, and dropped what she was carrying. As she bent to gather it all again, she tossed an angry glance toward a large house behind a high stone wall. It was the residence of the local magistrate, Joshua Windsor, whose niece Verity had that day been seated on the riverbank with her needlework.

The witch's hazel eyes darkened as not for the first time she sensed that golden-haired Verity posed a threat to her plans. She didn't know in what way, just that the threat was there. The magistrate's niece would have to be dealt with, but not tonight, for May Eve was reserved solely for Nicholas Montacute.

Judith crossed the stepping stones, then hurried past the vicarage and the churchyard, and out of the village along the Ludlow road. Bluebells grew in the verges, and unseen beyond the mist the waning moon was a thin sickle among the stars. The river curved sharply away into thick woodland, and was soon lost from view, but a few hundred yards before reaching the gates of Wychavon Castle, she left the road to follow an overgrown track that led deep into the trees.

A minute or so later she emerged into a secluded oak grove where a ruined watermill loomed darkly beside the harnessed water of the river. This was where the unfortunate admiral had been sacrificed by drowning in the pool and where, two centuries earlier, his vengeful bride had perished in flames for practicing her evil. It was a place that was shunned by local people, who rightly believed that Hecate had saved her servant by incarcerating her spirit in the standing stone in the center.

Known as the Lady, the stone was all that remained of the circle the third Lord Montacute had destroyed. The other twelve stones had been cast into the millpool, but the Lady could not be dragged out of the ground, and when Meg was burned, Hecate had entombed her spirit in the granite. There she had remained until freed by the Halloween thunderstorm.

Two hundred years earlier, it had been a quest for vengeance over the circle that led to Meg's downfall. Infuriated by the sacrilege, she and Hecate had turned their dark forces upon Lord Montacute, cursing to death his wife and unborn child, and attempting to do the same to him. But Meg had been arrested and condemned in time to save him, so now it was handsome Nicholas Montacute, the innocent ninth lord, who would suffer the ultimate reprisal instead. But first he had to be beguiled from London, where the diversions were all-absorbing to a gentleman whose wealth, looks, and eligibility made him one of society's leading players. Through his seal, however, he'd be *compelled* to return.

Judith crossed the damp grass to the mill, where the tools of her wickedness were hidden in a cavity beneath the rotting staircase. The building was dark and gloomy, the sound of water was all around, and the decaying wheel creaked in the foaming race as she put down the things she had brought with her, then removed her cloak.

She shivered because the night air was chill upon her naked body. She was very lovely indeed, and in spite of her red hair, had flawless skin. Her full lips were sensuous and pouting, and her firm-breasted figure was that of a twenty-five-year-old woman, but an ancient evil shone in her hazel eyes as she opened the staircase hiding place.

She took out five iron candlesticks, a carved elderwood wand, and a jar containing an ointment made of hemlock, nightshade, aconite, and opium, which she rubbed all over her body. Then she went out to the grove again, and with the wand drew a circle on the ground around the Lady. A new black candle was put in each candlestick and placed at even intervals outside the circle. The censer containing the herbs and seal she laid in front of the stone like an offering.

The preparations complete, she stretched her arms up, and whispered prayers to Hecate. The ritualistic words concentrated her mind, focusing her thoughts on the ceremony ahead, and as a trancelike calm descended slowly over her, she gazed intently at the Lady and called out.

"Come, dark queen of witches, goddess of the dying moon, dweller in the void. Come to thy servant and grant power to her purpose."

Suddenly the river ceased to flow through the race, and there wasn't a sound, not even the whisper of leaves. Then, in the distance, she heard hounds baying. The dog was sacred to Hecate, and Judith smiled, for the sound began to draw nearer, as if a hellish hunting pack coursed toward her along the valley. Louder and louder it became, until at last it echoed all around the grove, but the hounds remained out of sight in the shadows, howling at the sickle moon.

As the clamor reached a crescendo she pointed her wand at the first candle. "Hecate, light me!" she cried, her voice almost inaudible in the racket. The candle flickered into green flame, and the other four followed suit as she pointed at them in turn, then the hounds fell silent.

The ghostly green light swayed over her, shining in her eyes as she gazed in anticipation at the Lady. The granite seemed to breathe, then it sighed, and a fiendish female face appeared on its suddenly fleshlike surface.

Judith prostrated herself on the grass. "Hecate, I serve thee!" she cried. "I offer this seal to bring Nicholas Montacute into thy power, that thou might be avenged for what his forefather did. I implore thee to enchant it, that it will be a powerful amulet to bring its owner to me, to suffer the fate he deserves."

A snakelike curl of fragrant smoke began to rise from the holes of the censer. It twisted and turned anticlockwise around the perimeter of the circle as if dancing, and Judith got up to dance with it. She cast no shadow, and soon the ointment warmed intoxicatingly on her skin. Her senses began to swim, reality receded, and she felt weightless, as if floating on air.

She caressed herself sensuously as she drifted in the green haze of magic. She stroked her nipples and thighs, whispering Nicholas' name as if he were the one who touched her so intimately. The smoke began to collect in the center of the circle, gradually building into the handsome shape of the master of Wychavon Castle.

Power began to flood through Judith, and her eyes turned vivid emerald green as she stood before the phantasm. Exhilaration vied with triumph. After two hundred years, complete vengeance was at last within her grasp!

"Hecate hath made thee mine now, Nicholas. Thou must return from London before another day passes, thou must desire me with all passion, and be unable to put me from thee. Thou must make me thy wife, the sharer of thy life and wealth, the poison in thy heart, and destroyer of thy happiness."

Obediently the apparition turned toward her, but as she touched it, she was jarred by a sickening pain. A spectral wind swept the smoke away, and the candles were snuffed, plunging the grove into misty darkness once more. The hellhounds fled snapping and snarling along the valley, and with a cry of fury, Hecate disappeared from the Lady. After a moment the river again began to trickle slowly through the race, gradually gathering force until at last it foamed against the wheel as if it had never been still.

Judith sank to her knees in bewilderment. She felt lightheaded and dazed, and it was several moments before she could collect her wits. What had gone wrong? Something had destroyed the magic, and yet she'd done everything she should. Her gaze fell on the censer, and with a gasp she snatched off the lid to look inside. She stared at a bed of burned herbs, but of the seal there was no sign. Where was it? Then she remembered tripping on the embroidery thread. The seal must have fallen out then, and she hadn't noticed!

She scrambled to her feet. If she could find the seal, there was still time to complete the spell before dawn.

Chapter Two

It was more than just the dropping of the seal that had spoiled Judith's dark magic, for if it had simply lain unnoticed on the village green, all would have been well. But someone else picked it up at the precise moment it became enchanted, and thus innocently purloined all the power Judith had sought for herself.

Verity Windsor had decided to test whether her old nurse, Martha, was right to claim that dew gathered on May Eve was a sovereign cure for freckles. She knew Uncle Joshua would be very displeased with her if he learned she'd crept out in the middle of the night for such a purpose. He'd say that at twenty-three she was old enough to know better, but she hated the freckles on her nose so much she was prepared to try anything to get rid of them.

She paused by the gate in the wall to peep out at the deserted green. Her eyes were the same shade as the lilacs brushing her shoulder, she was of medium height, and her hair was a mass of long golden curls. Beneath her mantle her figure was the ideal willowy shape for the flowing muslins and lawns that were the fashion. Her oval face was considered pretty, although the largeness of her eyes sometimes gave her a rather solemn look, and if it weren't for the dusting of freckles, she'd have been well pleased with the physical attributes the Almighty had seen fit to bestow upon her. But those freckles were the bane of her life, she loathed them so much she'd resorted to every cosmetic preparation she could find, all to no avail. Hence the May Eve dew.

Seeing no one around, she raised the hood of her blue mantle over her loosely pinned hair and hurried toward the willows along the riverbank. She knew that one of them had a hollow where dew might collect, but before she reached it she trod on something hard in the grass, and with a cry of pain bent to see what it was.

To her surprise she saw a desk seal. Gold-mounted, with a tiger's eye quartz handle, it was clearly of considerable value. What was it doing on the village green? To her further astonishment, it started sparkling with strange green lights. Her curiosity aroused, she picked it up.

This was the moment Judith's spell went wrong, for Verity touched the enchanted seal at the very second the witch reached out to the phantasm of Nicholas Montacute. The magic that should have flooded through Judith, entered Verity instead. The green lights leapt from the seal and scattered all over her hand and arm. Her lilac eyes turned fleetingly green, the scent of burning herbs drifted on the air for a moment, then all became normal again, and the seal was just a seal.

Thinking she must have imagined anything odd, Verity turned the seal over. She recognized the double-headed phoenix of the Montacutes, but Lord Montacute had been in London for months now, so what was his seal doing here on the green? Warm color entered her cheeks, as always happened when she thought of Nicholas Montacute, but then an owl hooted in the willows, and with a start she pushed the seal into her mantle pocket before hurrying on to the tree she was sure would contain dew.

Climbing up, she felt inside the hollow. Sure enough, there was a small pool of moisture. She dipped her fingers in, and rubbed the dew over her face. "Freckles go away, Freckles go away, Be gone from me from this May Day," she whispered, then scrambled down again and fled back to the house without anyone knowing she'd been out.

A third person had been affected by the magic in the oak grove, and that was Nicholas Montacute himself. As Judith cast her spell, he was just leaving White's club in St. James's Street with his close friend, Oliver Henderson. Both men wore evening clothes, and had spent a profitable few hours at the hazard tables. They tapped their top hats on in unison, flexed their fingers in their white gloves, then strolled toward Piccadilly with their canes swinging.

The ninth Lord Montacute of Wychavon was thirty-two years old, tall, athletic, and strikingly handsome. His profile was said to be the most classically perfect in England, with a strong but not prominent jaw, a straight nose, and firm lips. His thick dark hair was wavy rather than curly, and his long-lashed gray eyes gave him a rather cool air, but when he chose he had a charm so winning few could refuse him; at such times his smile was all that was warm and engaging.

Oliver was two years Nicholas's senior and stockily built, with sandy hair and a complexion that flushed easily. He had light brown eyes, a good-natured face, and he was so happily married he believed a wife could be the making of Nicholas too. But the only liaison of consequence his friend had enjoyed recently had ended rather abruptly the previous autumn, and was most definitely a forbidden topic of conversation.

He glanced at Nicholas and observed his rather withdrawn expression. "What's the matter, Nick?" he asked lightly.

"The matter? Nothing, why do you ask?"

"Because I know you. Something's been up recently, and I think you should get it off your chest."

"Nothing's up."

"Yes, it is. You've been oddly quiet, and I can't help wondering if, well, if it has something to do with the young lady you ceased seeing last fall?"

Nicholas halted. "I don't wish to discuss it, Oliver."

"Damn it, Nick, why are you bottling it up like this?"

"I'm not bottling anything up."

"No?"

"No!"

The sharpness of the response made Oliver shift uncomfortably. "Very well, if you insist."

"I do. And I want you to promise that Anna won't attempt to matchmake on my behalf. I've had enough of amours for the time being."

"I'll do my best, but you know Anna. She thinks you're long overdue for matrimonial bliss. I think the same, as it happens."

"I know, but I'll marry in my own good time, thank you."

Nicholas smiled then. "Besides, who's to say marriage would make me as nauseatingly happy as you?"

Oliver was a little offended. "I resent your choice of adjective."

"Would deliriously suit better?"

"Yes." Oliver was mollified. "Is it so wrong to still be head over heels in love after seven years together? There's only one thing that could make us more complete, and that's a child, but after all this time I fear we must resign ourselves to the inevitable."

"Don't give up hope."

They walked on, and after a moment Oliver glanced at Nicholas again. "How long do you intend to remain in town?"

"I've no idea."

"I'm not complaining, it's been good to have you around for so long."

"I'm glad to be of service." Nicholas halted suddenly, staring at something just ahead on the pavement. "That's odd."

"What is?"

"Can't you see it? There's a peculiar green light just in front of us."

Oliver glanced around. "Hanged if I can see anything."

"You *must* be able to, it's like a damned green lantern! There's a strange smell too. Like woodsmoke. No, more like herbs. Yes, that's it, burning herbs."

Oliver sniffed, and then shook his head. "No, I can't smell anything either. Look, dear fellow, if you can see green lights and smell mysterious smells, perhaps it's time you toddled back to Shropshire for a rest. London's clearly too much for your delicate constitution."

He was only joking, but Nicholas's eyes brightened immediately. "By Jove, you're right," he declared.

"Eh?"

"You're right, it *is* time to go home to Shropshire. In fact, I'll leave tonight."

Oliver gaped at him. "You're mad!"

"Maybe, but it's what I want to do." Nicholas turned as a hackney coach rattled along the cobbles behind them. "Hey, there, coachman!" he called, waving his cane aloft.

The coach drew to a standstill, and Nicholas glanced at Oliver. "Why don't you and Anna come too?"

"What, now? In the middle of the night?" Oliver was dumbfounded.

"It isn't just any night, dear boy, it's Walpurgis Night," Nicholas replied with a grin.

Oliver glanced at the hackney coach. "Your broomstick, I presume?" he observed dryly.

"Maybe. Look, joking apart, Oliver, I'm sincere in the invitation. There's nothing I'd like more than to have you and Anna join me at Wychavon. Come whenever you wish, my door's always open to you."

"I—I'll think about it."

"Do that." With a quick grin, Nicholas stepped into the waiting coach and instructed the driver to take him to his house in Grosvenor Square.

The whip cracked, and the horse came up to a reluctant trot, leaving an amazed Oliver behind on the pavement.

At that moment in Wychavon, Judith was searching diligently for the seal. She found the yellow thread still wrapped around the reeds, but no sign at all of the precious seal, which she knew was now a very powerful charm. Why wasn't it here? Could she have dropped it somewhere else on the way to the grove? She didn't see how that was possible. This was the only likely place.

She swung her cloak tightly around her shoulders, her hazel eyes glittering furiously. She *had* to have the seal, for it would give her full control over Nicholas Montacute. She'd have to look again in daylight.

Trembling with rage, she made her way back toward the manor house, the yellow embroidery silk still in her hand.

Chapter Three

The following morning Verity was awakened by the blast of the first May Day horn as the village made ready for the celebrations. The overnight mist had gone, and sunlight poured in through a crack in the cream brocade curtains, revealing an elegantly furnished bedroom with gray-and-cream striped silk on the walls. There was a mahogany wardrobe, dressing table, washstand, a comfortable fireside chair, and an oval cheval glass that stood in a corner. A vase of lilacs occupied the hearth, and a large glass-domed clock dominated the mantelpiece between two silver candelabra.

Suddenly she remembered her freckles and reached hopefully for her hand mirror. But to her dismay there were as many as ever. So much for May Eve dew! She might just as well have remained faithful to Gowland's lotion. She got out of the silk-canopied bed, and after a quick wash went to the window.

The garlanded maypole soared against a clear blue sky, its ribbons fluttering gently in the light breeze, and there were boughs of greenery and bunches of flowers everywhere. Trestle tables had been set up, and some men were rolling casks of ale and cider across the grass. More horns began to sound around the village, and a man in a hobby horse pranced on the green. Morris dancers practiced to the music of a fiddle and hurdy-gurdy, and the village women laughed and chattered as they carried food to the tables.

The sound of hammering drew her attention to a cottage door, where two men were nailing up traditional boughs of hawthorn. When they finished they moved on to the manor house, carrying more hawthorn up through the topiary garden, but when they reached the door the butler came out to wave them off. The men protested, but the butler was adamant, and after a while they carried the hawthorn away again.

Verity was puzzled. Everyone in Wychavon had hawthorn on May Day, because apart from being a colorful custom, it was supposed to be a good-luck charm to deter witches, and yet Judith Villiers had clearly issued instructions that none was to be fixed to her door. Verity pulled a face, for she didn't like Judith very much. It was very sad that Admiral Villiers had died so suddenly, but there was something about his widow she simply couldn't take to.

The clock on the mantelpiece began to chime behind her, and she turned with a dismayed gasp. She was going to be late for breakfast! She was between maids at the moment, her last one having left to be married and a replacement not having been engaged yet, so she was having to dress herself. It wasn't the clothes she found difficult, just her hair. With so many long curls, it was a task and a half to pin them up adequately.

She hurried to the dressing table, hastily doing what she could to achieve some semblance of style, but then settling for tucking everything up beneath a lace day bonnet. It wasn't an elegant coiffure, but would have to do. Next she stepped out of her nightgown and into a neat cherry-and-cream-spotted lawn gown, but before going down she returned to the wardrobe for the seal, concerning which she intended to consult with her uncle. Should she send it to the castle, or to London, where Nicholas had been for so long?

There were no strange green lights this time, nor any whiff of herb smoke, but just as she was about to slip it into her gown pocket, she had a vision of Nicholas himself. He was seated in a fast-moving traveling carriage, and his eyes were closed, but suddenly they opened and he seemed to look directly at her and smile. She was so startled she almost dropped the seal, then the gong echoed through the house, and the image vanished as suddenly as it had appeared. She drew a long breath to steady herself, for the illusion had been so vivid it had seemed real. Then she told herself off crossly. This was all nonsense, just as the green lights and scent of herbs had been last night! For some reason she was allowing her imagination to run away with her, and it just wouldn't do. Taking another deep breath, she hurried from the room.

The dining room was at the front of the house directly below her bedroom, and her uncle was standing before the long-case clock, comparing its time with that of his fob watch. He was a stout, balding, rosy-cheeked man, and wore a maroon paisley dressing gown over a shirt and nankeen legwear. The tassel on his cap trembled as he pocketed the watch and turned to eye her.

"You're a little late, miss," he said reprovingly.

"I'm sorry, Uncle," she replied, hurrying over to kiss his cheek.

He smiled fondly. "How are you this morning? In fine fettle for the festivities?" He drew her chair out attentively.

"Oh, yes, I love May Day!" she said, sitting down and arranging her skirts.

The window stood slightly open, and the fragrance of wallflowers and peonies drifted into the room. Sparrows chirped in the lilacs, and beyond the high wall were the sounds on the green. Joshua sat opposite her, and glanced out. "Well, at least the weather's fine this year, last year was one long deluge, as I recall. If this keeps up, we'll soon be able to have breakfast in the summerhouse."

"And strawberries," she added with relish, thinking of the plump fruit ripening in the greenhouse.

He nodded. "Strawberries for breakfast are very civilized. Actually, I examined the greenhouse a short while ago. I believe the first fruit will be ready tomorrow."

"How very precise," she said with a smile.

"Strawberries should be consumed at the perfect moment. Oh, by the way, talking of tomorrow, I have to leave for Ludlow first thing."

She looked at him in surprise. "But it's Sunday tomorrow."

"There's a magistrates' meeting in the afternoon, and a banquet in the evening. I shall stay at the Feathers, and return on Monday."

"From which I take it you intend to overindulge," she said tartly.

"I merely do not wish to travel back late at night," he replied firmly, then said no more because the door from the kitchens opened and two maids came in, one with two plates of scrambled eggs and bacon, the other with warm bread rolls and a coffeepot.

It was several minutes before Verity placed the seal on the table in front of her uncle. "I found this on the green," she said, prudently omitting to say it had been the middle of the night at the time.

He scowled as he recognized the double-headed phoenix. "Montacute's? What in the devil was it doing on the green?"

"I really don't know. The thing is, what should I do with it?"

"I can't see any problem, you simply send it to the castle," he replied, reaching for a roll and breaking it so that crumbs cascaded over the table.

"Yes, but Lord Montacute is in London, and has been for some time. It's just that the seal is clearly quite valuable, so I wondered if it had been stolen from the castle. Maybe we should send it to him in London?"

"If there'd been a robbery at the castle, we'd have heard about it. No, I suspect Montacute dropped it himself when he was here."

"A fob seal, maybe, but one for use on a *desk*?"

He shrugged. "No matter what its purpose, the fellow's managed without it all these months, so I hardly think it's vital to his existence. Send it to the castle, and have done with it."

"Why do you dislike Lord Montacute so much?" she asked bluntly.

"You know why," he replied, applying himself to his breakfast in a way which precluded further discussion.

"I don't know anything of the kind, Uncle, so I wish you wouldn't keep saying that."

"If I've told once, I've told you a hundred times, I deeply resent his interference over that highwayman fellow."

Verity sighed and fell silent. Relations between the two men had never been all that warm because they were politically opposed. Then, as fellow magistrates, they'd differed bitterly over the sentencing of a highwayman, but last autumn her uncle's attitude toward Nicholas had suddenly changed for the worse. The highwayman had long since ceased to have anything to do with it, there was something else, but no matter how hard she tried to find out what it was, she got nowhere.

She sipped her coffee, her thoughts returning to Nicholas's prolonged absence. Clearly Wychavon was far too dull a place for a gentleman of his standing, only London was good enough now. She wished it were otherwise, for no matter what her uncle's opinion of him might be, *she* found the ninth Lord Montacute uncomfortably to her liking. She always had. Maybe it was his devastating smile. Yes, it probably was. . . .

Joshua interrupted her musings. "What time shall we join the jollifications on the green?" he asked, helping himself to more bacon from the platter the maid had left on the table.

"I don't really mind," Verity replied watching him in concern. "Uncle, you really should remember your dyspepsia. Dr. Rogers said—"

"Plaque take Dr. Rogers," he interrupted.

"Nevertheless—" She broke off as he pointedly ate a whole rasher. "Oh, on your own head be it," she murmured resignedly. He never seemed to learn that his digestive system wasn't what it had been, and that the number of nights he spent in discomfort was increasing because he refused to eat sensibly. His philosophy appeared to be "never be confined to two rashers if six were there for the taking."

He finished his plate and then mopped his lips with his napkin. "By Gad, that was a splendid start to the day," he declared.

"Let's see if you still think the same tonight."

"Oh, fiddlesticks," he muttered, then he sat back and eyed her. "We'll sally forth at about two, mm?"

"Whatever you wish."

"Actually, what I *wish* is that this afternoon you take the trouble to be kind to poor Mrs. Villiers. I happen to know she intends to participate a little, which I think is very brave of her so soon after her tragic loss."

"Brave? Some might say it's disrespectful," Verity replied uncharitably.

He frowned. "Come now, Verity, that's hardly Christian."

"I just don't care for her, Uncle, and I'd much rather *not* speak to her, if you don't mind."

"But I *do* mind, miss. She's a charming woman, and all that's suitable for a young chit like you to be seen with."

"She's decidedly strange," Verity replied flatly, thinking that whenever she encountered Judith Villiers she was reminded of stepping out of sunshine into shadow.

"Strange? In what way?"

"Well, even you have to admit that it isn't many a young woman who's found naked in a garden in the middle of a Halloween thunderstorm, claiming to have lost her memory."

"Amnesia is a medical fact, my dear," Joshua replied patiently.

"Maybe so, but those who are thus afflicted don't usually rush into marriage, least of all with old admirals almost three times their age."

"What has age got to do with it?" Joshua asked a little huffily. "Admiral Villiers fell in love with her, and she with him."

"And after a few weeks of wedded bliss he conveniently fell from his horse and drowned, leaving everything to her. What on earth possessed him to go riding to the oak grove anyway? He never rode at all because of his arthritis, yet suddenly he galloped off like a twenty-year-old. I thought it strange then, and I still do," Verity said, not meeting his eyes because she knew she was shocking him. "And you must have thought the same, even if you aren't shabby enough to say it. Well, I *am* shabby enough. I don't believe she ever lost her memory, and I don't believe she's in the least griefstricken. She's an adventuress, no more and no less."

"I'm ashamed of you, miss."

Verity's jaw set stubbornly.

He cleared his throat. "Perhaps we'd better change the subject."

"Yes, perhaps we had."

"But I still want you to speak civilly to Mrs. Villiers this afternoon."

It was an instruction, and she knew it. "Yes, Uncle," she replied resignedly.

"And since it's sunny today, please be so good as to remember your parasol, or I'll be obliged to pay for even more Gowland's lotion than I already do."

She colored. "Yes, Uncle."

He sighed. "Well, given your lack of charity toward poor Mrs. Villiers, I'm almost disinclined to tell you my good news."

"Good news?" She looked at him.

"I think it so. It's time you were married off, miss, and since it's clear you'll never find a husband in a backwater like Wychavon, I decided some months ago to do something about it." He sat back for dramatic effect. "I've planned it all with infinite care, and can now tell you that at the beginning of June we are to remove to London for the Season," he announced.

It was a bolt out of the blue, and she could only stare at him.

Chapter Four

The announcement left Verity thunderstruck. "Go to London for the—the *Season*?" she repeated incredulously.

"That's what I said," he murmured, pleased with the impact his news had had.

"But, isn't that a little *grand* for someone like me?"

He chuckled. "Grand? Certainly not. My dear Verity, you have expectations, what with the sum your parents left you and my estate too, therefore a proper husband must be found, someone whose fortune matches or preferably exceeds your own. So the Season seems the obvious thing. It isn't beyond my means, or contacts," he added.

She lowered her eyes, for any mention of her parents always upset her. They had died in a fire five years ago, and she still missed them terribly. That was why she was equally upset when her uncle spoke of the fortune she would inherit when he passed on too. He was all she had now, and because she loved him so much, she didn't like being reminded of his mortality.

Joshua leaned across to pat her hand. "Don't be sad, my dear, for we must be practical. You do have expectations, and it's up to me to see that the right thing's done about it. Or maybe you'd rather not go to London, mm?" This last was said in a teasing tone.

Her eyes flew to his. "Of *course* I want to go!"

"I thought so. It's settled then, which is as well, since I've, er, anticipated somewhat."

"Anticipated? What do you mean?"

"I've leased the Dover Street house of my good friend, Lady Sichester."

Lady Sichester was more than just his friend. It was Verity's suspicion that he and her ladyship had once been closer than they should have been, but it was no more than a suspicion. She looked at him. "Doesn't Lady Sichester require the house herself?"

"Not this year. She and her daughter Amabel left for Geneva last week. For her ladyship's health, I, er, believe." He cleared his throat, and fidgeted with his cup.

Verity looked curiously at him. "Is something wrong, Uncle?"

"Eh? Oh, no, nothing at all. Now where was I? Ah, yes, the house in Dover Street. What will you think of a Mayfair address, mm? Very superior. And we'll have all the furnishings, servants, etcetera, to say nothing of Amabel's French maid for you."

"The maid hasn't gone with Amabel?" she asked in surprise.

"Er, no, I understand not."

"Why?"

"I have no idea. Anyway, when I decided on this a few months ago, I successfully entreated Amabel to choose a suitable wardrobe for you. She's a very fashionable young woman, and, so I'm told, is exactly the same size as you. I'm therefore delighted to tell you that a bang-up-to-the-mark set of togs and accessories awaits your arrival. I'm assured you'll be fit for Carlton House itself."

Verity didn't know what to say. Delight rendered her speechless.

He smiled fondly. "It would appear I've done something to please you greatly, miss."

"Oh, yes!" Suddenly she got up and rushed around the table to hug him. "Thank you, oh, *thank you*!"

After breakfast she went to the kitchens to discuss the evening meal with the cook, but on the way encountered her old nurse, Martha Cansford, whose advice concerning freckles had proved so unrewarding.

Martha had a crooked back and straggly gray hair which she always tugged back into a tight bun beneath a crisply starched mobcap. She was a spry seventy-year-old who'd never married because the only man she'd ever loved had been a soldier who died at the battle of Bunker Hill in far-off America. Gifted with herbs and potions, she was the village wisewoman, turned to in preference to Dr. Rogers, whose charges were beyond the purse of most local people.

Because it was May Day, she was wearing her best brown gown, and there was a multicolored knitted shawl around her thin shoulders. Her blue eyes were sharp and bright as she smiled at Verity. "Good morning, Miss Verity."

"Good morning, Martha. I have a bone to pick with you. May Eve dew does *not* dispose of freckles. I did everything you told me to, and this morning have as many of the wretched things as I did before."

Martha eyed her. "Miss Verity, did I at any time state that the freckles would disappear in an instant?"

"Well, no, but—"

"All in good time, my dear. You must be patient. If you followed my instructions, your freckles will soon begin to fade. You have my word on it."

Verity smiled. "You always have an answer, don't you." It was a statement of fact, not a question.

"Yes, I do, and in the meantime I suggest you apply horseradish, which is also very efficacious for freckles."

Verity smiled again. "Ah, but will it work before next month?"

"Next month?"

Verity told her about the forthcoming visit to London. "So you see, I can't possibly embark upon such an adventure with my nose looking like this," she finished.

The nurse eyed her. "Your nose is perfectly charming, Miss Verity, as any young gentleman worth his salt will be at pains to tell you."

"From which I take it I'm doomed to have freckles when I'm away," Verity observed dryly.

"Maybe, maybe not," Martha murmured, her mind clearly on other things. "Well, I must be on my way now, for I have much to do."

"What's wrong, Martha?" Verity asked, detecting a worried note in the other's voice.

"I fear I must visit my sister Sadie."

Sadie Cutler was a widow who lived in a cottage across the

green with her orphaned eight-year-old grandson Davey, a carrot-haired imp who could only be described as a handful. "You *fear* you must visit her? Is she unwell, Martha?" Verity asked solicitously, for she liked Sadie.

"Sadie's well enough, Miss Verity, it's Davey who's ill."

"What's wrong with him?" Verity asked in surprise. Davey was the sort of child who was never unwell.

Martha hesitated, her old fingers creeping to a silver chain around her neck, upon which hung a dainty pink-and-azure stone, uneven but highly polished so that its colors were clear and bright. Verity had never seen it before. The nurse looked at her. "I—I don't know. No, that's not strictly true, let's say, I'm not sure. He woke up feeling poorly about a week ago, and hasn't left his little bed since. He just hasn't got any strength, and is wasting away before our eyes. There doesn't seem to be anything I can do for him, I've administered every salve and potion I can think of, but nothing does the trick."

"Oh, Martha, I'm so very sorry," Verity said with concern, trying to think of something that would cheer the nurse up, and help Davey too. "I know, I'll ask Uncle Joshua if I can have some strawberries from the greenhouse. I know how much Davey likes them because I seem to recall him being caught raiding them last year."

"You're very kind, Miss Verity. I'm sure some strawberries will tempt his poor little appetite." Tears filled Martha's eyes. "Oh, how I wish he were up and about again, even raiding greenhouses, for I'd far rather see him getting in trouble than lying there like a ghost."

"Would you like me to send Dr. Rogers? At Uncle Joshua's expense, of course," Verity ventured cautiously, knowing that as the village wisewoman Martha might be put out by such an offer.

But Martha wasn't offended. "I know Sadie'd appreciate that, Miss Verity."

"I'll see to it directly."

"If there's no improvement soon, as a last resort I'll have the men carry him around to the Lady. I know it's Meg Ashton's resting place now, but many believe such standing stones to have healing powers."

"A last resort? Oh, Martha, surely you don't think Davey's

that bad?" Verity was quite upset. "Oh, I wish there were something else I could do."

"It's very kind of you to do that much, Miss Verity. Many would not bother at all." The nurse blinked the tears determinedly away, then looked at Verity with a different kind of urgency. "May I say something concerning Mrs. Villiers?"

Verity was startled by the apparent change of subject. "Yes, of course."

"I advise you to avoid her if you can."

"Why do you say that?"

"Because it's my belief that Davey's illness may not be natural. He may have been overlooked by Judith Villiers."

Verity's lips parted. "Overlooked? I—I don't understand."

"She has the evil eye, Miss Verity."

"The what? Oh, that's nonsense!"

"You may think so, but we country folk know about such things. I've tried everything I know to make Davey better, but nothing works. Now it's a fact that the day before he was taken ill, he fell foul of the admiral's widow. He splashed her gown at the ford, it was an accident, but she took exception. I saw her that night, outside Sadie's cottage, staring at Davey's window. A long time she stood there, then she walked away. I believe she overlooked the poor child. So be warned, where the widow is, there also is wickedness."

Verity shivered. "Please don't say things like that, Martha."

"Just think of what day it was when she came among us."

Verity's lips parted. "Halloween . . ."

"Yes, my dear, Halloween, when witches and all manner of other evils go abroad." Martha held her gaze. "So just think on what I say, Miss Verity, and don't cross her. I intend to do all I can to work against her wicked magic, and that is why I've begun to wear this snakestone." She indicated the necklace.

"Snakestone?"

"It is called that because if you look closely into it, the shape of the azure color resembles a writhing snake."

"But what is its significance?" she asked.

"The Welsh people called them Maen Magi, and believe the original one was fashioned by the great magician Merlin to protect his mother from black sorcery. The stone was broken into six and given to wisewomen who were versed in good magic.

This one has been in the Cansford family for hundreds of years, being passed from mother to eldest daughter, and that is how it comes to be in my possession now. It must not be used lightly, and I have never worn it before, which is why you've never seen it."

"If it protects against witchcraft, why haven't you used it to protect Davey?"

"Because it only protects women."

Verity gazed at the stone and then into Martha's eyes. "You really do believe that Judith Villiers is a witch, don't you?"

"Yes, my dear, that is indeed what I believe."

The nurse walked on then, leaving Verity to gaze uneasily after her.

Chapter Five

It was evening, and Wychavon's annual May Day junketing was almost over. The horns had ceased to blow, and the children had woven the maypole ribbons into the traditional plaited pattern for the last time. The morris men lounged on the grass with tankards of ale and cider, and the empty hobbyhorse was propped against a tree.

The sun was beginning to sink as Verity took a final stroll along the riverbank. She carried her yellow silk parasol and wore a cream jaconet gown with a wide blue satin sash around the high waist. Her straw bonnet was adorned with a posy of fresh bluebells and cowslips, for everyone was expected to wear flowers on May Day.

She hadn't been called upon to heed her uncle's instructions concerning Judith Villiers—or Martha's startling warnings, for that matter—because the admiral's widow hadn't attended the celebrations after all. But now she was intensely dismayed as she brushed past some low-hanging willow fronds and saw the lady concerned only a few feet in front of her.

Judith was dressed elegantly in the mourning clothes that became her so well, with her chestnut hair swept up beneath a stylish hat with a net face veil. She seemed to be searching for something in the grass, and before Verity could draw discreetly away again, she suddenly whirled about. "Why, good evening, Miss Windsor."

"Good evening, Mrs. Villiers. I—I trust I find you well?"

"You do."

"I wondered if you were indisposed."

"Indisposed?"

"I—I saw your butler turn the hawthorn men away from the door this morning, and when you didn't attend the celebrations either, I just presumed you were unwell. A headache, maybe."

Judith's eyes flickered. "As you see, I'm in perfect health."

"Yes." Verity managed a weak smile. She wanted to hurry away, but for Uncle Joshua's sake felt she shouldn't, although right now, looking past the net veil into Judith Villiers' uncomfortably steady gaze, it was only too possible to believe the woman *had* put the evil eye on poor little Davey Cutler. Almost immediately Verity drew herself up sharply. Young ladies about to embark on a London Season simply did *not* believe in the evil eye! So, to change the subject, she glanced down at the grass where Judith had been searching a moment before. "Have you lost something?"

"I've mislaid an earring."

"Shall I help you search for it?"

"There's no need."

"This appears to be the place for losing things," Verity observed lightly.

"I don't understand."

"Last night I found Lord Montacute's seal in almost this very spot."

Judith became very still. "Lord Montacute's seal?" she repeated levelly.

"Yes."

Cold rage seethed through the witch. So *that* was what happened. This simpering nonentity had found the seal and interfered with Hecate's magic!

Verity didn't notice her reaction. "Well, I, er, must find my uncle," she murmured, inclining her head and turning to walk away.

Judith spoke quickly. "What have you done with the seal?"

Verity paused in surprise. "Oh, nothing yet, but I'm going to send it back to the castle. Why do you ask?"

"I can take it if you wish, I have to go there tomorrow."

"You have to go to the castle?" Verity was even more surprised, but before she could say anything else she was distracted as a traveling carriage entered the village from the south and drove around the green toward the ford. It was a splendid vehicle with a phoenix crest emblazoned on the doors, and the dwindling May Day festivities came to a startled halt as everyone realized Lord Montacute had returned.

Judith was shaken by his arrival. Verity Windsor's meddling had ruined the spell, and yet he'd *still* left London in the prescribed time. How could that be? If she had the seal she'd be in no doubt of the reason he'd come back, and she would be certain of maintaining power over him from now on. Instead, because of Verity Windsor, she couldn't be sure of anything. She needed that seal, it was the first and therefore the most powerful amulet for controlling Nicholas Montacute. Everything else in her repertoire of magic paled into insignificance in comparison.

Verity forgot Judith's curious offer to take the seal to the castle, and hurried over to her uncle, whose face had assumed a distinctly choleric hue the moment the carriage appeared. She linked his arm firmly. "Come on, let's go back to the house," she said as if nothing untoward had occurred.

But to her dismay the carriage drew to a standstill, and Nicholas alighted. He was immaculate in a charcoal coat, white breeches, and a kingfisher waistcoat, and nothing could have been more perfect than the complicated knot of his starched neckcloth. He paused to don his top hat, then glanced around at the sea of faces on the green.

Verity had to concede that everything about him was excellent. He remained the most handsome man she'd ever seen, and she was conscious of a secret shiver of excitement. He hardly knew she existed, but she was drawn to him like a pin to a magnet.

Joshua had been about to let her usher him from the green, but the moment the carriage halted he dug his heels in.

She pulled his arm. "Please come home, Uncle," she pleaded.

"No, my dear, I'd like to know why his lordship has deigned to return after all this time."

"Does it really matter?"

"It does to me."

"Oh, Uncle . . ."

"The actions of Lord Montacute are very much the business of the people of Wychavon."

Her gaze returned to Nicholas and with a start she realized he was wearing the clothes she'd "seen" him in that morning when she had taken the seal from her mantle pocket!

A cool finger ran down her spine, and she stopped trying to persuade her uncle to leave.

Nicholas toyed self-consciously with his cuff. He still didn't know why he had left London, and as he looked around at the astonished gathering, he wished he hadn't. Arriving unannounced at Wychavon after a long absence seemed to be almost as heinous a crime as arriving at Almack's superior assembly rooms in the wrong togs!

He drew a heavy breath, reflecting that he would spend much more time on his estate if it weren't that he found the castle so damned lonely. Being the last of one's line meant there were far too many empty rooms and passages, and as he stood there looking beyond the village at the rolling Shropshire hills, the endless acres of dark woodland, and the brilliance of the dying sunset, he felt more alone than ever, for all the people surrounding him on the green, he might be a thousand miles from anywhere.

The silence seemed to hang, and he was relieved when the vicar, a plump, bespectacled man whose powdered wig concealed a completely hairless head, prudently instructed the morris men to dance again. Within moments the celebrations had resumed, and Nicholas felt less glaringly conspicuous as he commenced a brief but polite circuit of his tenants. He acknowledged everyone he knew and had been thus engaged for nearly fifteen minutes when he came face-to-face with Verity and her uncle

Joshua accorded him a stiff bow. "Welcome back to Wychavon after all this time, my lord," he said acidly.

Nicholas's gray eyes flickered. "Mr. Windsor," he murmured, inclining his head slightly. Then his glance moved to Verity, and the influence of the seal swept forcefully over him as he found himself gazing into eyes of a most arresting and wonderful shade of green. He was taken aback, for he seemed to recall her eyes were lilac, as indeed they were, of course, but he was bewitched by Hecate's magic, and to him they were now the green of the candle flames that had burned in the grove.

How could he have forgotten such a striking color, he wondered? And how could he also have failed to realize how very fetching the rest of her was? It was as if he were meeting her for the first time. He drank in the sheen of her hair, the bluebells and cowslips adorning her bonnet, and even the sprinkling of freckles on her nose. She was enchanting, he thought with unknowing accuracy.

Judith's spell engulfed Verity as well. She'd been at sixes and sevens from the moment she realized she would have to speak to him, but now the attraction she felt toward him increased dramatically. Her pulse quickened, and her heartbeats became so frantic she wondered no one could hear. She stared at him, her lips slightly parted, her cheeks flushing with embarrassment as at last he took her hand and raised it to his lips.

"Miss Windsor," he said softly.

His touch electrified her, and she had to snatch her fingers away. "L-Lord Montacute . . ."

He gave a slight laugh that revealed how disconcerted he was too. "I confess I thought your eyes were lilac," he said, for it was all that came into his head.

"But they are," she replied in puzzlement.

He looked inquiringly into a gaze that was indisputably emerald and wondered why she denied it.

Joshua coldly interrupted the exchange. "Well, my lord, I trust you're in good health?" he said in a tone that conveyed he trusted the complete opposite.

Nicholas tore his attention from Verity. "I'm rather afraid you do, sir," he answered a little drolly.

"I thought it could only be extreme ill health that kept you in London so long," Joshua remarked acidly.

"I note your disapproval, sir."

"Your responsibilities lie here in Wychavon, my lord," Joshua declared.

Verity became uneasy. "Please, Uncle . . ."

He ignored her and pressed stubbornly on. "Or have you dispensed with those responsibilities, Lord Montacute?"

Nicholas flushed. "No, sir, I haven't, as you well know. My agent has attended very properly to everything in my absence."

"An agent is hardly adequate."

Verity was appalled that her uncle seemed intent on provoking a public quarrel. "Uncle Joshua, *please* stop!"

But Joshua had been wanting to confront Nicholas for too long to give up easily. "Is this what we must expect of a Tory landlord?" he demanded.

"What have politics to do with this, sir? Or is it just that your Whig tendencies deprive you of civility?"

"My Whig tendencies will make certain that I watch whether or not you observe your duties now you've deigned to return," Joshua declared airily.

"Oh, I'll observe my duties, sir, even to attending court to see that justice is *properly* dispensed."

Joshua flushed. "Is that a criticism?"

"No, why should you think that?" Nicholas inquired.

There was no mistaking that their dislike went far beyond any disagreement over a highwayman, and Verity stepped anxiously between them. "Please stop this, sirs," she begged. "Today is May Day, a time of celebration, and certainly no time for rancor."

Nicholas gazed into her eyes again. "You're quite right, Miss Windsor. Forgive me, for I would not distress you for the world."

A maelstrom of emotions swirled over her, alien emotions she'd never experienced before. She was conscious of a deep longing, an unidentified craving that upset her composure far more than his confrontation with her uncle.

Feeling he had lost this opening skirmish, Joshua decided to bring the meeting to a close. "Come, Verity, we were about to go home," he said firmly.

She lowered her eyes. "Yes, Uncle."

Nicholas raised her hand to his lips again. "Good-bye, Miss Windsor," he murmured.

"Good-bye, Lord Montacute."

He gazed after them as they made their way back toward Windsor House. What on earth had come over him? He felt like a gauche schoolboy beset by the first pangs of adolescent infatuation! And all because of Joshua Windsor's hitherto uninteresting niece!

But as he stood there he was suddenly conscious of someone watching him. He turned to the willows on the riverbank, where he saw an elegant woman dressed entirely in black gazing in his direction. He didn't know who she was, but guessed it had to be old Admiral Villiers' widow. News traveled, especially startling news, and his agent had told him of the goings-on at the manor house. Who would have thought the old seadog would rush to the altar with a beautiful amnesiac found in his garden in the middle of a Halloween storm?

He continued to look at her, and quite suddenly it seemed her clothes just fell away. His breath caught, for she appeared totally naked. Her mane of red hair tumbled in abandon over her shoulders, and he could see every contour of her body, even the tiny shadows cast by her nipples. But she was fully dressed, he *knew* she was! As he stared, she pursed her lips into a kiss that seemed to reach across to caress his mouth. Then she was clothed again, once more the demure, dignified widow.

Nicholas was shocked. "Dear God above . . ." he whispered.

"I beg your pardon, my lord?" said the vicar, who had just come over to speak to him.

Nicholas turned. "Oh, er, Reverend Crawshaw . . ."

The clergyman peered curiously at him from behind thick-lensed spectacles. "Are you all right, my lord?"

"Er, yes, quite all right, thank you. Tell me, who is the lady in black?" Nicholas nodded toward the willows, but the woman had gone.

"Admiral Villiers' widow is the only lady in black at the moment, my lord."

Nicholas glanced around, but couldn't see her anywhere.

The vicar spoke again. "Are you back here for long, my lord?"

"Mm? Oh, er, I don't really know." Nicholas made himself put the startling widow from his mind, and concentrate on the clergyman. "I haven't decided yet, Reverend."

"I trust we will see something of you?"

"I trust so too." Nicholas managed a smile. "Tell me, how have things been in my absence? Is there anything you think I should know?"

"Well, my lord . . ." The clergyman launched upon a lengthy list of parish matters, and as Nicholas listened politely, from the corner of his eye he caught another glimpse of the admiral's widow. She was by his carriage, which still waited by the ford, and she seemed to be looking down at something in the damp earth. Then she walked away toward the manor house.

* * *

It was twilight half an hour later when Nicholas drove on to the castle. Judith held a lace curtain aside to watch his carriage negotiate the ford before turning on to the Ludlow road. She smiled, knowing he had seen her naked, just as she had hoped he would. It was reassuring to know her command of the black arts was powerful enough to influence him a little, even though Verity now possessed the seal.

Her malignant gaze went toward the ford and the spot where the carriage had waited. The imprint of a fashionable London boot was plainly visible in the mud, and her lips curved into another cool smile.

It was a smile that would have faded in an instant if she'd realized the extent of Verity's intrusion into her magic, and the effect the magistrate's niece was already having upon Nicholas Montacute. But the sorceress didn't realize. Not yet anyway.

Chapter Six

That night Verity awoke with a start, frightened by a dream that fled the moment her eyes opened. Her heart was beating uncomfortably fast, and she felt so hot she had to fling the bedclothes aside.

The dream's influence waned, and as she lay there she became aware of her uncle's restless pacing in his room across the passage. Dyspepsia, she thought. Well, she had tried to warn him. . . .

With a sigh she got up and went to the window to draw the curtains back and stand in the cool draft that crept in beneath the raised sash. It was a beautiful night. The stars were like diamonds against the inky sky, and she could smell the wallflowers beneath the dining room window below.

She gazed toward the crescent moon. How low it was, almost as if it were touching the treetops near the old mill. . . .

As Verity looked out of her window, Judith was in the oak grove casting a second spell before the Lady. The mill loomed silently above the pool, and as the water ceased to flow through the race, the unearthly howling began in the distance. Green candlelight swayed over the witch's body, and as the hellhounds' baying reached a peak, Hecate's face appeared on the suddenly pliable stone. Then there was silence again.

Judith danced anticlockwise around the circle, intoxicated by the ointment on her warm skin. Reality became blurred, and soon she could no longer feel the grass beneath her feet. Incantations whispered on her lips, and her eyes were closed as she conjured Nicholas into her thoughts. In her mind's eye she saw him. He was walking on the castle terrace, above the beautiful azalea gardens, where pink and carmine blooms were turned to crimson and mauve by the pale light of the moon. He paused by one of the stone urns that stood beside the flight of steps leading down from the terrace.

Judith stroked herself. "Hecate, fill him with passion for me tonight . . ." she breathed, sighing as she rubbed trembling fingertips over her breasts.

Still she could see him. He descended the steps and along the path between the azalea beds. Fountains splashed as he neared the laburnum walk, which folded in a tunnel over the path. At the leafy entrance he paused again, turning as if he sensed the supernatural force directed from the grove.

Judith slid her hands between her thighs. "Hecate, let me go to him, let him be denied of the will to resist. Now, Hecate, now . . ."

She felt her body changing. She was no longer human, but animal, a hare, wild, agile, and swift as she bounded from the grove toward the castle.

Nicholas had been too restless to sleep. He was exhausted after the journey, and he had had several large measures of postprandial cognac, but still he couldn't relax.

It was pleasant by the laburnum walk, where the cool of the night seemed to release the scent of a thousand flowers. Behind him the castle was a romantic battlemented outline against the sky, and in front the valley stretched away toward Wychavon, where the church spire reached up above the trees. The primitive ways of the countryside had never seemed more close, and London more distant. On a night like this it was possible to believe in magic, old wives' tales, and folklore.

And only too possible to dwell on the unfathomable depths of Verity Windsor's compelling emerald eyes . . . He was almost resigned to the train of thought, for she had hardly been out of his mind in the hours since his return, and yet before today he'd been completely indifferent to everything about her. All of a sudden he had a fancy for Joshua Windsor's niece! Why? *Why* was he suddenly seeing her so differently?

There was a sound behind him, like a cat running down the path, but when he turned he was shaken to see a naked woman approaching. It was the admiral's beautiful widow, and she cast no shadow as she came toward him. Her hair flowed in profusion over her shoulders, and the motion of her body was seductive. A beguiling sense of otherworldliness began to settle over him, like invisible shackles tightening around his limbs. He wanted to speak, to back away, but he couldn't move at all.

A strangely alluring scent filled the air, making him feel light-headed and almost euphoric. She seemed to lack all substance as she slipped her slender arms around his neck and raised her lips to his, but the sweetness of her kiss was real enough. Her tongue flicked between his lips, and her body pressed excitingly to his. He couldn't resist, he didn't want to, for she was temptation so carnal and persuasive that he felt himself becoming aroused.

She sighed, slipping a hand down to the front of his breeches, and stroking him through the silk. Her fingers were knowing, exploring his erection until he felt he would explode with excitement. This couldn't be happening, it couldn't. He was dreaming . . . She seemed to coil around him drawing out his very spirit with her kisses, and all the while caressing him to the edge of climax.

But Verity was about to unwittingly interfere again. She was still at her bedroom window, and suddenly noticed the seal on the sill, where she had placed it earlier. Puzzled by the way the moonlight seemed to glow green through the tiger's eye quartz, she picked it up, and immediately destroyed Judith's magic for a second time.

In the castle garden, Judith felt a stab of pain as the spell was rent in two again. As she cried out, and fell back, Nicholas felt the invisible shackles unwinding. His desire was extinguished, and the helpless euphoria faded into revulsion and shocked disbelief. Her tantalizing perfume suddenly became a vile stench that seemed to choke his breath, and he stumbled away, his senses reeling unpleasantly. When he glanced back again, she had gone, but he thought he saw a small fleet-footed animal darting away toward the terrace steps.

Judith had felt all control drain instantly from her. She was a hare again, bounding helplessly back to the grove, where she fell exhausted and confused before the Lady. Hecate's face had gone, and wisps of smoke still rose from the candles. The river was flowing through the race, and she could hear the creaking of the mill wheel.

For a moment she was weak with nausea, but as the unpleasant sensations died away, she resumed human form and sat up, clenching her fists tightly. Her face was ugly with rage as intuition told her that Verity had intruded again. The magistrate's niece would pay for this, and pay dearly!

Nicholas was bewildered by what had happened, if indeed it had happened. Common sense told him no one could appear and vanish as swiftly as his mysterious seductress. It also told him he was as unlikely to have really experienced her astonishingly abandoned approaches as he was to have seen her clothes simply fall away on the green. It was all nonsense, and probably the result of the overgenerous measures of cognac he had taken after dinner.

He ran his fingers through his hair, and closed his eyes for a moment. He was suffering from a lack of tender female company and an overactive imagination, it was as simple as that. Taking a deep breath, he turned to retrace his steps toward the castle.

His equilibrium began to return, and he pondered why it was the admiral's widow upon whom his fantasies appeared to center. Why not Verity Windsor, who seemed far more to his liking at the moment. Ah, yes, Verity of the emerald eyes. Now if *she* were to come to him with her virginal charms naked and her heartstopping eyes wanton with desire, he wouldn't hesitate to initiate her into the pleasures of the flesh!

He laughed to himself, imagining old Joshua's reaction if he were to discover the lascivious thoughts Lord Montacute entertained toward his precious niece. Nelson's bombardment at Trafalgar was nothing to the broadsides that would be directed at the master of Wychavon, who would sink without trace, the remains of his manhood tied in a reef knot!

He paused at the top of the steps to look back over the gardens toward the church spire in the distance. "Sleep tight, sweet Verity," he murmured, then went into the castle.

Judith was at that moment passing the churchyard on her way back to the manor house. She still shook with fury and frustration, and her flowing cloak was tossed around her like a shroud. Her thoughts were savage, and at Sadie Cutler's little cottage, opposite the vicarage, she halted as she noticed candle-light flickering at one of the bedroom windows. Sadie's shadow moved against the curtains as she bent over her sick grandson.

Judith breathed out slowly. She regretted cursing the boy because, if her instinct didn't deceive her, it may have alerted his busybody of a great-aunt to the possibility of overlooking. So far it was only a feeling that the village wisewoman might suspect sorcery, but such intuition was often only too well founded. Judith exhaled slowly, for if anyone should have been overlooked, it was Martha Cansford, not the child.

The cottage door opened suddenly, and Judith drew back out of sight in the vicarage gateway as Martha herself emerged after several hours doing what she could to help her sister nurse the ailing child. Judith watched the old woman step out into the roadway and then pause to glance around as if she felt the witch's eyes upon her. Judith froze, hardly daring to breathe as Martha put a hand to the polished stone on the silver chain around her neck and raise it to her lips for a moment before walking away toward the ford.

The witch's eyes turned to flint as she felt the amulet's aura reaching out to her. A snakestone, the old biddy had a snake-stone! The witch recoiled in the darkness, for why would Martha Cansford wear such powerful protection if it were not that she suspected there was sorcery in Wychavon? Maybe she even suspected who was behind it!

A nerve flickered at Judith's temple, for while the old woman was protected by the snakestone, no evildoing could harm her. She was shielded by no less a wizard than the great Merlin himself!

Verity was still at her window and had observed how Judith drew out of sight as Martha left Sadie's cottage. Now, hearing the nurse coming up the staircase, she put the seal down on the sill again and hurried to open the door.

"Martha?" she whispered, keeping her voice low because her uncle's pacing had ceased and she was sure he had gone back to bed.

The old woman gave a startled gasp, and her lighted candle

shivered so that shadows leapt over the walls. "You startled me, Miss Verity!"

"I'm sorry. How is Davey?" Verity asked before mentioning anything else.

Martha gave a sad smile. "He'll be carried to the Lady at dawn."

Verity put a gentle hand on her sleeve. "I'm sure he'll recover after that, Martha."

"I hope you're right."

"Dr. Rogers will visit him tomorrow, and Uncle Joshua says that of course I can take some strawberries." She hesitated. "Martha, I think you're right about Judith Villiers." She described what she had witnessed from the window. "She was just standing there, staring at Davey's window, until you came out, then she hid by the vicarage. She saw you kiss the snakestone, although I don't know if she realized what it was."

Martha smiled a little. "Oh, she realized, Miss Verity, for every witch recognizes the snakestone. She now knows I protect myself from sorcery, and that will tell her I suspect there to be such a thing here in Wychavon."

"Martha, I—"

"It's time we both went to our beds, Miss Verity," the old woman interrupted quietly.

Verity stared at her for a moment, then obeyed. As the door closed, Martha lowered her gaze thoughtfully. Something would have to be done before the admiral's widow perpetrated any more evil. But what? What power did Martha Cansford have that was strong enough to counteract the magic of a witch like Judith Villiers? The answer was simple. She had no such power at all.

Chapter Seven

After two broken nights in a row, it was hardly surprising that Verity overslept the next morning. The sun was shining yet again, the church bells were ringing for Sunday service, and her uncle had already left for Ludlow by the time she had dressed and finished laboring over a suitably elegant coiffure for church, but he had remembered the strawberries for Davey, and a full basket waited on the hall table.

Verity had to dispense with breakfast in order to attend morning service, where the Reverend Crawshaw's sermon was taken from Romans, chapter twelve, verse twenty-one—"Be not overcome of evil, but overcome evil with good." A singularly appropriate text, she thought, glancing toward Admiral Villiers' pew, which hadn't been occupied since Judith's memorable Halloween arrival in the village. Given what she now knew, she supposed it was hardly surprising, since witches weren't likely to attend church, and with hindsight there seemed much more to Judith's insistence on a special license and marriage ceremony at the manor house, than had appeared at the time. The admiral had wished to marry in church, but his unusual bride had been responsible for changing his mind.

Nicholas didn't come to church. The ornate Montacute pew was as empty as the admiral's, a fact upon which much comment was made as the congregation began to leave. He was expected to observe the customary duties, of which attending church was but one, and Verity wished he had complied, but not for the same reasons.

Now that he had returned to Wychavon, she longed to see him again, and apart from that, in the cold light of day she was sure the dream that had awoken her during the night had concerned Nicholas in some way, although she still couldn't recall any details, just that he'd seemed to be in danger. What she did know, however, was that she found it difficult not to think about him.

She was one of the first to leave the church, and waited by the lychgate for Martha and Sadie in her neat white lawn gown, navy blue velvet spencer, and matching bonnet. She had the basket of strawberries ready to give to Sadie, but was ashamed to admit that at the moment it was once again the ninth lord of Wychavon Castle who occupied her thoughts, not poor little Davey Cutler.

Her feelings had been in chaos since Nicholas had looked into her eyes on the green the previous evening. Too late she realized that a good deal of her excitement about going to London was due to his presence there, now that he had returned to Wychavon, the Season was less enticing. She was cross with herself for being so affected by him, after all, it wasn't as if he'd *ever* danced attendance on her, in fact he had always been a little cool because of her uncle.

Her thoughts broke off as she heard hoofbeats approaching along the Ludlow road, and her heart lurched as she saw Nicholas himself riding toward her, the brass buttons on his pine green coat shining in the May sunshine. At first she thought he was arriving late for church after mistaking the time, but this soon proved not to be the case as he rode on past. He only recognized her at the last moment, but as he began to rein in to speak to her, some more of the congregation left the church, and to her disappointment he quickly rode on after merely doffing his hat.

She gazed after him, feeling hugely self-conscious, for she was convinced he'd been able to read her thoughts from her face. What if he now realized how she felt toward him? Oh, it would be too embarrassing for words. But even as these dread fears swept over her, she began to dismiss them as complete nonsense. How could he *possibly* read her thoughts! Her cheeks went red even so, a fact she realized when Martha and Sadie emerged beneath the lychgate behind her and exchanged glances on seeing how flustered she'd become because Lord Montacute had passed by.

Sadie Cutler was very like her elder sister, but much more rosy and embonpoint, as Lady Sichester would say. She also possessed a much more open personality, lacking Martha's quiet intensity, but because of her grandson's illness her usually cheerful face was tired and anxious.

A little guiltily, Verity took her plump hand. "How is Davey?" she asked gently.

"Not at all good, Miss Verity."

"Was he taken around the Lady this morning?"

Sadie nodded. "He was, miss, but so far there hasn't been any change."

Martha broke in. "There won't be, not until later today. This evening maybe, if it's going to make any difference."

Verity pressed the basket of strawberries into Sadie's hands. "Maybe these will cheer him up a little, Sadie. My uncle picked them himself this morning."

"Oh, thank you, Miss Verity, Mr. Windsor is very kind." Sadie's eyes filled with tears.

"Not at all. Dr. Rogers should come soon as well, and you're not to worry about his bills, for they're to be sent to Uncle Joshua."

Sadie was quite overcome. "I—I don't know what to say, Miss Verity," she whispered gratefully.

"Don't say anything."

"Will you take tea with Martha and me?"

Verity declined tactfully, feeling that the presence of someone from one of the village's "big houses" would probably provide a further damper on the sisters' already low spirits.

Returning to Windsor House, she decided that Nicholas was right to go for a ride on a day like this, so she changed, took her horse from the stable, and went out as well. Her riding habit was made of royal blue silk, and with it she wore a top hat with a white gauze scarf around the crown. In her laced-edged neckcloth she wore one of her most prized items of jewelry, a black pearl pin that had once belonged to her father.

She'd been out for about an hour when the weather changed, becoming overcast and humid. Maybe she would have been wiser to stay at home after all, she thought, reining in on the tree-covered ridge above the valley. The Shropshire countryside shimmered in a haze, and in the distance it was difficult to tell where land became sky. Everything was very quiet, except for a skylark tumbling high overhead, where storm clouds were beginning to gather.

Sound traveled a long way, and she heard a tilbury driving smartly along the Ludlow road. It was Dr. Rogers on his way to visit Davey. She hoped he would be able to do something, although she doubted it. Medicine wasn't going to be any good against witchcraft, if that was indeed what was the cause of the child's illness. She still hoped not, but everything seemed to point to it. She became cross with herself then, for the fact that Martha believed all that superstitious nonsense was no reason for her to do the same. There was no such thing as witchcraft! She sighed then, for if that was true, why did she feel an irresistible urge to cross her fingers?

From here she could look down on Wychavon Castle. With its lawns, terraced gardens, deer park, and peerless views of the surrounding hills, it was one of the most beautiful estates in the county, but it had originally been a medieval stronghold. The whole area had been the scene of many border skirmishes between the English and Welsh, for this was marcher country, wild and in some ways still untamed, but Nicholas's father had employed Mr. Wyatt, the brilliant architect, to turn Wychavon Castle into a romantic fantasy that brought to mind Camelot itself. Camelot, Merlin, the snakestone . . . Her thoughts began to run on, and she cut them off sharply.

A flash of lightning made her gasp, and she glanced up to see the clouds had thickened menacingly. She was going to be caught in the first thunderstorm since last Halloween! Suddenly it seemed she could feel Judith's shining gaze upon her, and with an uneasy shudder she kicked her heel and urged her horse down toward the valley. Thunder rolled intimidatingly across the sky, the air was breathless, and not a leaf moved. It was as if the land were waiting for the imminent deluge.

She reached the road as two virtually simultaneous flashes of lightning split the daylight, followed almost immediately by thunderclaps that made the ground vibrate beneath her horse's hooves, and as she passed the imposing phoenix-topped gates of the castle, the first drops of rain began to fall. The air stirred at last, and the smell of damp earth and bluebells filled her nostrils as the rain suddenly increased to a downpour that immedi-

ately began to soak through her riding habit. Ahead she saw the
track that led to the oak grove. The ruined mill was nearer than
the village, so without hesitation she turned her horse from the
road.

Lightning clicked audibly overhead, and as a tremendous
crash of thunder echoed over the lowering sky, the rain became
a cloudburst. Rivulets of water gushed down the track as suddenly the trees splayed back, and she was in the grove, where
the Lady stood out starkly in another blinding flash of lightning.

The mill rose desolately beside the rain-dashed pool, and for
a moment Verity was more afraid of the place than the storm,
but then more thunder cracked across the heavens, and her hesitation vanished as she urged her horse the final yards and dismounted to lead the animal into the ruined building.

The gloomy mill closed over her, and the odor of rotting
wood and crumbling stone was heavy as she made the reins fast
to a post. She glanced relievedly back at the doorway which
framed the Lady's endless vigil in the center of the grove. She
thought of how the village men had carried poor little Davey
here this morning, but suddenly forked lightning illuminated
the granite, making it seem to breathe, and her breath caught
nervously as one of the oak trees was struck. A branch was sev-
ered, and fell in a shower of leaves and splinters across the
track, right where she'd ridden only seconds before.

Nicholas spoke quietly behind her. "Don't be afraid, Miss
Windsor, for I'm sure we're quite safe in here."

With a stifled cry, she whirled about, searching the shadows
to see where he was. As her eyes became accustomed to the
light, she saw him getting up from the steps where, if either of
them had realized, Judith's tools of wickedness were concealed.

He sketched her a bow. "I'm sorry if I startled you, I really
didn't mean to."

"Nevertheless you did," she managed to say, noticing his
horse tethered nearby and wondering how on earth she hadn't
seen it when she entered.

He gave a faint smile, silently thanking fate for bringing him
someone so delightful to share his shelter. "It would seem we
are two minds with but a single thought," he murmured, noting

again how unexpectedly attractive he found her freckles, and how very green her eyes were. Deeply, mysteriously green . . .

"Yes," she replied lamely.

He didn't know what to say next because she affected him so much. His glance roamed approvingly over her figure, outlined so daintily by the tight-waisted jacket of her riding habit. He liked the tilt of her head, and the jaunty angle at which she wore her little top hat. There was even something charming about the frothiness of her neckcloth and the sheen of the unusual black pearl pin adorning the knot. God damn it, *everything* about her was pleasing! He turned away, shaken by the force of feeling running through him.

His open scrutiny made her feel hot, and for something to do she reached up to remove her hat. She immediately wished she hadn't, for some of her painstakingly coiffured curls tumbled down, making her feel even more self-conscious, and therefore even more hot. Color flooded into her cheeks, and she toyed nervously with the scarf around the hat.

The magic purloined from Judith had begun to tighten its hold over them both, stealthily weakening their inhibitions and focusing their thoughts only upon each other. They didn't know what was happening, only that they felt very strange indeed. There was no green glow, no elusive fragrance of herbs, just the dank mill and the thunderstorm, but the atmosphere between them was as electric as the lightning that discharged across the sky.

Unspoken words and feelings instilled them both with a secret sense of anticipation, but neither of them gave a hint of it as they faced each other in the shadows of the ruins.

Chapter Eight

Verity was the first to think of something to say next. "Lord Montacute, I—I forgot to say last night . . ."

He cleared his throat awkwardly. "Yes?"

"I found your seal on the village green."

He looked blankly at her. "My what?"

"Your desk seal."

"On the village green, you say?" Right now he didn't give a damn about any seal!

"Yes, it was lying in the grass near the river. I—I'll send it back to the castle."

He ran a hand through his dark hair. "I can't imagine how it came to be there."

"Perhaps you should see if anything else has been stolen," she suggested."

"I will." Striving to bring a little normality to the conversation, he drew himself together and faced her. "If anything has been stolen, no doubt your uncle will say it's no more than I deserve for staying away so long."

"Possibly."

"Come now, Miss Windsor, he'd *definitely* say so."

"Uncle Joshua believes a landlord should be more conspicuous by his presence, not his absence."

"Do you support your uncle where I'm concerned, Miss Windsor?"

"He's my uncle, sir, whereas you . . ."

"Whereas I am nothing to you," he interrupted.

"Yes." Although I wish it were otherwise, came the unbidden postscript.

"Joshua Windsor is a fortunate man to have such a supportive kinswoman," he said then.

She held his gaze. "Why do you and my uncle dislike each other so?" she asked with a directness that surprised her.

It surprised him too. "How very frank you are, Miss Windsor," he murmured.

Her cheeks warmed. "Maybe, but you have to admit the coolness between you has become more pronounced."

"Has it? I hadn't noticed."

"Oh, come, sir, you *must* have detected his increased antagonism last night on the green. Not even he is usually accustomed to taking such a strong line."

He cleared his throat. "Well, I suppose we're at opposite poles politically, and when it comes to sentencing felons, your uncle considers my judgment to be far too lenient in the case of a certain highwayman."

The same old explanation, she thought in exasperation, and he watched the expression on her face. "I see my answer hasn't satisfied you."

"No, my lord, it hasn't, for it's plain to me that something important has happened since the business of the highwayman. My uncle will not say what it is, and neither, it seems, will you."

He glanced away for a moment. "Nothing has happened, Miss Windsor. How could it, when I've been in London, and he's been here? Unless, of course, it's simply his detestation of anyone who may be categorized as an absentee landlord?" He met her eyes again and smiled.

This was what she herself had wondered, and yet there was *still* something niggling at the back of her mind. "There has to be something else."

"I cannot help you, Miss Windsor," he murmured.

He was avoiding her eyes, she noticed, which meant there was *definitely* something else, and he was as determined as her uncle not to speak of it! But before she could say anything more, another dazzling flash of lightning lit the shadows, and she turned nervously as the mill shuddered to the following thunder. The cloudburst continued unabated, the water sluicing over the Lady until the granite shone like glass.

Nicholas realized how frightened she was. "Come away

from the door, Miss Windsor," he said gently, uncomfortably aware that he couldn't look at her now without desiring her. It was a feeling that was beginning to course potently through his blood.

She obeyed. "I suppose you think I'm very foolish," she murmured, more than a little embarrassed.

"Foolish? Not at all."

"I—I've always been afraid of storms."

"It's hardly a crime."

"Maybe it is for someone about to embark on her first Season."

He looked quickly at her. "You're going to London?"

She nodded. "At the beginning of June."

Dismay washed coldly over him. He didn't want her to spend one day away from Wychavon, let alone a whole Season!

She spoke again. "Lady Sichester is kindly allowing us the use of her house in Dover Street."

"Indeed?"

His tone was unmistakably abrupt, and she looked curiously at him. "Is something wrong, my lord?"

"Er, no."

She managed a smile. "I—I wondered if perhaps you disliked Lady Sichester."

"I hardly know her."

His manner was still odd, or so she thought. "Then have I said something untoward, Lord Montacute?" she asked.

"No, of course not." He made himself smile. Oh, God, he wanted to take her in his arms, and kiss her . . . He had to turn away, for his heart was beginning to beat more swiftly, and his whole body felt warm, as if he already held her.

She was scarcely less agitated, and cast around for something bland to say. Her glance fell on the Lady, which was suddenly very bright as more lightning sent the shadows reeling. She closed her eyes tightly until the accompanying thunder had rolled away, then she looked at the Lady again. "Do you believe in witchcraft, Lord Montacute?" she asked.

Surprised, he turned toward her again. "Witchcraft? Why ever do you ask that?"

"I—I was thinking about Meg Ashton, and the stone circle

that used to be here. They say her spirit is trapped in the Lady, did you know?"

"Yes, and right now it's invitingly easy to give credence to the legend, isn't it?" he said with a slight smile.

"Yes."

"Well, I don't know whether or not Meg was a real witch, but I do know she was responsible for killing the wife and unborn child of one of my ancestors. Whether by black arts or only too human hand may never be known. I take it you're of a superstitious nature, Miss Windsor?"

She gave him a slightly rueful smile. "If you had a nurse like Martha Cansford, you'd be a little superstitious too."

"Ah, yes, the wisewoman of Wychavon," he murmured with a hint of wryness.

Suddenly it seemed the storm was directly overhead, for more lightning pierced the gloom, and the crumbling building vibrated to another shattering clap of thunder which made the horses shift uneasily. Verity's eyes widened anxiously as dust fell from the ceiling, for all the world as if the mill were about to collapse. Without warning, panic rose sharply through her, and she gathered her cumbersome skirts intending to run out into the rain-swept grove, which inexplicably seemed a safer place than the mill, but Nicholas stepped swiftly over and caught her arm. "It's much more dangerous out there than in here," he said firmly.

She struggled a little, and he pulled her roughly back, putting his arms around her so she couldn't escape. "Stay inside, Miss Windsor, for if you go out, you run the risk of the same fate as the oak tree."

Another thunderclap jarred the sky, and with a gasp she hid her face against his shoulder.

He held her close. "It's all right, we're quite safe in here," he murmured, unable to help himself from sliding his ungloved fingers into the warm hair at the nape of her neck. From the moment he had touched her, he'd been conscious of an intensifying of desire. From being a constant ache in his loins, it became a fierce craving that pervaded his whole body. It went far beyond anything he'd ever experienced before, and was so strong it was all he could do to resist the temptation to tilt her face toward his.

But suddenly she raised her eyes to look at him anyway. It was a guileless gesture that dashed aside the vestiges of his restraint. Her lips were within inches of his own, and so sweetly parted they seemed to beg a kiss. Before he knew it, his embrace had tightened, he'd bent his head, and his mouth was upon hers in a way that left chaste pecks far behind. To his unutterable shame and shock, he found himself subjecting her to the sort of full-blooded kiss that was usually the prelude to far far more. It was as if the grove itself affected him, releasing something primitive and pagan that made him abandon his sexual principles. Normally he would never have taken such a liberty with any woman, let alone Joshua Windsor's niece, but now he felt almost compelled to do so. Arousal began to grip him, sweeping him along with a fervor that was exhilarating. Oh, Verity, Verity . . .

The top hat slipped from her fingers, and for a moment she was rigid with shock, but then wild feelings began to run through her veins too. They were deliciously hungry feelings she had never known before, and she knew she should resist by pushing him away, but instead her lips softened beneath his, and she succumbed to the attraction that had plagued her for so long. It was as if she were in a dream. It couldn't really be happening, she couldn't possibly be in his arms like this. . . .

Nicholas found her response as exciting as it was unexpected. Her body yielded warmly against his, and yet at the same time he could feel her hesitancy. She was unversed in such intimacies, and her innocence was as affecting as everything else about her. It was as if she were precious to him, and in that moment his thoughts were of her, not himself. He knew well how to give her pleasure without taking things to the ultimate conclusion, and he wanted her to know what that pleasure could be, so, with his lips still moving tenderly on hers, he pressed her gently to him so she could feel the arousal pounding in his breeches.

She was helpless but willing in his arms, a prisoner to her own emotions and the spellbinding atmosphere that pervaded everything. The thunderstorm had faded away to the periphery of her consciousness, and the only sound she could hear was the pounding of her heart. She could feel every sensuous line of his body, and the ironhard maleness pushing toward her through their clothes. She ached with need, and sank weakly against him as meltingly pleasurable sensations fluttered gratifyingly over her entire being.

Still he kissed her, moving his lips gently to prolong her pleasure. They were still two separate entities, unjoined in the full physical sense, but he'd never felt more in love and at one with anyone before. He could hardly believe their actions, breaking every rule and dashing aside as meaningless every reserve. A strange magic had them both in its grip, and its sorcery was indomitable.

Suddenly the rain stopped. One moment the downpour had filled the air with its noise, the next there was absolute silence. The draft from the doorway was unexpectedly cold and fresh, breathing soberingly over them both so that they suddenly drew apart, shocked by what they'd been doing.

Verity backed away in disbelief. Her eyes were huge with mortification, and she pressed her trembling hands to her lips as she stared at him.

He was equally as bewildered. "Verity . . ." he began, not really knowing whether to use her first name, or to resume their previous formality.

Covered with confusion such as she'd never felt before, she shook her head and turned swiftly to untether her horse.

"Please, Verity, you can't go like this!" he cried, stepping after her.

But she remounted and urged her horse out of the mill before he could seize hold of her bridle. She had to duck low beneath the door lintel, and the last pins in her hair gave up their grip. Golden curls fell heavily to her shoulders as she galloped away across the drenched grove. She felt the Lady's closeness, as if it were watching her, laughing at her, and she choked back a sob as she made her horse jump the fallen branch and then come up to a reckless gallop along the track, where rivulets still flooded down the ruts.

Blinded by tears, she galloped out of the track onto the road, right in front of an oncoming carriage. The coachman shouted in alarm, and the team whinnied, their hooves clattering as he tried to apply the brakes. Verity was thrown bodily into the verge, tumbling among the dripping bluebells.

Her senses began to fade, but in the few seconds before

blackness engulfed her, she saw a small ball of orange fire hovering at the entrance to the track. She knew it was a corpse candle, for Martha had told her all about them. They heralded death, and were followed by the churchyard watcher's ghostly cart, which was heard but seldom seen. Driven by the last person to die in the parish—it would be Admiral Villiers at the moment—it rattled around the countryside waiting for the candle to show the way to the next corpse. Someone was going to die here on this corner. Was it her? Was she dying?

Verity was frightened. Darkness seemed to be closing in, and the scent of bluebells was cloying. She thought she heard a spectral cart coming slowly up the track behind her, but there was nothing there. The darkness pressed in still more, and as she lost consciousness a woman's anxious voice cried out nearby.

"Have we killed her, Oliver? Oh, *please*, don't let us have killed her!"

Chapter Nine

Verity opened her eyes and saw a bed cornice that was richly carved with Montacute phoenixes. The gold-fringed hangings were mulberry velvet, and the room beyond was very grand and Gothic. And could only be part of Wychavon Castle!

Horrified, she tried to sit up, but a woman spoke immediately. "Please don't try to move too much, Miss Windsor, for you had a nasty fall."

Verity's glance flew toward the voice, but all she saw was a silhouette against the brilliance of a triple-arched window. The storm had gone, and it was sunset outside. Crimson and gold blazed like fire, as if through the stained glass of a church, and the woman's face, even the color of her gown, was distorted.

There was a rustle of taffeta, and the silhouette came into focus as the woman moved to the side of the bed and smiled down at her. She was about five years Verity's senior, with an hourglass figure that was shown off to great advantage in a fashionably low cut magnolia evening gown that was lavishly embroidered with little pink rosebuds. Shining brunette curls framed her heart-shaped face, she had gentle light brown eyes, and her diamond earrings flashed in the light from the window as she took Verity's hand. "How are you feeling, Miss Windsor?" she asked solicitously.

"Who are you?" Verity asked.

"Oh, forgive me for not introducing myself, my dear. I'm Mrs. Oliver Henderson, although no doubt that means nothing to you."

"No, I'm afraid not."

"My husband is Lord Montacute's friend. We were on our

way here to Wychavon Castle when you fell from your horse right in front of our carriage. There was a terrible storm, and I think your horse must have taken fright and bolted. Don't you remember?"

Verity looked away. Yes, she remembered being in the mill with Nicholas, and how she'd ridden away in unutterable dismay at the things that had happened between them. She also recalled seeing the corpse candle . . .

"Do you remember the accident, Miss Windsor?" Mrs. Henderson asked again.

"Er, yes, vaguely," Verity replied, wishing she were anywhere but at the castle. She could never look Nicholas in the eyes again, let along accept his hospitality!

"Oliver and I didn't know who you were or where you lived, so we brought you here. Nicholas—I mean, Lord Montacute—returned from his ride at the same time we arrived, and he recognized you right away. Actually, he'd found your riding hat! Anyway, the doctor—Rogers, I believe his name was—says you haven't broken any bones. You're just badly shaken and bruised, and in a day or so you'll be well enough to go home."

A day or so! She couldn't possibly stay another minute! Verity was appalled at the thought, but as she tried to get out of bed again, the room began to swim unpleasantly, and she had to lie back.

Mrs. Henderson smoothed the bedclothes. "I told you not to move too much, Miss Windsor, now perhaps you'll listen," she chided with a kindly smile.

"I—I'm sorry . . ."

"We've sent word to your uncle, but I understand he's in Ludlow until tomorrow. However, since he'll be obliged to drive past the castle gates on his return, the lodgekeeper has been instructed to look out for his chaise."

Have Uncle Joshua come to the castle for her? Oh, no! Verity became quite agitated. "It—it really would be better if I went home. Uncle Joshua and Lord Montacute don't like each other, and—"

"Don't fret about it, Miss Windsor," Mrs. Henderson interrupted swiftly. "I don't profess to know the cause of the ill feeling, but I *do* know that if his lordship is in any way curmudgeonly toward your uncle, he'll have me to deal with."

"It's most kind of you to try to reassure me, but I really would much rather go home." Oh, you have no idea how much I'd rather be at Windsor House right now than here beneath Nicholas Montacute's roof. . . .

"I won't hear of it. Besides, I already feel bad enough about this, without having any further mishap to you on my conscience."

"You feel bad? But why?"

"Because if I hadn't insisted we drive with all speed through the storm, the accident might have been avoided. I feel it's my fault."

"Please don't blame yourself, if anyone's at fault it's me. I shouldn't have been riding so quickly."

Mrs. Henderson smiled and sat on the side of the bed. "Perhaps we should share culpability, Miss Windsor."

Verity returned the smile. "Yes, I think that's best."

"Now I feel able to beg a favor of you."

"Of me?"

Mrs. Henderson nodded. "If you stay here until you're better, you'll be providing me with much needed female company. You see, although I love coming to Wychavon, it's rather lonely for me. Oliver and Nicholas amuse themselves with a little riding, shooting, etcetera, but apart from strolling in the gardens, reading, and playing the spinet, it can be very dull for me. I know it's unfair to blackmail you like this, but apart from obliging you to obey the doctor's instructions, it really would please me. And there is the added incentive that I will be able to tell you all about the Season. You *are* about to go to London, aren't you?"

"Yes, but—"

"No buts, Miss Windsor. It will be a bargain, will it not? You will be relieving me of unutterable boredom, and I will be repaying your kindness by regaling you with all you need to know about the *beau monde*."

Verity still didn't want to stay, but found it impossible to hold out against such charming coercion, so—very reluctantly—she gave in. "How can I possibly refuse, Mrs. Henderson?"

The other smiled. "I'm afraid I have no shame when I want my own way. Oliver tells me I'm quite a bully, and maybe I am, but in spite of that, I rather think we'll get on famously."

Verity had to smile, for her new companion was very likable indeed.

Mrs. Henderson looked inquiringly at her. "Have you been to London recently?"

"Not since childhood, when I used to stay with my uncle. He had a house in Mount Street until he tired of the social round," Verity explained.

"So you won't be staying at Mount Street this time?"

"No. Lady Sichester is allowing us to use her house in Dover Street."

"Lady Sichester?"

"She and my uncle are old friends."

"I see."

"Do you know her?" Verity asked, thinking her tone as odd as Nicholas's had been.

"Er, yes. A little. She's friendly with your uncle, you say?"

"Oh, yes," Verity replied. "They've known each other for years, and although he doesn't go to London now, they still correspond regularly."

Mrs. Henderson fell silent and then got up briskly. "I'll, er, go and tell Oliver and Nicholas that you've woken up. I'm sure they'll be eager to speak to you—"

"Oh, no! Please! I'd much rather not see anyone right now," Verity exclaimed quickly.

Mrs. Henderson paused in surprise, but then smiled understandingly. "Of course, my dear, if that's what you wish. To be truthful, I suspect that I'd feel the same way in your place. One prefers to be properly prepared to meet gentlemen. I'll just tell them you've woken up, but wish to rest. Will that do?"

"Yes. Thank you." Verity was relieved. She knew it was a case of putting off the inevitable, but right now she knew she couldn't possibly find the fortitude to confront Nicholas.

The magnolia taffeta rustled as Mrs. Henderson went out, and Verity glanced unhappily through the window at the sunset. If only she hadn't decided to go for a ride today, if only she hadn't taken refuge at the mill, if only she hadn't so far forgotten every standard of proper behavior as to indulge in such deplorable misconduct with Nicholas Montacute . . .

Her eyes closed in shame. How *could* she have done it? What on earth was she going to say to him when the time came—as come it soon would, there was no doubt of that.

Nicholas and Oliver were in the solar, by which name the castle drawing room was known. It was a lofty chamber, vaulted like a cathedral, with exquisite tapestries depicting scenes from *Le Morte d'Arthur*. The arched doorways were flanked by rich green arras curtains, and there were wheel rim chandeliers and floor-standing candelabra, some of which were already lit because the windows faced east.

Oliver lounged back on a chair, a glass of cognac in his hand. He was dressed for dinner, and smiled as he glanced across at Nicholas. "Well, we've commenced our visit in fine style, getting caught in the mother of all storms, and then almost killing a village damsel."

Nicholas nodded and leaned his head back. He was also dressed for dinner, and the signet ring on his finger caught the candlelight as he swirled his glass.

Oliver studied him. "What's up?" he asked at last.

"Mm?"

"Well, your mind's hardly been on anything I've said."

Nicholas shrugged, and sipped his drink.

Oliver raised an eyebrow. "Who is this Miss Windsor?" he asked suddenly.

"I've already told you, her uncle is a tiresome old codger of a magistrate who gets under my skin with very little effort."

"I'm not interested in the uncle, dear boy, just tell me about the young lady. How did you come to have that hat?" Oliver pressed.

"I just found it. There's nothing more to tell."

"Nothing at all? Nick, your face was a positive picture when you realized who it was we'd nearly run over! You looked as if one of Zeus' thunderbolts had caught you between the shoulder blades."

Nicholas eyed him. "You're wrong."

"No, I'm not. This Miss Windsor means something to you."

"She doesn't. Look, Oliver, will you *please* leave the subject alone? You're like a damned dog with a bone!"

"Because you're being mysterious. What is she to you, Nick?"

"Nothing!"

Oliver pursed his lips. "If that's true, it's a great pity, for she's dashed attractive. In my opinion far more attractive than—"

"That's enough, Oliver," Nicholas interrupted sharply.

"For heaven's sake, why are you being so touchy? I was only going to observe that—"

"I know what you were about to observe, and I'd thank you to keep it to yourself. My private life is just that—mine—and I'd be obliged if you'd refrain from poking around in it."

Oliver pulled a face at him. "I loathe you when you're on your high horse."

"You'd be on your high horse if I kept on at you about something you'd rather not discuss."

Light footsteps approached, and Oliver's wife came in. She waved to them both to remain seated, and her skirts rustled as she came to sit on the arm of her husband's chair. "Miss Windsor is awake and well," she announced then.

Oliver slipped an arm around her waist. "What's she like, Anna?" he asked, with one eye on Nicholas.

"Quite charming. I vow I shall enjoy her company, although it was a struggle to persuade her to stay." Anna looked across at Nicholas. "Are you the local ogre, sir?" she inquired.

"The what?"

"Local ogre. You must be something of the sort, for she was all of a scramble not to partake of your hospitality."

Nicholas colored a little. "I don't know what you mean."

"No?"

"No," he replied with forced patience.

Anna smiled. "Is there something you're not telling us, Nicholas?"

"Not you too! No, there isn't!" he snapped, getting up to pour himself another cognac.

She watched him. "You're a terrible fibber, sir," she murmured. "By the way, did you know that she and her uncle will be staying at the Sichester house in Dover Street when they go to London?"

Oliver's jaw dropped. "Is that so?"

Nicholas turned. "Yes, apparently it is."

Anna's eyes sparkled mischievously. "What a coincidence, mm?"

Nicholas slammed his glass down by the decanter. "If you'll excuse me, I have things to do before we dine . . ." he muttered, and strode from the room.

Anna and Oliver exchanged glances and then she drew a long breath. "All very curious, don't you think?"

"I do indeed. So what's the enigmatic Miss Windsor really like?"

"Refreshingly untemperamental. I like her immensely."

"So, I fancy, does friend Nick," Oliver murmured, pulling her down onto his lap.

She linked her arms around his neck. "I wouldn't have thought she was his type," she said after a moment. "Let's face it, he's always gone for hothouse flowers."

"And much good it's done him. Besides, who's to decide what types anyone should go for? Look at you and me. I'm a dashing hero of a fellow, whereas you are such a nondescript mouse of a thing that—"

She pretended to poke him on the nose. "How dare you, sirrah!" She laughed.

He hugged her. "I adore you, Mrs. Henderson," he murmured, putting his lips to her throat.

She closed her eyes with pleasure. "Oh, I *am* looking forward to tonight, and that huge, huge bed," she whispered.

"You're a forward hussy, madam."

"I know. Aren't you lucky?" she said, kissing him.

Chapter Ten

That same Sunday, while Verity was so reluctantly detained at Wychavon Castle, Judith waited in growing perplexity for her to return from the ride.

The witch had been standing at a manor house window for some time now, her foot tapping impatiently as her temper worsened. Oh, where *was* the magistrate's odious niece? The thunderstorm had come and gone, but of the loathed figure in the royal blue riding habit there was no sign at all.

Judith's gaze went to Verity's room. Now that daylight was fading, she could pick out the telltale green glow of the seal on the windowsill. So near, and yet so very far. Retrieving it was of paramount importance, and to that end she had called at Windsor House in the early afternoon, only to be told the old man had gone to Ludlow and Verity was out riding. Now it was dusk, and *still* the tiresome creature hadn't returned!

Suddenly a foolishly obvious thought struck Judith. What if Verity had already returned, but to the back of the house? Snatching up her shawl, the witch hurried from the room, and soon emerged into the cool of the May evening. Everything was fresh after the storm, and puddles shone on the road as she made her way to Windsor House, where moisture fell from the lilacs as she pushed open the gate.

She knocked at the door, and the sound seemed to echo through the entire building. After a moment a maid hastened to answer. "Good evening, Mrs. Villiers."

"Is Miss Windsor at home yet?"

"No, ma'am, she—she . . ." The girl's eyes filled with tears.

"She's had a riding accident, ma'am, and has been taken to Wychavon Castle."

Judith was shaken. "To the *castle*?" she repeated.

"Yes, ma'am."

"Has she been badly hurt?" Judith asked, wishing Verity had broken her interfering neck.

"No, ma'am, but she'll have to stay there for a day or so, I don't know exactly how long."

"I'm so sorry to hear it," Judith replied insincerely, swiftly collecting her thoughts. "Actually, I've come for Lord Montacute's seal. Miss Windsor requested me to return it to him, so perhaps you could give it to me?"

The maid looked blankly at her. "Lord Montacute's seal?"

"That's what I said."

"I—I don't know anything about it, ma'am."

"Perhaps you could look for it?" Judith hinted, keeping a tight hold on her patience. The seal had only to be taken from Verity's windowsill, so if she could just persuade this village dunderhead to do as she wished, the spell could be recast this very night!

The maid was dismayed. "But I wouldn't know where to begin, ma'am."

"I believe it's on her windowsill, and since I'm about to leave for the castle now, it's really quite urgent that I have it."

But she had pressed a little too much, and the maid suddenly became uneasy. "I'm afraid I cannot take anything without Miss Verity's or Mr. Windsor's express instruction, ma'am, and besides, I'm sure Mr. Windsor will wish to return it when he visits Miss Verity on his return from Ludlow."

There was nothing Judith could say to this, so she gave a false smile and turned to walk away, but her fists were clenched and she was so furious she slammed the gate behind her. The lilacs shivered and scattered drips all over her.

She didn't hear the Reverend Crawshaw riding toward her on his large new cob, and knew nothing until there was a sudden clatter of hooves and a startled cry. "Have a care there, madam!"

She looked up in startlement and saw the cob shaking its head impatiently only inches from her. The vicar leaned reproachfully forward in the saddle. "You walked right out in front of me, Mrs. Villiers."

"I, er, wasn't concentrating." Judith took a handkerchief from her pocket and dabbed her eyes. "I—I was thinking of the poor, dear admiral . . ." she added in a convincingly broken whisper.

"Oh, dear lady," he exclaimed, and with difficulty dismounted from the cob, which was a very large and difficult animal for someone of indifferent riding skills. Then he took Judith's hand and patted it sympathetically. "Grief must run its course, Mrs. Villiers, and eventually it will become bearable."

"Yes, I—I'm sure you're right," Judith replied, striving not to snatch her fingers from all contact with a man of the cloth. To her relief the cob was impatient to be off again, dancing around on sharp hooves and shaking its bridle. The vicar held the reins tightly and gave Judith a rather sheepish look. "I fear my new mount is rather a handful," he declared with masterly understatement, for the sight of his equestrian endeavors had caused endless amusement in the village.

Someone hailed him at that moment, and they turned to see the church verger hurrying across the stepping stones. "Reverend Crawshaw, oh, Reverend Crawshaw, something dreadful has happened!" he called.

The vicar was alarmed. "Whatever is it, Mr. Tipton?"

"I've only just found out that lightning struck the vestry roof during the storm, and there's a great deal of damage. You really must come and see without delay. I fear the repairs will be costly."

Reverend Crawshaw was dismayed. "I'll come immediately!" he cried, and touched his hat to Judith. "Forgive me, madam, but I must attend to his unfortunate matter." He began to haul himself back into the saddle, and the cob danced around mutinously before at last allowing him to urge it toward the ford. The verger hurried after him.

Judith watched them sourly. What fools they were, she thought, fixing the cob with a dark look. She was rewarded by the animal's sudden start and the vicar's cry of alarm as for a moment it seemed he would be deposited in the river. The verger teetered across the stepping stones, and only just managed to reach the other side in safety.

The witch turned to walk back to the manor house. At that moment she wouldn't have given a fig if either man had drowned, for she was too concerned with how to lay hands upon the seal so that Nicholas could begin paying the full price for his forefather's crimes.

She cast a vitriolic backward glance at Verity's bedroom window, where she could still see the faint green glow of the seal. This was all the magistrate's niece's fault, she thought. If it weren't for dear, sweet Verity, by now Nicholas Montacute would be under the spell. She paused. The fact that he had left London proved that to some extent he was already influenced, but how much, that was the question? Could he be susceptible enough for her to proceed anyway, even without the seal?

Her thoughts began to race and without further ado she decided to go to the grove. It was almost dark, and with Hecate's aid she'd be able to slip unseen into the castle tonight. There she'd soon find out how much sway she held over the ninth Lord Montacute! With a faint smile, she set off across the stepping stones and along the Ludlow road, where long shadows now merged into the gathering gloom of twilight.

She had passed Sadie's cottage when the door opened and Martha came out. The old nurse was close to tears because Davey still showed no sign of improvement. Carrying him around the Lady didn't seem to have been beneficial at all, and Dr. Rogers hadn't proved very helpful either. He had left some medicine and had instructed Sadie to light a fire in the child's bedroom, even though the cottage kitchen ensured that the small building was already warm throughout. Something had been said about applying leeches the next day, and then he had climbed back into his tilbury and driven off again.

Martha returned to Windsor House. She already knew about Verity's accident, for word had been sent to her at the cottage, but she didn't know that Judith had called twice. The seal's importance was apparent to her the moment she learned of the witch's interest in it.

She hastened up to Verity's bedroom and found the seal still lying on the windowsill. It just seemed to be an ordinary enough object, she thought at first, turning it over, and looking deep into the tiger's eye quartz. Hecate's magic hadn't touched her, so there weren't any strange green lights, but even so she began to sense enchantment.

Her thin fingers closed slowly over the seal. If the witch wanted this so badly that she was prepared to come openly to the door and ask for it, then it was something she must not be allowed to have. And there was one hiding place no witch would dare to go—the church!

Later, when evensong was over and everyone had gone home, she would place it beneath the great silver-gilt cross on the altar.

There were two reasons why dinner at Wychavon Castle had proved a restrained affair that night. Firstly, Oliver and Anna were both very tired after the journey, and secondly they'd both attempted to question Nicholas again about his acquaintance with Verity. His reluctance to discuss it merely fueled their curiosity, but he refused to be drawn about something he didn't really understand himself, and thus both the conversation and the meal dragged to an unsatisfactory end. After that, Oliver and Anna decided the wisest thing would be to bring the whole evening to a close by retiring.

Nicholas was too restless to do the same. Verity's close proximity rattled his equilibrium, and try as he would, he couldn't stop thinking about those few outrageous minutes in the mill. Outrageous and exquisitely pleasurable. He was still shaken by the eroticism that had seized them both and knew that he should try to speak to her alone. What her reaction might be was in the lap of the gods, but he had to see her, and there was no time like the present, when the rest of the castle was quiet.

Steeling himself for a meeting that was a completely unknown quantity, he went up toward her room. There were few lights now, and shadows reared all around him. Suddenly he felt as if someone were watching from behind a pillar. There was no one there when he went to look, but then he heard a sound, like a small animal—a cat maybe—bounding away toward the great hall.

After a moment there was silence again, and he continued up the broad stone staircase that curved between Norman pillars to the oak-ceilinged gallery on the second floor.

Chapter Eleven

Candlelight glowed beneath Verity's door, but there was no sound from inside to indicate if she was awake. He became suddenly irresolute again, and paced slowly up and down. He still wanted to speak to her alone, but was her bedchamber at night the proper place! What if she were to misunderstand? He might be accused of grossly improper conduct toward a young woman who was, strictly speaking, under his protection. But if they *could* talk, maybe . . . Maybe what? His own feelings were still so confused he had no idea what he really wanted. In fact, *everything* seemed to have been confusing from the moment he and Oliver had left White's on May Eve. Yes, that was when his whole world had seemed to start turning upside down!

He faced the door again, and after taking a deep breath he tapped lightly upon the carved oak surface. "Miss Windsor, may I speak with you?" he called softly. There was no reply, so he called again, but still there wasn't a response.

The last thing he should have done was open the door, but he pushed it ajar a few inches, and looked into the dimly lit room beyond. She was asleep, her hair pouring in golden ripples over the pillow. He knew he should close the door and walk away, but there was something so very beautiful and alluring about her, that instead he went to stand by the bed.

He was conscious of the now familiar sexual enthrallment sweeping over him again. It was as if he'd stepped inside an invisible ring where strange forces robbed him of his customary moral code, and him prey to an alien new immorality. Desire spread through him anew as he gazed down at the thickness of her lashes, and the way her lips curved as if her dreams were pleasant. The bedclothes silhouetted her figure, so relaxed and defenseless in sleep, and as she moved slightly, the nightgown she'd borrowed from Anna parted over her breasts, revealing one dainty nipple. Its upturned pinkness seemed to invite his lips, and excitement gathered at his loins, pulsing imperatively with a force that was visible beneath the white silk of his breeches.

Dear God, he wanted to fall on her, ravish her, arouse her into a passion to match his own . . . Bewildered by the power of the attraction he felt for her, he had to turn away. His heart was pounding, and he felt hot. The scent of herbs seemed to drift over him, urging him to take her, but instead he stumbled from the room and closed the door behind him. Then he leaned back against it with his eyes closed. Was this bewitchment? For as God was his witness, that was how he felt. Verity Windsor had cast a spell over him, and he was at her mercy.

Then he opened his eyes a little ashamedly. Wasn't that the excuse of man throughout the centuries? He accused woman of using black arts to enslave him, when all the time the culprit was his own sexuality. He exhaled very slowly, and then straightened. He couldn't blame anyone but himself for the way he felt now. He wanted Verity Windsor, and that was all there was to it. He didn't know why it had suddenly happened like this, but she'd aroused the sort of hunger he hadn't felt in far too long. Scales had fallen from his eyes, and he was seeing her properly for the first time; and what he saw he wanted with a ferocity he found hard to cope with.

There was a sound along the passage, and he turned guiltily. The last thing he wanted was for one of the servants to see him outside Verity's door! Quickly he walked away in the opposite direction, taking a circuitous route to his own apartment, which faced over the gardens toward the distant village.

The rooms were lit by a single candle which shivered as he closed the door behind him. Gray velvet curtains were drawn across the arched windows, and on a table, with a glass and decanter of cognac, stood the portable escritoire he took with him wherever he went.

He crossed to the adjoining dressing room and took off all his clothes before dousing his face with cold water from the jug. Then he ran his fingers through his hair and went to fling himself on the bed. He stared up at the canopy. He'd never thought of himself as a lustful man, but where Verity was concerned, he suddenly seemed to be ruled by his loins!

The sound he'd heard outside Verity's door was audible again now, and his gaze flew toward the nearest window. Someone was there! He sat up warily. "Come out, whoever you are," he commanded.

The curtains moved slightly, and Verity stepped from behind them. She was naked, the curves of her body soft and sensuous in the dim light. Her hair fell in a golden glory around her shoulders, there was a tempting smile on her lips, and her lilac eyes were warm and seductive. Lilac eyes, not emerald . . . The thought was only fleeting, for as she approached the bed, he knew she intended to make love to him.

"Verity?" he whispered.

For a moment he thought her eyes flashed with anger, but then she smiled again. "I want you, Nicholas," she murmured, kneeling on the bed and slowly putting questing fingers over his manhood.

He lay back as helpless need thundered through him. His gaze moved over her, drinking in the perfection of her breasts, the slenderness of her waist, and the firmness of her thighs. She was so beautiful, and so very very desirable . . .

She gave a low laugh, and knelt beside him on the bed before bending to kiss the tip of the shaft she'd aroused so effortlessly. He felt the gentle touch of her tongue, then her lips enclosed him. Oh, God, oh, God, this was ecstasy. A sigh shuddered from him and he closed his eyes as she took him fully into her mouth.

His body quivered with excitement. How could she know of such things? Where had she learned? Dizzy pleasure rippled over him, and he had to pull away for fear it would end too soon. He put a hand up to touch her hair. "Oh, Verity, my love," he breathed, sliding his fingers adoringly into the heavy golden curls.

She raised her face to look at him, and for a moment his pleasure checked. She didn't seem like the Verity he'd been with at the mill, there was something different about her. It wasn't just her eyes, it was as if she were a different woman. . . .

She smiled. "Do you want me, Nicholas?"

The doubt faded. "Yes, oh, yes . . ."

She knelt up and then moved astride him, easing herself down onto his erection.

He gasped as her warmth sheathed his whole length. He stretched his hands up to clasp her breasts, and felt her nipples thrust into his palms as she began to move up and down on him. She took her time, and every tiny movement afforded him such exquisite pleasure he thought he would pass out. He wanted the rapture to go on and on, but was approaching climax. He closed his eyes as wonderful feelings raced from his loins and along his veins, then he cried out as the final moment came.

Wild joy scattered over his entire body, and he opened his eyes again. But it wasn't Verity who rode his manhood with such voluptuous abandon, it was the admiral's russet-haired widow! Shock engulfed him as he stared up into her willful hazel eyes, then he pushed her away and leapt up from the bed, but when he turned, she was nowhere to be seen.

The curtains moved, and he ran to wrench them aside and breathe deeply of the cool night air. The window was open, and he gazed out into the moonlit night. The gardens stretched away below, too far down for anyone to have jumped, and the only thing that moved was a hare that leapt away beneath the laburnum walk before disappearing.

He felt sick and shaken. What in the devil had just happened? How could Verity have turned into the Villiers woman? And how could anyone disappear like that?

He went to the table and poured himself a cognac, which he drank in one gulp. There was no doubt he had just made love with someone. He had thought it was Verity, but common sense told him it couldn't possibly have been her. He'd left her asleep, and anyway, she couldn't possibly know the things his mysterious seductress had known. Verity was untouched, he'd stake his life on it; the woman who'd just come to him had been very experienced indeed.

He poured himself another glass. This was the second time he'd believed himself to have received uninvited attentions from the enigmatic Mrs. Villiers, and both times she'd seemed to just disappear afterward. He swirled the cognac. Something strange had been happening lately, and he couldn't begin to understand it all. One thing was certain, he didn't intend to say anything about it, for who would believe him?

* * *

Bitter fury gripped Judith as she hurried into the village. What a fool she'd been not to realize the extent of Verity's interference, but she'd known it clearly enough when she had stepped from behind those curtains and it was the magistrate's niece he saw, not Judith Villiers!

The seal's importance now simply could not be underestimated, but until it had been regained, there was nothing that could be done except keep trying other magic.

Chapter Twelve

At the castle the following morning, Verity insisted on getting up, even though the doctor had instructed her not to, and Anna did all she could to dissuade her. The riding habit, although dried and cleaned after the fall, wasn't suitable for sitting around in, so Anna insisted on providing her with a morning gown from her own wardrobe.

It was a very fashionable confection of flimsy black-spotted white muslin, with a ruff at the throat and flounces around the hem. The full sleeves were gathered prettily at the wrists, and the high waistline was marked by a thin red velvet belt with a gold buckle. Anna's maid dressed her hair up into a Grecian knot trimmed with red ribbons, and all in all Verity had to concede that she looked very well indeed.

When the maid had gone, Verity gazed at her reflection in the cheval glass and wondered what her London wardrobe would be like. She didn't know Amabel Sichester all that well, having only met her a few times, but on those occasions she had thought Lady Sichester's daughter very *à la mode* indeed. Verity couldn't help hoping as much thought had been put into her wardrobe as Amabel would have put into her own!

Verity went to the window to look out over the park toward the village, but then she heard a man's footsteps approaching the door. She turned in dismay, for she didn't doubt it was Nicholas. He knocked, and she sat down quickly on the window seat, arranging her skirts and clasping her hands in her lap in what she hoped was a relaxed manner. Then she answered, "Come in."

As he came in, she saw he wore a plain charcoal coat, a blue brocade waistcoat, and white cord trousers that vanished into gold-tasseled Hessian boots. His unstarched neckcloth sported a gold pin in the shape of the Montacute phoenix, and it shone in the light from the window as he paused to sketch her a bow.

Guilt seized him in those first few seconds. He still didn't understand what had happened to him during the night, and he hadn't said a word to either Oliver or Anna. Maybe he had dreamed the whole damned business after all! All he knew for certain was that for a while he had believed this enchanting young woman had come to him. In the end he'd known she hadn't, but while the illusion concerned Verity, it had been the most exquisitely pleasurable experience of his life. The more he thought about it this morning, the more convinced he was that it had all been a trick of sleep—a manifestation of his deepest sexual yearnings! It was the only rational explanation.

He closed the door. "Good morning, Miss Windsor," he murmured, looking directly into her eyes.

"G-good morning, Lord Montacute."

"I, er, think we should talk, don't you?"

She looked away. "There's nothing to say, my lord."

"How can you say that?"

Her cheeks warmed awkwardly. "Perhaps what I'm saying is that I'd *prefer* to say nothing, sir."

"You wish to forget what happened at the mill?"

Her face was on fire. "Yes."

"That's easier said than done."

"But not impossible." She kept gazing steadfastly out of the window. "I—I'd regard it as a mark of your honor if you were to put the whole incident entirely from your mind."

"And I'd regard it as a mark of my *dishonor* if that were to happen," he replied quietly.

Her eyes flew unwillingly back to him. "Please, Lord Montacute . . ."

He interrupted. "Miss Windsor, I was the one who instigated events at the mill. I took advantage of the situation, and I'm truly sorry, but I can't possibly put it from my mind."

She rose slowly to her feet. "Let's be strictly honest here, sir. You may have instigated things, but I did absolutely nothing to discourage you. I abandoned modesty completely, and if my uncle were to discover how I behaved . . ." She couldn't finish, for her uncle's reaction didn't bear contemplation.

He wanted to touch her, but remained where he was by the door. "Is that really why you regret what happened? Because of your uncle's disapproval?"

"Yes. No. Well, partly. Oh, I don't know . . ." She toyed nervously with her sleeve. "Lord Montacute, we both behaved lamentably, and I really do want to consign all thought of it to the past, so I'd be most grateful if you obliged me by—"

"I can't do that, Miss Windsor," he interposed quietly.

"Why not?"

He plunged into the wonderful green depths of her eyes. "Because I don't want to forget what happened. I enjoyed every moment I spent with you yesterday, and if the same opportunity were to present itself again, I'd repeat every action."

She stared at him.

He held her eyes. "I don't know what it is about you, but since my return I've found myself unable to think of anyone else. I want to hold you close again now, and if you only knew how difficult it is for me to stand here and not even touch you . . ."

"You—you shouldn't say such things, my lord," she whispered.

The yards separating them seemed like miles, and yet he knew he could cross them in a single step. . . . With a huge effort he stayed by the door. "I know I shouldn't say anything, but I'm being truthful. I find you the most bewitching creature I've ever met, and I desire you with all my heart."

"Please—"

"Tell me you don't feel the same. Tell me you felt nothing when I kissed you yesterday, and I'll leave this room without another word."

She looked away. "You should leave anyway, Lord Montacute," she said quietly.

"My name is Nicholas."

"I couldn't possibly address you so familiarly!"

"Not even after yesterday's intimacies?"

She felt her hard-achieved poise beginning to slip inexorably away. "You're not being fair," she whispered.

"I know." He went toward her at last, taking her hand and

raising it to his lips. "You affect me as no other woman ever has, Verity, and I just want you to admit that I affect you as well."

"You—you know you do . . ."

She tried to pull her hand away, but his fingers tightened. Her perfume seemed to fill his nostrils, and her eyes were so compellingly attractive that he found himself bending his lips toward hers.

"No!" she cried, drawing sharply away, but he still held her, and after a moment she stopped struggling. "Please, don't," she pleaded softly.

"I must, Verity," he whispered, his lips brushing hers.

She closed her eyes as her senses betrayed her again. Waves of tantalizing attraction tingled through her, and as he kissed her more lingeringly, her mouth softened helplessly beneath his.

With a moan he slipped an arm around her waist and kissed her more passionately. Her lips parted, and she shivered with pleasure as the tip of his tongue slid slowly against hers.

She abandoned all pretense, suddenly linking her arms around his neck and kissing him with the same fervor as the day before. She molded her body to his and was rewarded by the hard mound at his loins. Forbidden pleasure stole through her veins, delicious pleasure that tightened her breasts and ached between her legs. Her fingers curled yearningly in his hair as she leaned her head back for him to kiss her throat. She felt his fingers brush her nipple through the thin muslin of her borrowed gown, and more pleasure swept unstoppably through her.

His lips were gentle on her neck, and he pressed her more tightly against his erection. Desire throbbed urgently through him. He wanted her, oh, God, how he wanted her. . . .

Suddenly the door opened behind them, and Joshua's outraged voice bellowed a furious exclamation. *"What* is the meaning of this?"

They leapt apart as if stung and turned to see him standing there with Oliver and Anna. Verity could have wept with mortification. It had been bad enough to fall by the wayside in the privacy of the mill, but to have done so all over again in front of others was awful beyond belief.

Nicholas was equally dismayed. The fire of passion died instantly away, and he closed his eyes for a moment. How on earth was he going to explain this away? He managed to find his voice. "Mr. Windsor, I, er . . ."

But Joshua was beside himself with rage. "Don't attempt to excuse your monstrous conduct, sir, for there cannot be any mitigating circumstances!" he advanced into the room, brandishing the ivory-handled cane he always took with him when traveling.

See that he intended to strike Nicholas, Oliver stepped hastily after him and caught his wrist. "That's not the way, sir!"

"Let me at the blackguard!" Joshua cried.

Verity dissolved into tears, hiding her ashamed face in her hands and turning away from everyone.

Joshua strove to wrench free of Oliver's restraining grip. "I will punish him!" he shouted.

Oliver relieved him of the cane. "Words are a wiser weapon, Mr. Windsor," he said firmly.

Joshua took a steadying breath and at last mastered himself sufficiently to look more rationally at Nicholas. "Well, sirrah? What do you have to say?"

"I realize my actions are less than acceptable, sir, but—"

"Less than acceptable? They're damned well contemptible!" Joshua cried.

"Your anger is justified, sir."

"You're a scurvy cur, Lord Montacute! A base scoundrel without any morals or principles!"

Oliver was appalled. "I say, sir, can't we keep the insults to a more becoming minimum?" he suggested tentatively.

But Joshua wasn't in the mood to be reasonable. He held Nicholas's eyes. "You and I both know why your present conduct is particularly despicable, sir. I have as low an opinion of you as it is possible to have, and if you touch my niece again, so help me I'll call you out!"

Verity turned with a horrified cry. "Uncle Joshua!"

"Silence, miss!"

"But—"

"Enough!" he shouted.

Tears shimmered on her lashes, and she fell silent. She had never seen him like this before. He was quite beside himself with passion, and his personal hatred for Nicholas was so evident that it was almost written on his face.

Oliver ventured to pour oil on the troubled waters. "Perhaps we gentlemen should adjourn to the solar, and leave Anna to comfort Miss Windsor?" he suggested, glancing at his wife.

But Joshua was having none of it. "My niece isn't going to remain beneath this iniquitous roof a moment longer! Come, Verity!"

"But, Uncle, I—"

"Come!"

She flinched and without another word gathered her skirts to hurry from the room. She halted in confusion in the passage to look back at Anna. "Your gown . . ."

"Send it to me. I'll have your things sent to the village," Anna said gently, putting a sympathetic hand on her arm.

Joshua glowered at Nicholas a moment longer. "You, sirrah, are a stain on the rank of nobleman. It seems there is no depth to which you will not stoop in the pursuit of your selfish pleasures, but you will not embroil my innocent niece in your depravities, d'you hear?"

Nicholas didn't trust himself to reply. Joshua was justified in his anger, and the moment was hardly appropriate to try sweet reason. Better to leave tempers to cool, his own included.

Joshua stomped from the room, snatching his cane from Oliver as he passed and then ushering Verity ignominiously along the passage and down the staircase. Oliver hurried after them, feeling that someone should observe what was left of the usual courtesies.

Verity had never felt more humiliated and ashamed. Her cheeks were aflame, and more tears began to wend their way from her eyes. This was the most dreadful moment of her whole life, and she would never live it down. Never. Keeping her head bowed, she hurried ahead of her uncle to the courtyard, where his chaise was waiting. She climbed inside without waiting for one of Nicholas's footmen to assist her, and then she lowered the blind and turned her face away as Oliver helped Joshua in behind her.

A second later the whip cracked, and the chaise drove smartly out of the courtyard, across the lowered drawbridge, and then through the park toward the lodge and phoenix-topped gates.

Anna faced Nicholas in Verity's bedroom. "Why did you do it, Nicholas?"

"Because I want her."

"Want?"

"Desire, need, long for! How else can I say it?"

She raised an eyebrow. "I notice the word 'love' doesn't figure," she murmured.

He fell silent.

"Nicholas, Verity Windsor isn't a common whore, she's a properly brought-up young lady who's about to have her first London Season! You can't treat her like a strumpet!"

"I didn't!"

"From where I was standing that's *exactly* what you were doing," Anna replied sharply. "What on earth possessed you? You *knew* her uncle was going to be brought here when he returned from Ludlow!"

"Joshua Windsor was the last person on my mind."

"That was obvious enough."

"Anna, you don't understand . . ."

"You're right, I certainly don't." She searched his face. "There's a great deal I haven't understood about you recently, Nicholas."

He stiffened a little. "If you're about to say what I think you're about to say, I'd rather you saved your breath. You don't know the half of it, and I don't intend to enlighten you, so the whole thing's better left."

"Well, you would say that, wouldn't you? I mean, heaven forfend that, romantically or morally, Nicholas Montacute might be in the wrong!"

"As I said, you don't know the half of it."

"Nor will I ever, unless you elucidate."

He shook his head. "No, Anna."

"Then I trust you'll understand if I think the worst of you."

"That's up to you."

"And to Oliver," she answered, "for he thinks the worst as well."

"I know."

"You can be very aggravating at times, Nicholas."

The ghost of a smile touched his lips. "It's part of my irresistible charm," he murmured.

"That's not how I'd put it," she said tartly. "And don't be facetious, for under the circumstances it's not in the least becoming or amusing!"

"I'm not the scoundrel I've been branded, Anna."

"No? Forgive me if I find that hard to believe. After all, I now have the evidence of my own eyes, do I not?"

He gave another wry smile. "You'd be ill-advised to jump to conclusions about anything, Anna."

"I'd like to think that, truly I would, but right now the scales of justice seem to prove your guilt." Anna drew a long breath and adjusted the lace at the cuff of her blue lawn gown. "You were manifestly in the wrong before, Nicholas, and where Verity Windsor is concerned, history does seem to be repeating itself. Please take my advice and leave her alone."

"I don't know whether I can," he replied softly.

Joshua's face was like thunder as the chaise drove smartly along the road toward the village. His gloved hands were clasped tightly over the handle of his cane, and he stared straight ahead.

His heavy silence did nothing to lighten Verity's misery. She knew she had let him down, indeed she had let herself down by not only allowing Nicholas to make such advances a second time, but by enjoying them a second time too!

At last Joshua broke the silence. "How could you fail me like this, Verity?"

She bit her lip and blinked as even more tears stung her eyes. She had nothing to say in defense, for nothing could excuse her weakness.

"If I hadn't arrived when I did, you'd have been completely ruined! You do realize that, don't you?"

She couldn't speak.

"Montacute is an unprincipled monster, and it grieves me to think he so nearly added you to his ignoble list of conquests."

She looked intently at him. "What really lies between you and him, Uncle?"

"Nothing I'm at liberty to say."

"Uncle—"

"I don't intend to speak of it, Verity, nor do I intend to allow you to stay within his reach. We're going to leave for London without further delay."

"Leave? But—"

"My mind is made up. By this time tomorrow we'll be on our way."

She was shocked. "By this time tomorrow? But we haven't even begun to pack!"

"Half the luggage will suffice, the servants can send everything else on. And anyway, your wardrobe awaits you at Dover Street, does it not?" He said this last on a rather odd note, then looked out of the window as the chaise splashed across the ford.

Chapter Thirteen

Verity was as ready as she ever would be to set out on the journey. She wore a shell pink lawn gown and a matching frilled pelisse, and her hair was tucked up beneath a leghorn bonnet, with a single ringlet falling down past the nape of her neck. Her face was pale and drawn, and her eyes tearstained, a fact that even the skillful application of her Chinese cosmetic papers couldn't hide.

She couldn't bring herself to go downstairs until the last moment, and so she sat on the edge of her bed to wait. She had forgotten all about the seal and certainly didn't notice that it was gone from the windowsill. All she could think about was the awful events of the day before. How she wished none of it had happened, but it was too late now.

There was a tap at the door, and Martha peeped sadly in. "Mr. Windsor wishes you to come down now, Miss Verity."

As Verity rose resignedly to her feet, the nurse came closer and held something out to her. "Take this with you, Miss Verity."

Verity stared, for it was the snakestone. "Oh, I couldn't possibly—" she began.

"Take it," Martha interrupted. "And be sure to keep it with you at all times, for it will protect you from all evil."

Reluctantly Verity put it around her neck, where its beautifully patterned stone went very well with her shell pink clothes.

"Promise me you'll never set it aside, Miss Verity," Martha pressed anxiously.

"I promise." Verity searched her eyes. "But what of you? You were wearing it because you felt in danger."

"I've taken some communion wafers from the church," the nurse replied reassuringly. She knew that holy wafers weren't as powerful as the snakestone, but she was more worried for Verity than for herself. Anyone who directly interfered with Judith's spells, whether innocently or not, was bound to be in considerable danger. Verity knew nothing about shielding herself from witches, and Martha would feel a great deal better knowing she had the very best protection possible.

"Are you absolutely certain you wish me to have it?" Verity asked again.

"Beyond all doubt." Martha looked intently at her. "Please tell me what happened yesterday, my dear," she urged gently, for the complete silence on the matter made her feel very anxious.

Verity shook her head, color flooding instantly into her cheeks. "I—I'd rather not, Martha."

The nurse was concerned, but could say no more. She brushed the awkward silence over. "Your riding habit has been sent from the castle. I put it in one of the trunks. It's been very neatly repaired after your fall."

"Thank you." Mentioning the fall jogged Verity's memory. "Martha, I saw a corpse candle yesterday when I fell from my horse."

Martha's eyes swung swiftly to hers. "A corpse candle? Are you sure?"

"Well, I've never seen one before, but I can't think what else it could be." Verity described the little ball of orange fire. "I—I thought it had come for me," she finished with a rueful smile.

"No one sees their own corpse light, my dear," Martha said quickly and then glanced toward the window. "So, the churchyard watcher's cart will soon be heard in the village again. It came for the admiral, now *he* will come for someone else."

Joshua's impatient voice echoed up through the house. "Verity!"

"Coming, Uncle!" She hugged the nurse and then hurried from the room.

Judith was watching Windsor House from beneath the willows on the green. A little earlier she had noticed that the telltale emerald glint had vanished from Verity's window, and she had been using her witch's powers to try to ascertain where the seal had gone when Joshua's traveling carriage was brought around to the gate. As the first trunk was carried out from the house, she had been startled to realize that the rumors her servants had heard that morning were actually true, the magistrate and his niece really were leaving suddenly for London.

Her first fear was that for some reason they were taking the seal with them, but as she concentrated on the luggage that was loaded on the carriage, she detected nothing. Gradually she realized the seal was no longer anywhere near the house, although it *was* somewhere in the village. Where, though? And who had taken it away? Her eyes flickered then, for it was easy enough to guess who was responsible, she thought, glancing up at Martha, who now appeared at Verity's window.

Judith watched as the last hastily packed trunk was carried out. A small crowd of village children had gathered by the gate, but then the vicar rode up on his cob and ordered them all back before reining in to talk to the coachman. The witch's gaze was pensive. There clearly hadn't been any travel preparations in hand yesterday when she had tried to persuade that fool of a maid to hand over the seal, but now, quite suddenly, the departure was imminent. Why? She smiled. What did it matter why? Verity Windsor was about to go far away to London, leaving the seal—and Nicholas Montacute—in Wychavon.

Joshua and Verity emerged from the house, and Judith noticed how very pale and tense the latter appeared. Something was definitely up. Oh, to know what it was. As Joshua paused to speak to the vicar, Verity turned to wave good-bye to Martha, and the witch realized she was wearing the snakestone. So the old woman thought her mistress would need protection in London, did she? Foolish Martha, for Verity was no longer of any interest at all now that she was conveniently leaving Wychavon. But Martha herself was a different matter. By pitting herself against someone of infinitely greater power and knowledge than herself, the interfering old biddy had become very irritating indeed.

Joshua helped his niece into the carriage, and the vicar's cob danced nervously around, almost unseating him as the children raced noisily after the departing vehicle. At that moment, from the direction of the castle there came the distant report of shooting practice.

Judith smiled a little as she emerged from beneath the willows. It was time to remind his lordship of her existence.

Nicholas and Oliver were firing pistols at a target in the park and had been at their sport for some time when at last Oliver flung himself wearily on the grass to rest a while. They had brought a wicker basket of food and drink with them, and he selected a bottle of wine, which he opened to pour into two glasses.

Nicholas glanced at him. "Isn't it a little early for wine?"

"It's never too early for wine."

Nicholas smiled and took aim at the target, squeezing the trigger slowly. The pistol fired, and the distant jolt of the target told him he'd scored a bull's-eye.

Oliver surveyed him. "What do you intend to do about the delightful Miss Windsor?" he asked suddenly.

Nicholas turned. "I don't know."

"Damn it, Nick, you compromised her completely yesterday!"

"I'm well aware of that, but you saw her uncle. He'd as soon put a bullet in my brain as allow me near his niece again."

"But do you *want* to be near her again, that's the question?"

Nicholas smiled a little. "Oh, yes, there's no doubt of that," he murmured.

"Well, I trust you mean to do it in a civilized manner this time, because Anna's in a decided miff with you for treating a young lady with such disregard for the rules."

Nicholas joined him on the grass. "Anna's in a miff with me for more than just Miss Windsor," he said with a sigh.

"And rightly so," Oliver reminded him. "Last summer, you—"

Nicholas sat forward abruptly. "God damn it, Oliver, why must I be condemned for events last year? I have to say it grieves me just a little that you and Anna are always so quick to pass sentence on me. Why must I be the villain of the piece?"

"Well, whatever the truth of last year, yesterday's little episode didn't exactly bestow a halo upon your noble brow, did it?" Oliver pointed out coolly.

"Yesterday was different."

"Oh?"

"Yes, because yesterday I *was* guilty," Nicholas picked up his glass and drank a little.

Oliver's brows drew together then, and he nodded toward a copper beech about a hundred yards away. "Who's that?" he asked.

Nicholas looked where he indicated and saw a woman in black mounted on a gray horse. In spite of her veiled hat, he recognized the admiral's widow straight away.

Oliver glanced at him. "Well?"

"She, er, she's the widow of old Admiral Villiers, who died rather inappropriately on St. Valentine's Day."

"Old Admiral Villiers? I have to say his relict doesn't look elderly." Oliver studied the rider's curvaceous, fashionably clad figure.

"She isn't." Briefly Nicholas told him the strange tale of the admiral's bride.

Oliver's eyes widened. "Found naked in a garden during a thunderstorm on Halloween?" he repeated in disbelief.

Nicholas nodded. "Her memory as lost as her clothing," he murmured, his glance returning to the figure beneath the tree.

"My, my, Wychavon *is* an interesting backwater," Oliver declared.

"Oh, it's that all right," Nicholas said, thinking of his own recent experiences.

"So why does she have the freedom of the castle park?" Oliver asked then.

"She doesn't."

"Then isn't she presuming somewhat?"

"I, er, suppose she is."

Oliver glanced at him, thinking his manner a little odd. "First Miss Windsor, now a lady in black. *You* are a dark horse, and no mistake."

Nicholas frowned. "Damn it, I've never even been introduced to Mrs. Villiers, let alone . . ." He didn't finish.

"Then take my advice and get to know her, for a widow is a far safer bet than the Miss Windsors of this world. One can do as one wishes with a widow, if you follow my meaning."

Nicholas got up. "I don't want to know her," he said honestly, for there was something about the woman that made him shudder. He could feel her eyes upon him behind her veil, and he knew she was willing him to go over and speak. Suddenly something snapped in him. This woman had an uncanny knack of appearing and disappearing, and he had had enough of it. Thrusting his glass into Oliver's hand, he strode toward the tree.

Judith breathed out with relief as she saw him approaching at last. She had been exerting the full force of her will upon him and had begun to think it was to no avail. The effort made her tremble slightly, although she hid it as he reached her horse and seized the bridle.

"Madam, I fear you are trespassing," he said.

"I know."

"Then you will not mind if I request you to leave," he said, still uncomfortably conscious of her shining eyes behind the veil. Everything about her disturbed him in an unpleasant way, and he wanted her to go away.

"I'm sure you don't really wish me to go," she said softly, raising the veil to reveal her face.

Her beauty left him cold. "Yes, madam, I do."

Anger flickered through her as she became increasingly aware of his indifference, if not to say antagonism. "But will you wish it still if I come to you again tonight?" she asked.

Again tonight? The words shook him, for they disproved his theory about having dreamt events hitherto. He released the bridle as if it scorched him. "Who *are* you?" he breathed as a primitive unease suddenly welled sickeningly through him.

She smiled. "I'm whatever you wish, my lord," she whispered, leaning down to touch his cheek.

He moved sharply back out of reach. "I don't want you anywhere near me! Please go!"

Somehow she managed to maintain a tender smile, as if nothing he had said or done had offended in any way. "You will not wish to dismiss me," she promised softly. Then, before he could reply she turned her horse and rode swiftly away.

He gazed after her and was unable to suppress a shiver.

Chapter Fourteen

Joshua and Verity broke their journey at the Royal Oak Hotel in Cheltenham. Her uncle had said very little on the road or at dinner, and his silence made her feel so guilty she was glad to retire to her room.

But trying to sleep didn't make things any easier, for as she lay there in the darkness, her thoughts were all of Nicholas. Whenever she closed her eyes, she was with him again, either at the mill or in the room at the castle. She could feel his arms around her, and his lips on hers. She could smell the southernwood on his clothes and taste his kisses.

She tossed and turned. If only she weren't so susceptible to him now. It had been so much easier when he had virtually ignored her, for then she'd been at liberty to adore him from a distance. Now it was very different, and her whole existence was in confusion. Where he was concerned, suddenly she seemed incapable of conducting herself with propriety, giving in to sexual temptation that only just stopped short of actual surrender! She'd never been kissed before, let alone kissed the way he had kissed her! And she had certainly never experienced the astonishing feelings that resulted from pressing her body to his.

Feeling hot and bothered, she sat up in bed and pushed her tangled hair back from her flushed face. The room was lit by a solitary candle, and the glow curved gently over the cream-papered walls. She drew her knees up and clasped her arms around them. That she was hopelessly and irretrievably in love was a fact she could no longer ignore, nor was the fact that she didn't really know what he thought or felt.

All she could be certain of was that he was attracted to her, but did he feel anything more than physical desire? Was his heart engaged, as hers was? He hadn't said anything when Uncle Joshua caught them virtually in flagrante delicto. Was that because the whole thing meant nothing to him? Or was it that he didn't feel the moment was right? There were so many questions spinning around in her head, all of them unanswered.

Tears stung her eyes as she rested her forehand against her knees. "Oh, Nicholas, I love you so much," she whispered, as a nearby church clock struck midnight.

The midnight chimes of the church clock in Wychavon carried on still air to the grove, where Judith danced around the Lady. Green light shone on her body, and smoke curled from the censer as dried mud from Nicholas's footprint burned among the herbs. Hecate's demonic face had appeared on the stone, the river was still, the spectral hounds howled, and the moon hung low above the trees, but tonight there was a watcher among the trees at the edge of the grove.

Martha had been leaving Sadie's cottage when she saw the witch slipping out of the village, and so she had followed. Keeping out of sight, she saw Judith emerge naked from the mill with the candles, wand, and censer. Now she watched as the witch performed her sinful rituals.

The nurse fingered the holy wafers in her pocket as she guessed to whom the demonic face on the stone belonged, for everyone knew that Hecate was the goddess of witchcraft, and that a stone circle dedicated to her had once stood here in the grove. At these thoughts, Martha suddenly realized who Judith might really be. Meg Ashton had been Hecate's handmaiden and had worshipped the goddess in this place, practicing diabolic black arts until retribution finally overtook her. Now Judith Villiers served Hecate here too. The old woman gazed fearfully at the face on the Lady. Hecate was believed to have imprisoned her loyal servant in the stone two hundred years ago, but had that servant been freed last Halloween? And if so, what was her purpose?

The nurse shrank back among the bushes at the edge of the grove as the hellhounds suddenly fell silent, and the green light increased to an unearthly glow. Judith disappeared, and all Martha saw was a brown hare leaping away in the direction of the castle. Hecate's face remained on the Lady, and the candles swayed gently, for there was no breeze, but of the witch herself there was no sign at all.

Martha's heart thundered as she stared toward the castle. Did all this have something to do with Nicholas Montacute, whose seal was clearly of such consequence? Back in Tudor times, Meg Ashton had tried to wreak revenge upon the Lord Montacute who had offended both her and her grim mistress, and she had succeeded in killing his pregnant wife before being caught and sent to the stake. That was all the nurse knew of the story. She wished she possessed more details, but only the bare outline had been handed down over the centuries.

The wisewoman's gaze returned to the center of the grove. Judith *had* to be Meg Ashton returned, for only a witch as powerful as Meg could transform herself into a hare. A cold finger traced down the nurse's spine. There was great evil abroad again in Wychavon, and no one in the village was of sufficient knowledge to fight it. Her own powers were inadequate for confronting Hecate and her kind.

Suddenly a new sound carried on the still air from the direction of the millpool. It wasn't the gurgling of flowing water, but a heaving and splashing as if something large were hauling itself up onto the bank. Then there was the creak of wheels, and the slow clip-clop of hooves, as well as the occasional flick of a whip, but nothing was visible.

But Martha knew what was there. It was the churchyard watcher, and as she looked she saw the faint marks left by cart wheels trundling relentlessly across the grass toward the track that led up to the road. The Lady and the witch's circle lay directly in the path of the invisible cart, but the watcher served a higher power than Hecate, and had no cause to show respect.

The wisewoman pressed back in the tree. Her mouth had run dry and her heart was now pounding so fast she couldn't count the beats. She knew old Admiral Villiers was at the reins, for this was where he'd gone to his death. Now he was preparing to collect the next soul. Whose was it? She prayed it wouldn't be Davey's.

The ghostly cart entered the witch's circle, passing within inches of the Lady, and knocking the black candles and censer aside. Hecate shrieked with fury and vanished from the granite, and the hellhounds fled yelping into the night. The watcher drove on without check, and the sound of his cart gradually diminished as it made its way resolutely up the track toward the corner where Verity had seen the corpse candle.

Martha looked back into the grove and with a start saw Judith lying senseless in the remains of the circle. Her red-gold hair was spread in tangled profusion over the grass, and her eyes were closed. Thin traces of smoke still rose from the scattered candles and the censer, and gradually the deathly silence was broken by the sound of the river beginning to flow again.

As the water filled the race, making the ancient mill wheel creak, Martha emerged cautiously from the bushes and went toward the witch. A cursory glance told her Judith wasn't dead, merely unconscious. The nurse gazed down at her, and whispered, "Tonight you turned into a hare, and I, Martha Cansford, saw it with my own eyes. I know you for a witch."

Taking some communion wafer from her pocket, the old woman crouched down to press it to Judith's arm. There was a hissing sound, and a red mark appeared as the witch's flesh burned.

Martha straightened again, and hurried fearfully away. She was out of her depth and didn't know what to do. Clutching her shawl around her, she made her way up the track in the wake of the watcher's cart. Then she halted with a startled gasp, for the corpse candle Verity had seen now hovered in front of her as well.

The nurse's eyes filled with tears as she stared at its flickering orange flames. "Have you come for Davey?" she whispered, but the question remained unanswered as the ball of fire disappeared as suddenly as it had come.

Then a vixen shrieked somewhere in the woods, and the uncanny sound echoed over the whole valley.

At the castle, Nicholas hadn't felt Judith's brief touch before the churchyard watcher shattered her magic, and she had been flung back into the grove. But the scream of the vixen disturbed him, and he sat up with a start.

His first thought was of Judith, and he glanced uneasily around the room, but soon sensed no one was there. Relieved, he flung the bedclothes aside and went to the window, which he

opened to let the cool night air into the room. He shivered a little, for he had nothing on, but the chill felt pleasant as he gazed
toward Wychavon church in the distance. He knew Verity
wasn't in the village, but had gone to London, for news like that
traveled as quickly as old Joshua himself! The magistrate's un-
seemly haste had caused talk, and everyone was hazarding a
guess as to why he'd whisked his niece away so suddenly.

Nicholas ran a hand through his dark hair. He wished he
could put Verity Windsor from his mind, but he couldn't. She
seemed to be all around him still. Judith Villiers might be here
and very available, but he felt nothing for her—except perhaps
distaste. For Verity, however, he felt the very opposite. He
wanted her so much it was a pain that sounded through him like
a bell. But she'd gone to London for the entire Season, and God
alone knew when she'd return. . . .

He turned from the window, and his glance fell upon the little table, and the portable escritoire with its London correspon-
dence. A slow smile came to his lips. There was nothing to keep
him here in Wychavon, he could return to London if he chose.
And choose he did. Old Joshua might think he'd successfully
plucked his niece from the clutches of a dastardly scoundrel,
but he hadn't, for the scoundrel intended to give chase!

Judith regained consciousness in the grove. Her head was
swimming unpleasantly, and as she sat up she retched. She saw
the candles lying on the grass and the crushed censer, and then
the wheelmarks in the grass. Her eyes widened, and she got up
slowly, putting out a hand to the Lady to steady herself.

What had happened here? Her eyes followed the marks toward the track in one direction, and then to the edge of the
millpool in the other. A sense of deep horror spread through her,
for she knew of only one vehicle that could come out of the
depths like that—the churchyard watcher. The admiral! Fear
settled over her as she thought of the husband she'd murdered
through her dark powers, for suddenly he didn't seem so safely
and finally dispatched. She began to tremble and put her arms
around herself, wincing as she touched the burn on her arm.
She stared at the red mark, which was clearly visible in the thin
light of the moon. How had she been burned? Had she fallen on
one of the candles? Her disquiet increased, and quickly she

gathered her things together and hastened into the mill, where she hid them under the staircase. Then she flung her cloak around her shoulders and ran out of the grove.

The corpse candle didn't appear as she reached the road, but she detected a strange atmosphere that made her halt warily. She glanced all around, shivering a little as a slight breeze stirred through the trees. The vixen screamed again, and there was a rustling in the undergrowth, but that was all. After a moment she hurried on, and the flowers in the verge swayed in the draft from her billowing cloak.

But as she passed the lychgate, she glanced toward the church and didn't see the little pothole in the road. Her foot caught, her ankle twisted violently, and with a gasp of pain she stumbled to her knees. Tears sprang to her eyes, and her fingers trembled as she examined the ankle. It throbbed agonizingly, and she had to close her eyes.

Then she glanced uneasily around. The vicarage was to one side of her, and Sadie Cutler's cottage a little further along on the opposite side, yet she didn't dare call out for help. Somehow she had to get back to the house without anyone knowing she'd been out at such an hour, for beneath the cloak she wore nothing except Hecate's garter!

Wincing as fresh waves of pain lanced through her, she managed to drag herself to the verge, where a sycamore tree that had been felled the year before had thrown up sturdy new growth from the stump. Almost fainting from the pangs from her ankle, she managed to break off one of the shoots to use as a walking stick. Then she began to make her painful way toward the ford.

It took her some time to cross, and by the time she reached the manor house gate she was exhausted, but at last she reached sanctuary. Once inside she tore off the red garter and hid it in a carved chest in the hall, then she commenced the final agonizing yards upstairs to her room.

Somehow she managed to hang her cloak in the wardrobe and put on a nightgown, then she eased herself weakly onto the bed and lay there in the darkness. Her ankle was throbbing and swollen, and she knew that at the very least she'd given it a savage wrench. Tears of frustration pricked her eyes, for this would halt her plans for the time being.

She couldn't do anything if she couldn't reach the grove. If she had the seal, it would be different, for then she'd be empowered to do a great deal wherever she was. But she didn't have it, and so she was temporarily reduced to virtual impotency. She clenched her fists and beat them furiously on the bed coverlet.

It was at breakfast the next morning that Nicholas announced his decision to return to London. Anna immediately put her cup down with a clatter, the lappets of her lace day bonnet quivering as she eyed him across the table.

"You intend to leave again *immediately*?" she repeated.

"Yes."

Oliver gave a sigh and sat back. "This is becoming rather wearisome, you know, Nick," he murmured.

Nicholas nodded. "Yes, I do know, and I'm sorry, but—"

Anna got up with an irritated rustle of rose taffeta. "There shouldn't be any buts, Nicholas!" she said sharply. "It doesn't take a great intellect to arrive at your reason for returning. It's Miss Windsor, isn't it?"

He avoided her eyes. "Anna, this really isn't any—"

"Of my business?" she interrupted. "I'm afraid it is, sir, when you invited us here to enjoy your company!"

"I'm sorry, Anna, but it's important to me."

She came around the table. "Honorably important? Or lasciviously important?" she demanded.

Oliver's lips parted. "I say, Anna, steady on . . ."

She ignored him, her bright gaze still upon Nicholas. "Well, sir?"

He met her eyes. "I fail to see why I should respond to such a question, Anna," he said quietly.

"Then I will draw my own conclusions. Oh, Nicholas, I'm gravely disappointed in you. I've always believed you to be a proper gentleman, but everything you do these days points to the opposite being the case."

"You're being grossly unfair to me, Anna."

"Prove it."

Nicholas looked up quizzically. "Prove it? How?"

"By staying here."

He got up slowly. "Why should I do that?"

"Because you should have other priorities than your breeches," she said frankly.

Oliver stared at her. "Anna!"

"It's true! Everything he's done recently has been ruled by his base male urges, and I think it's intolerable. If he wishes to retain any of my respect, he must behave more temperately."

Oliver raised an eyebrow and then looked at Nicholas. "What do you say to that, Nick?" he asked lightly.

Nicholas glanced at him. "I know what I'd *like* to say, but contrary to popular belief, I *am* a gentleman." He turned to Anna. "How long do you want me to stay here?"

"A month at the very least," she replied flatly. "Anything less and I will regale Miss Windsor with all manner of tales about you."

"You're a hard woman, Anna Henderson."

A light passed through her eyes. "Needs must, sir."

The ghost of a smile played upon his lips. "Very well, a month it is. I swear upon my honor—disputed as it is—that I will remain here at Wychavon until some time in June."

She raised her chin. "I'm going to hold you to that, Nicholas Montacute, for Miss Windsor is far too good to be pursued for shabby reasons. I'll have far more respect for your interest in her if you show a little restraint." With that she turned on her heel and left the room.

Nicholas glanced at Oliver, who shrugged. "Don't look to me for sympathy, Nick, old man, for I happen to agree with her," he declared, reaching forward to help himself to another warm bread roll.

But events were to conspire to keep Nicholas in Wychavon for longer than even Anna demanded. A combination of problems on the estate, and magisterial matters in Ludlow and Shrewsbury were to keep him occupied until the middle of July.

It would be July fifteenth, St. Swithin's Day, before he would at last set off for London.

Chapter Fifteen

The tradition of forty days of rain if the weather was bad on St. Swithin's Day seemed unlikely to be tested, for that day dawned as bright, clear, and endlessly sunny as most of the summer had been so far.

At the manor house, Judith took her usual lonely breakfast in the room facing over the garden and summerhouse where she'd been found during the Halloween storm. It was the first morning she'd been able to move around without the use of a walking stick, for she hadn't just twisted her ankle when she fell by the lychgate, she had broken it quite badly.

Now, after two months of hobbling, she was at last beginning to feel fit again. Not that her temper had improved. Being incapacitated just when her plans seemed likely to come to fruition, had put her in a constantly vile mood. Most of her maids had been reduced to tears, and the butler had actually walked out rather than endure any more of his disagreeable mistress.

Judith was indifferent to the wretchedness she caused her servants, for she was entirely without conscience whatever she did, and as the St. Swithin's Day sun beamed in through the window, her thoughts were of Nicholas and how she intended to resume her plan by going to the grove again that very night. There was something else she had to do at the grove. She still had no idea where the seal had gone, but could nevertheless feel its presence somewhere in the village, and she intended to call Hecate's wrath down upon Martha Cansford, who, she was convinced, was responsible for hiding it. If the old woman were to be sufficiently frightened, she would confess the seal's whereabouts.

Judith's fingers drummed on the white tablecloth as she brooded upon Verity's nurse, but then the drumming ceased as something made her glance up at the portrait above the mantelshelf. It was a full-length likeness of the admiral in dress uniform, looking splendid against a Caribbean background. Quite suddenly it seemed to the witch that his painted eyes were gazing bleakly down at her. A shiver ran over her as she remembered the spectral wheel marks running across the grove from the millpool, and for a moment it seemed she could hear the ghastly rattle of the watcher's cart. The sound was so real that she gave a frightened start as a maid gave a tap at the door.

"Madam?"

Judith's eyes flashed angrily. "What is it?" she demanded.

The maid came respectfully and timidly in. "Lord Montacute has called, madam," she explained.

Judith stared at her. "Lord Montacute?" she repeated.

"Yes, madam. He wishes to speak urgently with you."

An anticipatory smile crept to Judith's lips. Now why would he call upon her? She sat back in her chair. "Please show him in."

"Madam." The maid bobbed a curtsy, and hurried away again.

Footsteps sounded in the passage, then Nicholas entered the room and faced her. He wore a dove gray coat, amethyst waistcoat, white trousers, and Hessian boots, and his dark hair was slightly ruffled.

She smiled. "Good morning, Lord Montacute."

"Madam."

"To what do I owe this honor?"

"No honor, madam, for this is not a social call."

"Oh?" She searched his face.

"I'll come straight to the point. I wish to buy this house from you, and I'm prepared to pay well over the odds in order to do so."

She was taken aback. "But why do you wish to do that, my lord?"

"Because I want you out of Wychavon," he said quietly.

Her lips parted, and anger crept into her gaze. "How very ungallant, to be sure," she murmured.

"Ungallant, but necessary. I don't profess to know what your purpose is, neither do I care, but I *do* care that in the recent past you've made intimate and unwarranted intrusions into my privacy. In order to prevent further such occurrences, I've consulted a lawyer in Shrewsbury, and it is his advice that I make this offer, which, under the circumstances, I think more than generous."

Her eyes were cold. "It would seem you have forgotten how we made love at your castle, my lord," she murmured.

"Oh, no, madam. I haven't forgotten anything. I don't know what really happened that night, nor indeed do I understand the other occasion in the gardens, but I certainly know that I didn't want either even to occur."

She got up and came around the table. "Did you push me away?"

He didn't reply.

She smiled. "You made me yours in every way, my lord, and you cannot deny it. Or are you suggesting I forced you against your will?"

"I'm suggesting that there is something very strange about you, Mrs. Villiers, something that repels me completely. You have a way of appearing and disappearing, and of insinuating yourself on my property without permission. I'm returning to London now, but—"

Alarm rushed into her, and she interrupted him. "You're returning to London?"

"Yes. My carriage is at the door."

"Why are you going?"

Her voice had risen a little, and he drew back warily. "My reasons have nothing to do with you, madam."

"They have *everything* to do with me!" she cried, caught so completely by surprise and dismay that she was no longer rational.

He turned to go. "Please consider my offer, and then contact my agent when you decide," he said.

She rushed to place herself between him and the door. "Is this how the Montacutes treat defenseless widows? Using them and then casting them aside?" The words were hurried and uttered through clenched teeth as she tried to regain mastery of herself.

"With all due respect, Mrs. Villiers, defenseless is the last word I'd use to describe you."

"You can't leave!" she cried.

"Please step aside."

"No."

He caught her arm and drew her away from the door, then he walked past, snatching up his hat and gloves from the hall table before striding out into the sunshine.

Stumbling a little because her ankle was still weak, Judith ran after him. "You *have* to stay!" she cried.

A maid was in the hall, and she turned in astonishment at the sight of her mistress pursuing Lord Montacute. Judith tried to catch his arm, but he shook himself free and kept walking away.

Anna and Oliver's traveling carriage drove past at that moment, and they saw everything. Anna glanced at her husband. "What do you make of *that*?" she murmured curiously.

He cleared his throat. "I, er, don't know."

She eyed him. "Oh, yes, you do. I can tell by the tone of your voice. Who is the redheaded beauty?"

"Well, I can't be certain, but from her widow's weeds I'd hazard a guess she's a certain Mrs. Villiers." He told her what had happened when he and Nicholas had been at target practice.

Anna looked crossly at him. "Oliver Henderson, you've known this since the beginning of May and yet haven't said a single word to me? How *could* you!"

"I didn't think it was of any significance," he muttered, shifting uncomfortably on his seat.

"Not of any significance? Oh, *Oliver*!" She glared at him. "After all I said to him that morning he announced his intention to return to London, the least you could have done was confide in me afterward. Instead you let more than two months pass by, without so much as a syllable passing your lips."

"Oh, come on, Anna, it's hardly a heinous crime to forget what's probably a worthless titbit."

"Worthless? I've just seen Mrs. Villiers, don't forget," she said dryly, thinking of the beautiful red-haired woman who had pursued Nicholas from the manor house. "The lady appeared to me to be just the sort that a virile fellow like Nicholas Montacute would find to his taste."

"Anna, you're letting your tongue run away with you. I've

seen Nick speak to her on one occasion, that's all, and I promise you he didn't seem particularly pleased to see her."

"He wasn't particularly pleased when I challenged him to stay on in Wychavon, but he agreed to my request. Now I can see why!" Anna declared. "For the past two months, far from pining after Miss Windsor, he's been consoling himself with this Mrs. Villiers!"

Oliver ran his hand through his hair. "You're impossible," he murmured.

"Maybe, but I'm also right, am I not? Nicholas has been conducting a liaison with the admiral's widow?"

"I—I don't know, and that's the truth," Oliver admitted then, for he really had no idea what had been going on.

Anna smoothed the folds of her sage green silk pelisse, then retied the ribbons of her bonnet. "His conduct has really become quite intolerable, and I think I should call on Miss Windsor as soon as possible, to warn her about him."

"Do so, by all means, but don't be surprised if her uncle sends out your cards ripped in half!" Oliver replied.

"If he does, he does, but I have to try. I don't want Miss Windsor's ruin to be on my conscience, which it would be if I stood by and said nothing about this."

He held her gaze. "And what else will you feel obliged to tell her about Nick at the same time?"

"I—I don't know."

"Well, perhaps I should tell you that Nicholas claims to be innocent of the charge, so maybe you'll remember that it you feel the urge to blacken his name still further with Miss Windsor."

Anna flushed a little. "Well, Nicholas *would* claim innocence, wouldn't he?"

"But what if he is?"

"Oh, very well, I won't say anything about that other business, but I certainly will regale her about the admiral's widow."

"Can't you just leave well alone entirely, Anna?"

"It wouldn't be right."

Oliver gazed wearily out as the last cottages of Wychavon disappeared behind. Right now he wished they had never left London in the first place.

* * *

Judith stood in the dining room as Nicholas's carriage pulled swiftly away. She was in the grip of a fury so violent she was barely in control, and as her maid came timorously in to see if she was all right, the witch turned suddenly. "Leave me!" she screamed, her eyes wild with rage.

Terrified, the maid gathered her skirts to flee.

Judith's nostrils flared, and her whole body shook. She was so beside herself she could barely stand, and suddenly she seized the tablecloth and wrenched it away. All the crockery crashed to the floor, and Judith sank to her knees in the middle of it. Her fists were clenched and her knuckles white. The seal, she had to have the seal! Once it was in her hands again, nothing on earth would keep Nicholas from her.

"You'll take a witch to wife then, Montacute, and your death will be slow and very painful, just as mine was two hundred years ago," she whispered, her lips so stiff with bitter resolve that she could hardly say the words.

Chapter Sixteen

L ady Sichester's London residence was an elegant four-storied property, with dormer windows in the roof and a dark blue door with a semicircular fanlight. There were railings separating it from the pavement, and it stood on the east side of Dover Street, facing directly down the short incline of Hay Hill toward Berkeley Street and corner of the famous square of the same name.

Verity thought the house very pleasant and luxurious indeed, but she would have enjoyed it far more if it weren't for the circumstances that had prevailed in the two months since her arrival. There was no disputing that the facts behind the precipitate departure from Wychavon had taken the shine off her coming to London. She knew she had let her uncle down and now wanted only to forget about it if she could, but that was impossible when he continued to accuse her with silent glances. She was still an unconscionably long way from regaining his confidence, or his forgiveness.

The Season so far had been all she had expected, but it couldn't be enjoyed to the full when things stood the way they did. She and Joshua had attended the theater, various balls and assemblies, exhibitions, dinners, and a variety of other superior gatherings, for although he had lived out of London for some time now, many of his old friends still resided in town. Invitations certainly weren't lacking, nor was there any shortage of eligible gentlemen who found her of interest, but none of them could match Nicholas in her eyes, so she soon discouraged any hopeful overtures.

A week after St. Swithin's Day she stood at the window of

her bedroom waiting for the breakfast gong. She fingered the snakestone at her throat, for she had abided by her promise to Martha and had worn it every day since leaving Wychavon. Tonight she and her uncle were going to the theater, and tomorrow they were leaving London for a few weeks to stay with some of his old friends in Kent. She wasn't looking forward to either event, and as she touched the snakestone she thought of Martha and wished she were still at home in Wychavon.

She gazed down Hay Hill with a thoughtful expression in her eyes. At the bottom she could see the famous trees in the gardens of Lansdowne House, and they reminded her of Shropshire. She wondered if Nicholas even missed her. Perhaps he hadn't given her a second thought since her departure.

A gentleman on a fine chestnut Arabian rode into view in Berkeley Street, accompanied by two lean greyhounds. He wore a cherry red coat and reined in to look up the hill toward her. He was so like Nicholas that for a moment she thought it was him. Her pulse quickened, and she put a hand to the glass, but then he rode on out of sight again. She lowered her eyes. How foolish she was. Nicholas Montacute didn't care about her. She had been of interest for a while, but that was all. Perhaps she should be thankful things hadn't had time to go further, for by now she would have fallen completely from grace. Her cheeks warmed with embarrassment as she remembered some of the shockingly intimate caresses she had shared with the master of Wychavon Castle. From this distance she could hardly believe her conduct.

With a sigh she turned back into the room and then paused to study her reflection in the looking glass. Amabel Sichester had done her proud, she thought for the hundredth time since first inspecting her wonderful London wardrobe. The gown she had chosen today was made of muslin, thinly striped in maroon and cream. Its neckline and hem were trimmed with lace, and its full sleeves were gathered into tightly buttoned cuffs.

Her hair had been beautifully pinned by Amabel's French maid, a Parisian named Jeanne, whose knowledge of coiffures appeared to exceed that of most hairdressers. There was nothing rustic and Shropshire about the numerous golden ringlets that fell so daintily from beneath the lace-lappeted cap that was pinned just so on top of her head, and Jeanne had also applied rouge so prudently to her new mistress's cheeks that no one could possibly have known Miss Verity Windsor was in anything but excellent spirits. But the truth was that Verity Windsor was feeling very low and unhappy indeed.

The room itself—also Amabel's—was a frothy and very feminine chamber, with pink hand-painted Chinese silk on the walls and a deep carpet. Two silver brocade chairs flanked the white marble fireplace, and there was a rose damask bed of such flounced splendor that lying in it seemed reprehensible.

A dressing table stood against the wall next to the window, and there were japanned wardrobes of such vastness that they could surely hold sufficient clothes for three ladies, not just one. A bowl of hothouse roses stood in the hearth. They were large single blooms, not sprays like those in the gardens at Windsor House, and she thought they lacked the wonderful fragrance, but there was no denying their symmetrical beauty—if symmetry was what one admired in a rose.

The gong sounded at last, and she put a shawl around her shoulders to go down to the dark green breakfast room that overlooked the gardens at the rear of the house.

Her uncle was already there and rose from his chair as she entered. He wore a brown brocade dressing gown and matching Turkish hat, and he accorded her a civil if not exactly warm smile as one of Lady Sichester's gold-liveried footmen hastened to draw out a chair for her. "Good morning, Verity."

"Good morning, Uncle."

She selected a modest meal from the dishes the footman brought to the table, and when he had gone, she and Joshua ate in formal silence. After a while it became too much. She put her cutlery down with a clatter. "Can I say something, Uncle?"

"Of course you may, Verity."

"I know I disappointed you at Wychavon, and I'm deeply ashamed of it, but *please* can't we pretend it didn't happen? It was over two months ago now, and I've been all I should have been since arriving here. All I want now is to go back to the way we were."

He met her eyes a little unwillingly. "How can things go back to the way they were after you've proved such a sorrow to me?"

"That isn't fair. I was in Lord Montacute's arms, not his bed!"

"Verity!"

She lowered her eyes guiltily, knowing she shouldn't have said something so shocking. "I—I'm sorry, Uncle, but it's the truth."

"Maybe it is, but I suspect his bed would have been the next place I'd have found you if I hadn't arrived when I did!"

She colored.

"Yes, well you may blush, young lady. I'd dearly like to be able to trust you again, but after that appalling misconduct at the castle, it's very difficult. You must be able to see that."

"I know, but it won't happen again, I swear."

"An easy enough promise when the gentleman concerned is in Shropshire, and you are here," he said tersely, then searched in his pocket and took out a calling card which he placed before her. "Mrs. Henderson called yesterday. I informed her that I did not wish her to call again, and I told her that you would not be calling upon her."

Verity was dismayed, for she liked Anna. "Oh, Uncle!"

"She and her husband are Nicholas Montacute's allies, my dear, and I will not have you associating with them."

"But they were clearly as horrified as you about what happened," she pointed out, recalling their shocked faces at the castle.

"It makes no difference. You are not to see either of them, is that clear?"

"Yes, Uncle."

He proceeded with his breakfast.

She watched him for a moment and then spoke again, but tentatively. "Uncle, do we have to go to the theater tonight?"

"It is all arranged," he replied.

"But I really don't like *King John*, it's my least favorite Shakespeare."

"Mr. Kean is in the leading role, my dear," he said, as if this would make every difference in the world.

It didn't. "I know, but—" she began.

"We're going," he interrupted firmly.

"Yes, Uncle."

"Besides, it's Wednesday, so the audience will be quite thin, which means we'll be able to hear everything much more clearly than any other night."

"Yes, Uncle," she said again. Wednesday was the night of the Almack's subscription balls which were held for twelve weeks during the summer. Everyone who was anyone clamored for a voucher from one of the six lady patronesses who ran the assembly rooms in question, and to be excluded from the premises was a social calamity second to none. It was said that Almack's was of greater importance than the court, for to be sure London's high society was more dismayed to be turned away from the door in King Street than it was to be left out of a royal drawing room. All of which served to explain why on Wednesday nights it was much easier to acquire a box at the Theatre Royal, Drury Lane.

He glanced up again. "I trust you've packed everything you'll need for our stay in Kent?"

"Yes, Uncle."

"I suppose you don't wish to do *that* either," he remarked dryly.

"Of course I do," she replied untruthfully, for she thought the people they were to stay with were rather pompous, but they were his old friends, and so she wouldn't complain. Besides which, a society wedding of some importance was to take place during their stay, and the occasion promised to be very grand indeed.

It wasn't until breakfast was over that she realized that in spite of his stiff attitude during the meal, her uncle was actually beginning to forgive her, for as they left the table, he suddenly asked her if she'd like to go for a ride in Hyde Park.

Her eyes brightened. "Oh, yes, I'd love to!"

"Then ride we shall, provided the livery stable can provide us with suitable mounts," he said, patting her shoulder fondly.

The royal blue riding habit showed no signs of the mishap on the Ludlow road. The maids at Wychavon Castle had cleaned it and her tophat so perfectly, it was impossible to tell the skirt had ripped slightly when she fell. Verity therefore felt as stylish as all the other ladies as she and her uncle rode through Grosvenor Gate into the park to join the fashionable throng in Rotten Row. The sun shone on the black pearl pin in her neckcloth, and the gauze scarf from her top hat fluttered prettily behind her. The snakestone still lay against her throat, although hidden now beneath her shirt.

The water of the Serpentine was dazzling beneath the flawless blue sky, and the trees cast leafy shadows over the smooth green grass. The jingle of harness and the thuds of hooves upon turf was very pleasant to the ears, especially on yet another glorious summer day, and it was no small satisfaction to Verity that she was a better horsewoman than most of the other ladies, and even better than some of the gentlemen. She handled her spirited roan mare with ease, and was flattered to receive a number of admiring glances from members of the opposite sex.

Joshua bounced beside her on a stout bay hunter, frequently reining in to exchange greetings with friends and acquaintances. They made several circuits of the park, and at last he decided to halt by the Serpentine, where pleasure boats bobbed and children sailed toy galleons under the watchful eyes of their nurses.

It was while his attention was diverted by the exploits of two young gentlemen in a punt that a strange sensation came over Verity. One moment she was laughing with her uncle, the next she had turned in the saddle because she felt as if Nicholas was somewhere nearby. She scanned the faces all around and saw no sign of him, yet the feeling persisted. He was here somewhere, she was sure of it.

Suddenly she saw him, although he had yet to see her. He was mounted on a chestnut Arabian, with two greyhounds at his heels. The gentleman she had observed from her window! She stared in disbelief, caught totally off guard by seeing him again so unexpectedly.

At last he seemed to sense her gaze on him, for he reined in and turned. Their eyes met, and her heart lurched joyfully as he smiled, but then her uncle spoke. "We've rested long enough, so let's ride on, mm?"

Without waiting for her to reply, he urged his horse on once more. She had to follow, but as chance would have it, they became caught up in a considerable crush of other riders and were separated. She couldn't see her uncle anywhere, and then Nicholas maneuvered his mount alongside.

"Verity?" he said softly.

Her breath caught. "Please don't speak to me now, my uncle may see!"

He looked into her green eyes, and the spell enveloped him as tightly as ever. "I must see you," he said urgently.

"No!" She glanced around, fearing her uncle would suddenly ride up and catch them talking.

"Please, Verity."

"Don't call me that," she begged.

"Agree to meet me, and I'll go."

"No," she whispered, tears springing to her eyes because it wasn't what she wanted to say.

"Will you be at Almack's tonight?"

"No, we—we're going to the Theatre Royal."

"I'll see you there."

Her eyes widened. "Please don't! Uncle Joshua—"

He interrupted. "Your uncle will not know," he said, leaning across to put his hand briefly over hers. Touching her seemed to seal his fate. The green of her eyes beguiled him, and the curve of her lips reminded him of the sweetness of her kisses. He had to have her. . . . "Until tonight," he said softly, his voice almost lost in the noise of the riders all around them. Then he turned his horse and rode away, just as her uncle found her again.

"Ah, there you are, Verity! I've been looking all over."

She was all confusion, her cheeks crimson with guilt. "I—I thought I'd better say in one place, otherwise we might ride around in circles without seeing each other," she managed to say.

He shifted uncomfortably in the saddle. "Well, I've had enough of horseflesh for one day, and I sincerely trust you feel the same way now?"

"Yes."

"Excellent. Let's be off, then." He turned his mount toward Grosvenor Gate.

She accompanied him, but her mind was elsewhere with Nicholas. Part of her was overjoyed to know she would see him again tonight, but the other part was wretched with remorse for having so easily broken her word to her uncle.

Temptation had suddenly followed her from Wychavon, and now folly loomed on all sides again.

Chapter Seventeen

Grosvenor Square was the largest of Mayfair's squares, and was surrounded by handsome red-brick houses of very superior quality. A wide cobbled roadway separated them from the shady garden in the center, and as the sun set that evening, shadows lay darkly across the way as Oliver's gray tilbury drove up to Nicholas's residence in the northwest corner.

The vehicle halted beneath the arch in the railings, and Oliver alighted. He was splendid in evening attire—black velvet coat and white silk pantaloons, with white gloves, a black tricorn hat and a silver-topped cane—and he adjusted the lavish lace at his cuff before approaching the door. He doubted if Nicholas would even recall their arrangement to go to White's tonight, for they'd both been a little the worse for wear that last evening at Wychavon.

He knocked, and after a moment a footman answered. "Why, Mr. Henderson, please come inside, sir. I'll inform his lordship you're here."

Oliver stepped into the oval hall, where a seascape mural by William Kent graced the walls. The footman relieved him of his hat, gloves, and cane, and then hastened up the sweeping staircase.

Several minutes passed, and then Nicholas appeared at the columned balustrade at the top. He was dressed in evening clothes, and for a moment Oliver thought he had remembered after all, but his words soon put paid to the notion. "Oliver? What brings you here? I thought you'd be toddling off to Almack's tonight."

"Actually, I'm keeping our appointment, dear boy," Oliver replied dryly.

"Our what?" Nicholas's eyes cleared. "Oh Lord, I'd clean forgotten White's," he said, coming down quickly.

"So it seems." Oliver met him at the bottom and eyed his attire. "I take it Almack's is *your* destination, even if it isn't mine?"

"Er, no. The Theatre Royal."

Oliver raised an eyebrow. "Isn't Kean appearing there at the moment?"

"He is."

"But you can't abide the fellow! I seem to recall some very uncomplimentary remarks about his darting eyes and strutting manner."

Nicholas smiled. "Very true."

"Then why . . . ?"

"I just happen to be in the mood for him tonight."

"Don't humbug me, Nick Montacute, for it won't wash."

Nicholas pursed his lips. "Then let's just say it would be better if you pretended to be humbugged."

Oliver stared at him and then exhaled slowly. "Miss Windsor!"

"Just leave it, Oliver. Anna has made it abundantly clear that she strongly disapproves of me at the moment, so it's best all around if you know nothing of my, er, private life."

"Nick, it's also best if you know that Anna intends to apprise Miss Windsor with the details of your activities with the admiral's widow."

Nicholas's smile faded. "What activities?"

"Don't beat around the bush, Nick. We passed the manor house as we were leaving, and we saw the, er, scene."

"The late Admiral Villiers is well out of it, believe me, for his widow is quite mad," Nicholas replied with feeling.

"I wouldn't know, but I *do* know what Anna thinks. She may even tell Miss Windsor about that other business with . . . Well, with you-know-who."

"I sometimes wish your dear wife in perdition," Nicholas murmured with feeling.

"Unfortunately for you, she's only in Park Lane, and her fellow feminine loyalties are somewhat rampant at the moment, so be warned."

Nicholas groaned. "Heaven preserve me from crusading women."

"Have a care, Nick, for it's my wife you speak of."

Nicholas gave him a rueful smile. "I know, and in spite of the way she feels about me, I still have a great affection for her. Please impress upon her that I'm innocent of all charges, for as God is my witness, I've done nothing for which to reproach myself."

"Except when it comes to your dealings with Miss Windsor," Oliver said quietly. "Nick, please leave her alone, for unless you're serious about her—"

"Maybe I am," Nicholas interrupted.

Oliver searched his eyes. "And maybe you're not."

"I must see her again, Oliver. These past two months have been purgatory, and I can wait no longer. "

"Far be it from me to preach, but is a London theater the wisest place to conduct such a pursuit? There'll still be a lot of people there, even if it is Almack's tonight."

"I'm well aware of that."

Oliver shrugged. "I give up, for you're clearly beyond reason. I'll see you again soon, and in the meantime I sincerely hope you'll behave with some semblance of decorum."

"Good night, Oliver," Nicholas said wryly.

With a sigh, Oliver retrieved his things from the table and then left.

Nicholas went back upstairs. He knew he was still behaving reprehensibly where Verity was concerned, but he simply couldn't get her out of his head. He hadn't lied when he described the last two months as purgatory, for without her, that's exactly what they'd been.

The Theatre Royal, Drury Lane, was one of London's most prestigious theaters, rivalled only by the Italian Opera House in the Haymarket. It had recently been rebuilt after a fire, and was a rather severe building from the outside, but inside it was very sumptuous.

There was quite a crush of carriages as Verity and her uncle arrived in Lady Sichester's town carriage. They entered the foyer, which was decorated in the Chinese style, with little alcoves where oriental lanterns cast a delicate light. The babble of conversation was considerable, and in the background was the sound of music from the orchestra in the auditorium.

Verity was in a great state of nerves because of Nicholas, and she kept adjusting the folds of the lovely lavender satin gown she had selected for the occasion. It was cut very low over the bosom, with a jeweled belt that was matched by the comb in her hair, and it was the dainty gathers beneath the belt buckle that preoccupied her, for it seemed they simply wouldn't hang properly. A white feather boa rested over her arms, and a reticule and fan were looped around her white-gloved wrist. The snakestone nestled inside the reticule, with her handkerchief and vial of scent.

Beside her, Joshua was very impressive in the sort of full-skirted indigo brocade coat that was much favored by gentlemen of his generation. He wore a powdered wig, a tricorn hat was tucked beneath his plump arm, and the buckles on his shoes had been so highly polished it was possible to see one's face in them.

He glanced a little irritably at Verity as she fiddled with her gown again. "What *is* the matter with you? You've been doing that ever since we left the house!"

"I'm sorry, Uncle. I'm just nervous."

His face softened. "Forgive me. Of course you're nervous, for this is your first visit to a London theater. You'll enjoy it, I promise you."

She managed a guilty smile, for if he knew what was really behind her fidgeting, he would never forgive her.

They were conducted to Lady Sichester's private box, and Verity looked over into the vast auditorium, where jewels and military decorations flashed, and plumes waved. The heat was oppressive, and she opened her fan as she studied the faces in the other boxes, hoping to see Nicholas. But there was no sign of him. It was nearly time to raise the curtain, and as the patent lamps were dimmed, she began to relax. Maybe he wasn't coming after all.

The performance began, and she tried to concentrate on the stage. She didn't know what to think of Edmund Kean. He was much smaller than she had expected, and his eyes seemed to blaze from his pointed little face. She didn't doubt he was a genius, the greatest actor of the age, but she wished he were less intense. Everything he said seemed to be torn from his lips, and it wasn't long before she began to feel quite drained.

It was during the second act that she became aware of Nicholas entering a box opposite. She glanced across just as he took his seat, and her heart seemed to stop beating, for nothing could have been more devastating than the smile he gave her as he looked across directly into her eyes. Suddenly it was as if they were entirely alone in the theater.

She felt the relentless advance of folly, but common sense simply could not prevail where he was concerned. She wished it were otherwise, that she could look at him and then glance away again without feeling anything, but that was not so. When she looked at him, common sense flew out with the four winds.

The play became of no interest. She toyed with her fan and glanced constantly across the auditorium from beneath lowered lashes. At last the intermission came, and some of her uncle's old acquaintances joined them for a while, but their faces and conversation passed in a blur to her as she kept looking across at the box opposite.

The bell rang, and the performance resumed. Nicholas's eyes met hers, and he nodded slightly toward the curtain at the rear of the box, then he got up and left his seat.

She knew he wished her to do the same, and she also knew she should remain in her seat, but what she *should* do and what she *did* do where two different things. She leaned across to whisper to her uncle. "I—I have a slight headache and wish to go out into the passage for a while."

"Would you like me to accompany you, my dear?" Joshua asked concernedly.

"No, of course not. You stay and watch the play."

Nicholas was waiting outside. He didn't say anything, but just held out his hand, and she ran to him. He crushed her close, and their hearts beat together for a moment before he led her to a deserted anteroom nearby. As the door closed behind them, he pulled her into his arms again and tilted her willing lips to meet his.

The kiss was long, tender, and honey sweet with yearning. Her skin warmed, and her body melted against his. Wonderful feelings spread wantonly through her, flushing her with desire and consigning the remnants of common sense to the abyss. She felt weak and helpless, but at the same time so certain of her heart that she was strong. Nothing as good as this could be wrong, or so she told herself as her lips parted beneath his and her breasts became taut with arousal.

He held her to him, savoring the pressure of her body against his urgent manhood. Need flooded through him, and his kiss became more imperative, his lips hungry just for the taste of her. He felt close to the edge of control, swept along by sensations so forceful they almost commanded obedience. His hands roamed longingly over her, and the bewitching perfume of summer herbs filled his nostrils with heady delight.

He was beguiled by everything about her, and drawing back from the kiss was the last thing on his mind, but there was a burst of applause from the auditorium, and they both drew guiltily apart.

Alarm widened her eyes as she suddenly feared being caught in such a compromising situation. "I—I should return to the box . . ." she began.

He put a finger gently to her lips. "Please don't go yet," he whispered.

"But if we should be discovered . . ."

He knew she was right. "Say you'll meet me again soon," he urged, moving his fingers luxuriously over her neck and resting his thumb against the pulse at her throat.

She closed her eyes as the enervating desires began to return, and for a few moments she entirely forgot that the following day she and her uncle were leaving for Kent. She circled his waist with her arms, then raised her lips to meet his once more. They kissed slowly, their bodies caressing, and their need for each other rose to a tumult of irresistible pleasure.

He drew his head back and gazed adoringly down into her enchanting green eyes. "Meet me tomorrow," he urged. "Perhaps a casual encounter while out walking?"

Memory returned. "I—I can't . . ."

"Then the day after."

"I can't then either. Nicholas, we're going to Kent tomorrow, and will be away for several weeks."

He gazed at her in dismay. "Kent?"

"Dartley Place."

He nodded. "The Stratford wedding, I suppose."

She nodded.

He touched her cheek with his fingertips. "Well, no doubt it will do me good to wait a little longer before I'm able to spend some time with you." He searched her eyes. "You *will* meet me on your return, won't you?"

"I swear it."

"Send word to me at Grosvenor Square as soon as you come back. When I receive your message, I'll wait at the bottom of Hay Hill at eleven o'clock the next morning. We'll walk together."

She nodded. "I'll count the hours until then," she whispered.

"And so will I," he breathed, drawing his fingertips yearningly across her breasts. Temptation began to close in again, and he released her. "Desire for you will prove too much unless you go now," he murmured, then he kissed her a last time.

She gathered her skirts to hurry from the room. He waited only long enough for his desire to subside, then he followed.

The coming weeks suddenly seemed interminable.

Chapter Eighteen

Kent was very beautiful, a rolling landscape of orchards and villages, with the sea sparkling on the horizon, and Dartley Place was a very elegant house, but all Verity could think of was returning to London. She willed the days away, but as July slipped slowly into August, and the summer sun grew hotter than ever, it began to feel as if she would never see Nicholas again. His kisses burned on her lips each night as she lay in bed, and when she fell asleep, she dreamed of being in his arms again.

The occasion referred to as the Stratford wedding was splendid, and since a large portion of the *beau monde* attended the Canterbury cathedral ceremony, it was as if the Season had removed to the country for a week or so. Verity wasn't acquainted with either the bride or groom, but her uncle was an old friend of the groom's parents, whose property Dartley Place was.

As the end of the Kentish sojourn drew in sight, she was alarmed when at the last moment their hosts urged them to stay on a little longer, but to her relief her uncle politely declined, and on a misty morning that seemed to herald the oddly early onset of autumn, the traveling carriage set off down the drive, and on to the London road.

As soon as they reached Dover Street again, Verity sent a message to Grosvenor Square. If Nicholas remained true to his word, he'd be waiting at the foot of Hay Hill the following morning. How she slept that night she didn't know, for she was in such an agony of nervous suspense that she tossed and turned restlessly until nearly dawn. But at last it was the next day, and she got up to dress.

Joshua made it quite easy for her to go out, for he fell asleep over his newspaper after breakfast. She dressed with care, choosing a buttermilk lawn walking gown, a gray velvet spencer, and a pert little gray jockey bonnet from the back of which a long matching net scarf trailed as far as her hem. Most of her hair was hidden beneath the bonnet, but Jeanne had teased a frame of little golden curls around her forehead, and as she studied herself in the mirror before leaving, she decided she looked every inch the London lady of fashion.

But as she left word with the butler that she would be back in time for luncheon, and then slipped across Dover Street and down into Hay Hill, her polished Mayfair exterior hid the nervous country girl within. Remorse touched her for a moment as she glanced back at the house. She was deceiving Uncle Joshua very badly indeed, and doing her reputation no good at all if any of this should be discovered, but she could no more help herself than she could have flown around St. Paul's cathedral. She was captive to the overwhelming passion she felt toward Nicholas Montacute.

Suddenly he was in front of her, a tall, immaculate figure in a navy coat with silver buttons, white trousers, and gleaming boots. He carried a cane in one gloved hand and with the other moved his top hat to bow to her.

"Good morning, Miss Windsor," he said softly, his glance taking in every beloved detail of her appearance.

"Good—good morning, Lord Montacute," she replied, lowering her gaze quickly to the pavement. Her cheeks felt hot, and she was sure every curtain in the neighborhood was twitching with busybodies, although in her heart she knew that anyone who glanced out would only see what appeared to be a perfectly innocent encounter between acquaintances.

A lady and gentleman were strolling down the hill behind her, and Nicholas quickly offered his arm, addressing her in a loud enough tone for the approaching couple to hear. "Please permit me to escort you, Miss Windsor, for Curzon Street is on my way, and, with my protection, it will be safe for you to take the shortcut through Lansdowne Passage."

"You're most kind, Lord Montacute," she replied, feeling that her tone sounded so false that anyone with half an ear must realize it, but the lady and gentleman walked on by without giving them a second glance, so she rested her hand on his sleeve, and for a moment his gloved fingers brushed hers, then they began to walk down the hill toward Berkeley Street.

If they had looked back, they would have seen a tilbury conveying Anna Henderson drawing up at the house in Dover Street, but they didn't look back. She happened to glance down Hay Hill, though, and recognized them in the few seconds before they vanished from view.

Dismay rushed over her. Several weeks earlier, when Oliver had returned to the house that night without having gone to White's with Nicholas, she had wheedled the truth out of him. She had called at Dover Street the next day, only to learn that Verity and her uncle had gone to Kent, so she had waited until their return, and now called again. Her purpose was to warn Verity about Nicholas's connection with the admiral's flame-haired widow in Wychavon, and maybe about other things as well, so right now nothing could have been more horrifying to her than to see Verity slipping with him toward Lansdowne Passage. With a gasp she immediately ordered the tilbury to drive down the hill after them.

Lansdowne Passage was a subterranean way that passed between the gardens of Lansdowne House and Devonshire House. There were bollards across the entrance because in the past it had too frequently been used as a means of escape by highwaymen and other robbers, but footpads were still known to occasionally haunt its shadows, so ladies never went there alone, even though it was by far the quickest way across this part of Mayfair.

Steps led down from the Berkeley Street pavement, and the morning sunlight dimmed behind them as they continued to stroll for a while. As they realized there was no one else around, they halted, and Nicholas turned her to face him.

"If you only knew how much I've missed you," he said softly.

"And I you."

"Kent seemed as far away as the end of the earth."

She smiled. "It felt like it."

"You mean so much to me, Verity," he whispered, putting his fingertips gently to her cheek in the darkness, and with his other hand drawing her closer.

They found each other's lips in an adoring kiss, and the only sound they heard was the beating of their hearts, until the tap of light female footsteps made them pull apart in dismay.

Then Anna's voice rang out accusingly as she spied them in the shadows. "Nicholas Montacute, how *could* you!"

He stared at the newcomer in disbelief. "Anna?"

She halted a few feet away, her cerise gown and pelisse almost colorless in the dim light. Her closed parasol tapped on the floor as she eyed them both, and then she looked at Verity in particular. "I can't believe you're being so foolhardy, you'll have no character at all if this escapade should get out."

Verity lowered her eyes guiltily.

Anna looked at Nicholas again. "As for you, sir, I begin to think I don't know you at all. What has possessed you these past months? Have you no honor at all?"

He was angered. "Don't accuse me of dishonor, Anna, for it's a false accusation on every count except regarding Verity. As far as she is concerned, I admit my conduct is decidedly unbecoming to a gentleman."

"It certainly is," Anna replied tartly. Unwelcome revelations about him quivered on her lips, but before she could utter them, he turned to Verity and tilted her face toward his, and spoke.

"I offer no excuse for my conduct, save that I love you," he said quietly.

Verity met his eyes. "Oh, Nicholas . . ."

"I love you, and I want you to marry me," he said, hardly realizing the words were in his mind.

She stared at him, and so did Anna, who was so startled her parasol slipped to the floor with a loud clatter that echoed along the silent passage.

He took Verity's hand and raised it to his lips, then he looked into her eyes again. "Say you'll marry me, my darling," he urged again.

"But, you could have any bride in London . . ." she began.

"I don't want *any* bride, I want you."

"I'm hardly a great heiress . . ."

"What need do I have for more wealth? It's you that I want, Verity. Just you. Please say yes," he urged.

"Yes," she whispered.

As he gave a glad smile and enclosed her with a loving embrace, Anna continued to stare at them both as if she thought she would awaken at any moment. At last she found her tongue. "Are—are you both in earnest?" she inquired a little weakly.

They nodded, still gazing into each other's eyes.

She drew a long breath, still not entirely convinced that Nicholas was as committed as he appeared. "Nicholas, are you *quite* sure about this?" she asked, putting a meaningful hand on his arm.

He turned to her. "Never more sure in my life," he replied.

She searched his eyes for a long moment and believed him. Her hand fell away, and she looked at Verity again. "What of your uncle? I think we can all be certain of his vehement opposition to this match no matter how financially and socially advantageous it may actually be for you."

Nicholas drew Verity's fingers to his lips again. "Anna's right, my love. Will your uncle's opposition make a difference?" he asked her.

"It should, I know, but—but I cannot ignore the way I feel about you. If I were to refuse you because of his dislike, I wouldn't be being true to myself, or to you."

"Oh, my darling," he whispered, his heart swelling with such overpowering emotion that tears sprang to his eyes. Since May Day, she had become life itself to him, and he would defy the entire world to be with her, let alone one prejudiced old magistrate.

Anna looked from one to the other. "I take it there won't be a long engagement," she murmured resignedly.

Joshua's eyes darkened with outrage one week later, when at last he was persuaded to receive Nicholas in the Dover Street drawing room. "You *what*, sir?" he cried, gripping the back of one of Lady Sichester's prized cream-and-brown striped sofas.

"I wish to ask for Miss Windsor's hand in marriage," Nicholas repeated.

"Never!"

"Sir, I—"

"Never!" Joshua shouted, his knuckles white as his fingers dug into her ladyship's exquisite furniture.

Nicholas remained as calm as he could. "Mr. Windsor, I

swear that this is an honorable and sincere proposal. I love your niece, and wish with all my heart to make her my bride."

"If you were the last man on earth, I'd refuse to countenance a match between you and Verity." Joshua breathed, his whole body shaking with anger as he stepped across to the bellpull and tugged it so fiercely he almost tore it down.

Nicholas feared he might suffer a seizure. "Please, sir, it isn't my intention to upset you."

"But you have, sirrah! Oh, indeed you have!" Joshua cried.

"With all due respect, I'm hardly offering a misalliance," Nicholas pointed out, finding it very difficult to remain reasonable when what he really wanted to do was shake the old curmudgeon for his unremitting obstinacy.

"To me this is the greatest misalliance imaginable!" Joshua replied, turning as the butler hurried in. "Please show Lord Montacute out," he ordered.

Nicholas remained where he was. "Mr. Windsor, I ask you again to consider my proposal, for Verity and I are very much in love."

"Verity will never be your wife, sirrah," Joshua breathed. "You are a blackguard and a vile womanizer, and I would as soon see my niece in a nunnery than wed to you."

The butler stared.

Nicholas's eyes darkened. "No doubt you think you are justified in such insults, Mr. Windsor, but I promise you you aren't," he said, and strode out.

Verity had listened wretchedly from the top of the stairs, but although she called Nicholas's name as he snatched up his things from the hall table, he didn't hear. The door slammed behind him, and then there was silence. Gathering her skirts, she fled tearfully to her room, where she flung herself on the bed in a paroxysm of sobs.

Chapter Nineteen

Over the next two weeks, Nicholas swallowed his pride by calling again and again at Dover Street in an endeavor to make Joshua change his mind, but it was to no avail. The servants were instructed to turn his lordship from the door, and turned from it he was.

The twitching curtains Verity had feared so unnecessarily before, now twitched in earnest as Mayfair observed the frequent fruitless calls made at Lady Sichester's door by one of London's most eligible lords. Whispers began to spread, and soon the whole of society was rife with rumor. There was hardly a drawing room that didn't echo about the intriguing goings-on, and everyone was openmouthed with interest, with the unwelcome result that Verity's character rapidly became the subject of much debate.

The atmosphere at the Dover Street house was strained, for Joshua wouldn't even speak to his niece now, let alone forgive her this second monumental sin. He refused to allow her out of the house and snubbed all her efforts to reason with him. She had failed him so greatly now, that he couldn't find it in his heart to even try to meet her halfway, and seeing the Season through to its end was simply out of the question, so at the beginning of September he issued instructions for a return to Wychavon.

Throughout all this, Verity was unable to see Nicholas, and the only opportunity she had of being in the fresh air was if she sat in the garden. This is what she was doing on the last evening before the journey north, when at last Nicholas managed to speak to her again.

Shadows stretched across the lawns and flowerbeds, and the crimson sunset sparkled through the dancing waters of the raised fountain. There was a wrought-iron bench beneath a cherry tree, and the yellow of her muslin gown was warmed to apricot in the evening light. Her hair was tied simply back with a ribbon, the snakestone was around her throat, and there was a fringed white shawl around her shoulders because the coolness of approaching autumn was definitely detectable in the air now.

There was an open book on her lap, but she gazed blindly at the page because her vision was a blur of tears. She could hear the general sounds of Mayfair beyond the tinkle of the fountain and the flower girl right outside in the street. Horses shifted and whinnied in the stables, and then came the creak of the gate from the mews lane. . . . The gate? She glanced up, and with a start saw Nicholas entering the garden.

Her gaze flew back to the house, but no one was around, so she got up and ran into his arms. He drew her into the shadow of the coachhouse and kissed her achingly on the lips.

"Oh, my darling, my darling . . ." he breathed then, resting his cheek against her hair and stroking her throat with fingers that trembled to even touch her.

"We're leaving for Wychavon tomorrow," she whispered tearfully, raising her unhappy eyes to look at him.

"I know," he replied, then smiled. "Servants can be bribed for information. That's how I knew you sit out here in the evenings," he explained. His smile faded, and he took her face in his hands. "Don't go tomorrow," he urged.

"I—I have to."

"No, you don't."

"What are you saying?"

"That if you come to me, we can be married whether or not your uncle consents."

She stared at him.

His thumbs caressed her cheeks. "Come to me tonight, Verity. I've already secured a special license, which means you could be my wife before the day is out. You do love me, don't you?"

"You know I do."

"Then say you'll come," he urged softly, twining his fingertips in the chain of the snakestone.

Her heart felt as if it would burst with love for him, and suddenly she knew what decision to make, for there was only one. "Of course I will," she whispered.

"Oh, my darling . . ." he breathed, crushing her to him again. His hand curled desirously in the hair at the nape of her neck, and he wanted her so much he could hardly bear it. But tonight she'd be his at last and he'd make love to her until dawn. . . .

A door banged in the house, and he seized her hands as she looked anxiously toward the sound. "Verity, be ready at midnight tonight. I'll come here to the mews lane to take you directly to Grosvenor Square, where a clergyman will be waiting to conduct the ceremony. You'll be Lady Montacute then, and there won't be anything your uncle can do about it."

"I wish he weren't so intransigent, for I still love him so very much."

"He'll come around in the end," he reassured her.

"I hope so, oh, I do hope so."

He squeezed her fingers. "I'm afraid all this will make us the center of still more gossip, but it can't be helped. It's bound to be a nine-days' wonder, though, for the properness of marriage soon takes the edge off scandal."

He kissed her again.

As darkness fell in Wychavon, Judith set out for the grove. She was bitterly angry about the disappearance of the seal, and her inability to even begin to find out where it was. She had endeavored to put the eye on Martha, but the old woman was sufficiently protected by holy wafers to make her almost immune. The worst the nurse had suffered was an incapacitating headache that had confined her to bed for three days, but this wasn't punishment enough as far as Judith was concerned. Martha had to be *made* to divulge the whereabouts of the seal, and to this end the witch intended to seek Hecate's direct aid, but as she passed the lychgate, she came to a sudden halt.

Something drew her attention to the church door, which stood slightly ajar. It was strange that it should be open, because ever since the roof had been damaged by the storm, everything had been kept strictly locked to be certain the workmen's tools and equipment were safe from thieves.

The door seemed to almost be beckoning her, but as she went

cautiously to the lychgate, a warning wind stirred from nowhere to billow her cloak, for the forces of good were ever-vigilant, and the approach of a witch never went unnoticed. Normally she would not have gone a step closer, but something drew her toward the open door, and so she began to walk up the wide gravel path between the yew trees.

The wind increased, tugging at her hair and making the branches sway violently overhead, but she pitted her will against the outraged holiness that swirled all around her. Somehow she managed to reach the porch, where the wind buffeted furiously again as she clung to an iron rung that was sunk into the stonework.

The open door swung on its hinges, and her cloak flapped like a wild thing as she stared into the nave. The whirling draft of air swept through the church, riffling the prayer books and making the lanterns sway on their ceiling chains. She felt invisible hands trying to pull her away, but she held on tightly, her knowing gaze finally drawn to the altar, where moonlight shone thinly on the cross.

Suddenly the truth became dazzlingly clear. The seal was there! The wisewoman had been clever, for this was the one place no witch could enter. Unless . . . Determination surged through Judith, but as she tried to enter the church, the wind became a howling gale that flung her backward out of the porch. The church door slammed with a force that echoed through the night like a thunderclap, and Judith could do nothing but stumble helplessly toward the lychgate. Only when she had retreated into the road did the wind die down again, and the night become still.

The witch stood in furious impotence. She was so near to the seal, and yet so very far away! As she stared with loathing toward the church, she heard a door open at the nearby vicarage. The light of a handheld lantern swayed into view, and she drew back out of sight behind the sycamore that had provided her with a walking stick when she had broken her ankle.

The vicar appeared. He wore only his nightshirt and tasseled cap, and his Turkish slippers pattered on the path as he made his grumbling way toward the church. She saw that he was carrying the key and realized the slamming of the door had awoken him. He reached the porch, and she heard the heavy key turning in the lock, then he retraced his steps.

When he had disappeared back into the vicarage, the witch emerged from hiding. Flinging her dark cloak around her shoulders, she hurried on toward the grove. Even though she now knew where the seal was, she still needed Hecate's aid if she were to retrieve it from the house of God.

Midnight approached, and as Judith danced in the oak grove, at Dover Street Verity was nearly ready to leave. She had written a loving and apologetic note to her uncle, but knew he would see her action as a final act of betrayal. Joshua hadn't relented at all, and tonight had even turned his cheek away when she attempted to kiss him good night. There had been tears in her eyes as she hurried up to her room, for she didn't know when she would see him again, or if he would ever acknowledge her as his niece once she became Lady Montacute.

Stars shone in the cloudless night sky as she sat on the edge of her bed, willing the final moments away. The hall clock began to chime, and she put a pale blue velvet cloak over her yellow gown, picked up the small portmanteau she had packed earlier, and slipped from the room.

The moon cast a silvery light over the gardens as she hurried toward the gate, which creaked as she opened it. Nicholas's town carriage was waiting in the lane, and he alighted to take the portmanteau and put a protective arm tightly around her for a moment, before assisting her into the vehicle, but suddenly she felt the snakestone slip from her neck because she hadn't fastened it properly.

The precious amulet slithered to the ground, and she bent swiftly to retrieve it, but he picked it up first. He glanced at the unusual stone in the moonlight, and then handed it back to her. "It's very beautiful," he said.

"Martha gave it to me, it's supposed to be a lucky charm."

Another carriage returned to a nearby coachhouse, and Nicholas quickly assisted her into his own vehicle. "Don't let's waste time," he murmured, nodding at his coachman.

He climbed in and sat beside her, and the team strained forward, soon coming up to a smart trot over the cobbles to Grosvenor Square. A large dinner party was just breaking up at the house next door to Nicholas's. There were carriages drawn up at the curb, and a great deal of laughter and chatter as the fashionable quests took their leave. No one glanced at Lord Montacute's vehicle as it halted, or paid heed as the two occupants alighted and hurried into his house.

The door closed behind them, and in the cool gold-and-white entrance hall, where a magnificent French chandelier shimmered from a coffered ceiling, Nicholas turned her to face him. "I love you, Verity," he whispered, and an echo took up the words.

"And I love you."

He smiled and turned as his butler approached. "Ah, Charles, is everything ready?"

"It is, my lord."

"And the maid awaits Miss Windsor?"

"She does, my lord."

Nicholas looked at her again. "Charles will take you upstairs to prepare. When you're ready, he'll bring you to the drawing room. We'll soon be man and wife, I promise."

She nodded a little nervously, then the butler took the portmanteau and she followed him up the magnificent pink marble staircase that curved up between Corinthian columns to the upper stories.

The maid was almost as nervous as her new mistress, having suddenly been promoted from the post of parlor maid because she had some experience waiting upon ladies. She wasn't as nimble-fingered as Jeanne when it came to dressing hair, but she was anxious to please, and Verity liked her. Her name was Lizzy, and she was a Londoner, with a cockney accent and a friendly nature that soon came to the fore as she realized her new mistress wasn't as high and mighty as some ladies she had had dealings with.

Verity had brought an evening gown with her to be married in. It was made of plowman's gauze, cream with little pink satin spots that shone in the candlelight as Lizzy strove her best with comb and pins.

At last the maid achieved a creditable Grecian knot and stepped back to admire her handiwork. "Oh, you look lovely, Miss Windsor."

"I feel very nervous," Verity admitted.

The maid smiled at her in the mirror. "There ain't a woman in London wouldn't envy you right now, miss."

"Oh?"

" 'Is lordship's the most 'andsome man in the world."

"And I love him," Verity whispered.

Lizzy met her eyes again. "It's the most romantic thing I ever 'eard, miss, and to think that I'm your maid! Oh, I'll be crowin' like a country rooster after this, and no mistake."

Verity smiled and suddenly felt more relaxed.

"Are you ready then, miss?"

"I—I think so."

Lizzy drew her chair back and then smiled shyly at her. "Next time I address you, it'll be as Lady Montacute."

"Yes, I—I suppose it will . . ."

The maid hurried to a table where a little posy of white rosebuds was waiting in a dish of water. It had been tied with silver ribbons, which fluttered as she brought it to Verity. "This is from everyone belowstairs, miss."

"Why, thank you, Lizzy."

"We thought you might not 'ave any flowers, and every bride should carry flowers, miss."

Verity put the rosebuds to her nose and inhaled their perfume. "They're beautiful, Lizzy. Please thank everyone for me."

"Yes, miss." The maid went to the door and held it open for her. Verity's gown whispered softly as she went out to the corridor, where the butler was waiting to conduct her down to the drawing room.

Chapter Twenty

Footmen opened the double doors of the drawing room, and Verity entered a dazzling green-and-gold chamber that was furnished in the Greek style. Every chandelier and candelabrum had been lit, and all the servants were gathered as witnesses to the clandestine match which was bound to soon set the whole of London talking.

Nicholas had changed into evening clothes, and stood waiting with the priest. They both turned as she entered, and Nicholas came quickly over to her. "You look wonderful, my darling," he murmured, drawing her palm to his lips.

"I want to look perfect for you," she whispered.

"You always look perfect," he said softly, resting her hand over his sleeve and leading her before the priest, who took up his prayer book to begin.

The following minutes seemed to pass in a dream. She heard the priest's voice and gave her responses, but nothing seemed real, until the ring was slipped on her finger.

As they were pronounced man and wife and the servants applauded warmly, Nicholas kissed her on the lips. "You're mine now, Lady Montacute," he said, his gray eyes dark with promise.

The damask hangings of the bed were woven with the Montacute phoenix, and the sheets were scented with lavender. Candlelight was reflected in Verity's eyes as she lay in her nightgown waiting for Nicholas to come to her.

Fear of the unknown lingered secretly on the edge of excitement, as it had for every virgin bride since time began. Would it hurt? Would she disappoint him? Would the dawn come and find them both regretting the vows they had said tonight? Oh, please, don't let it all go wrong now, let this wedding night be as wonderful as any bride could wish. . . .

Nicholas was in the adjoining dressing room, and she gazed toward him as his shadow crossed the candlelight. His hair was ruffled, and he wore a navy silk robe with a single button at the waist. When he turned she could see the dark hairs on his chest.

As he extinguished the dressing room candle and came into the bedroom, she sat up slowly, her hair tumbling forward in a cascade of curls. She reached out to something she had left on the little table by the bed, next to his escritoire. As he approached the bed, she held the black pearl tie pin out to him.

"I—I didn't have a ring for you, but I want you to have this," she said. "It belonged to my father and is the most precious thing I own."

"I can't take it, Verity."

"Yes, you can. Please, Nicholas, for it's what I want." She pressed it into his hand.

"I'll wear it tomorrow," he promised, placing it carefully in a little compartment of the escritoire."

She blushed a little. "Maybe you won't want to by then."

"Why do you say that?" he asked, tilting her face toward his. "Because I may disappoint you tonight."

His thumb moved gently over her cheek. "You could never disappoint me, Verity," he said softly.

"But I don't know anything, Nicholas. I'm a green girl who can only prove very dull between the sheets."

He smiled. "Is that so? Well, then, it's up to me to teach you, is it not? Come the morning, if I'm a poor tutor, it may be that *you* will be the one who's disappointed."

"I do so want to please you, Nicholas," she whispered.

He held a hand out. "Come here, my lady," he murmured.

Hesitantly she slipped her fingers into his and he drew her from the bed. "Put your arms around my neck," he said gently.

She obeyed, and he put his hands to her waist, savoring her pliant warmth through the thin stuff of the nightgown. He pulled her toward him, and her eyes widened a little as she felt his arousal, so free and rampant now that he only wore the dressing gown.

He smiled, pushing gently against her. "You have nothing to fear, my love, for tonight I mean to introduce you to the joys of the flesh, not the terrors."

Her cheeks flushed, and her lips parted as all fear faded into oblivion. Excitement began to course into her veins, and she lifted her lips to meet his. He kissed her very tenderly, sliding his hands down to her buttocks and holding her to him. She trembled as she felt his erection pressing through her night-gown.

He drew back and gently undid the ribbons at her throat, so the gown slid from her shoulders to the floor. She stood there naked before him, her nipples upturned in readiness. The candle flame swayed over her body, sending light and shadow over her curves, and her breath caught with pleasure as he took her nipple between knowing fingers.

She closed her eyes as more and more pleasure washed over her. She wanted to touch him intimately, and she reached out hesitantly, then snatched her hand back in confusion, but he caught her fingers and drew them gently forward again, pressing them to the shaft that stood proud from his loins. She held her breath as she felt how hard yet warm and velvety he was. Her fingers curled around him, and his lips found hers in a more erotic kiss than before.

His hand moved to the hairs at her groin, and then slid gently into those moist places no one had touched before. She moaned a little as he caressed her in a way she'd never dreamed she could be caressed. Her hand trembled as she explored him too. His size and virility excited her more and more, and soon she found herself longing for the moment he would push deep into her.

He took off his dressing gown and then lifted her onto the bed. She lay there with her arms stretched up toward him, and he lowered himself into her embrace. As he sank down onto her, she felt his erection find its way between her parted thighs, and then its tip pressed urgently against that most secret place of all. For a moment her untouched body resisted, but the resistance was only fleeting, and he was permitted to enter. The pleasure was exquisite as he eased in inch by firm inch until he filled her completely. It was a wonderful feeling, close to ecstasy itself, but she knew the real ecstasy was yet to come.

He drew out slowly, and then penetrated her again. She arched with delight, her whole body quivering with feelings she had first discovered in the mill during the storm. Suddenly she was moving in rhythm with him, her hips swaying to his as desire cried out for climax. She was lost in a haze of pleasure, passing over thresholds of new experience that led her on and on toward something that her whole being craved. Her flesh felt as if it were melting, and her consciousness began to recede as at last she entered a fantastic realm where there was nothing but rapture.

As the gray of dawn found its way into the room, Verity lay cherished and contented in Nicholas's arms. She felt warm and complete and didn't regret anything. It had been right to run away to Nicholas, right to make clandestine vows in the middle of the night, right to surrender to him here in this bed. Had any bride ever had a sweeter initiation? Had any bridegroom ever shown more consideration, tenderness, and passion?

She leaned over him and kissed his mouth as he slept. He stirred, his lips responding before his eyes opened. Then he smiled and drew her down to him once more.

Joshua was just preparing to go down for breakfast when Jeanne found the note Verity had left for him. The maid couldn't read what it said, but the disappearance of its author and a portmantcau was sufficient evidence for the Parisienne who, like everyone else, knew all about Lord Montacute's persistent calls.

She was reluctant to be the bearer of such a communication, fearing she might be accused of complicity, and so she took it down to the kitchens, where all the servants exchanged glances. After some deliberation, it fell to the butler to convey the note abovestairs again.

Joshua read it, and then his lips pressed bitterly together. Slowly he crumpled the sheet of paper, tossed it into the hearth, and then he looked at the waiting servant.

"Have Miss Windsor's possessions sent to Lord Montacute's residence. I imagine you know his address?"

The butler avoided his eyes. "Er, yes, sir."

"See to it then."

"Very well, sir." The man turned to go.

Joshua spoke again. "My travel plans are not affected by this, I still intend to leave for Wychavon today."

"Yes, sir."

"That is all."

"Sir."

Chapter Twenty-one

Meanwhile in Wychavon, Martha was crossing the stepping stones on her way to the vicarage. She had dwelt long and hard upon what she had witnessed in the grove and was convinced that Judith was somehow connected with Meg Ashton. There had been the diabolical face on the Lady, the hare leaping away toward the castle, the ungodly green candles. . . . It all wreaked of the long-dead enchantress, but in order to find out more, the nurse meant to seek an interview with the Reverend Crawshaw, who she was sure would know a great deal about such an important part of the village's history.

As she approached the vicarage gate, she heard a familiar metallic thumping sound, like a tin drum, echoing along the Ludlow road toward her. She smiled and paused as a gaudy, heavily laden cart came into view. It was the Gypsy peddler who came every year at this time, and his arrival was always regarded as proof that summer was nearly over. He always set up camp on the village green, stayed for a few days, and then moved on to the next village.

The two-wheeled cart had a curved canvas top, and the peddler was walking beside the piebald horse, banging a wooden spoon on a saucepan to announce his presence. Baskets, kettles, and basins swung from hooks on the cart, and brightly colored ribbons fluttered from his hat. He repaired chairs and sharpened knives, made wooden dolls and other toys, and sold dress lengths, all manner of haberdashery, and an assortment of gewgaws to suit all tastes.

Martha stood aside to wave as he passed, but then she heard another cart behind, except that this one was invisible. Her smile faded and she shrank back against the gate as the church-yard watcher drove past as well. The supernatural sound drowned the noise made by the peddler, so that she could follow the spectral vehicle's progress toward the ford. There it halted, and for a terrifying moment she actually saw the cart very clearly indeed, with Admiral Villiers at the reins. He was dressed in full uniform, and he turned his ghastly face toward her, before he and the cart faded from view again.

The wisewoman felt cold in spite of the September sunshine. Everything seemed normal again, there was laughter on the green as the village children ran out to greet the peddler, and the breeze rustled through the willows as if all were well, but Martha knew there would soon be two deaths in Wychavon. One by the ford, where the admiral waited with his unearthly cart, and one by the track to the mill, where the corpse candle had appeared. For a moment her eyes fled fearfully across the road to her sister's cottage, where Davey still lingered halfway between life and death. "Not the boy, I beg of you, not the boy" she whispered, then turned to push open the vicarage gate and hurry up to the door.

The Reverend Crawshaw was not in the best of moods, for earlier that morning he had been informed by the workmen in the church that there was more lightning damage to the roof than had been realized. The whole building would now have to be permanently closed until the repairs were complete, and it was a situation he would have preferred not to have occurred. He was therefore a little disgruntled when Martha came in with her request concerning Meg Ashton, but he endeavored to be polite and helpful.

He cleared his throat. "Why, er, yes, Miss Cansford, in fact I can do more than just tell you about the sorceress, I can let you borrow a book that contains a chapter on her trial and death."

He went to a bookcase and took a slender leather-bound volume down, but as he held it out to her, she shook her head. "I do not read, Reverend."

"Ah, yes, I, er, wasn't thinking." He cleared his throat again. "Perhaps you'd be so good as to read some of it out to me?"

"Now?"

"If you please," she said politely, being so bold as to take a seat and clasp her hands attentively in her lap.

He drew a long breath, for reading to the village wisewoman hadn't figured in a morning schedule that was now much concerned with making alternative arrangements for services because the church had to be closed, but nevertheless he opened the book.

" 'A true and just record of the information, examination, and confession of the witch known as Meg Ashton, taken at Wychavon in the county of Shropshire in the year of our Sovereign Lady Queen Elizabeth, 1602. Trial held before Justice Henry Villiers . . . ' "

Martha sat forward. "Villiers?" she repeated.

He nodded. "An ancestor of the late admiral."

She sat back again. "Do go on, Reverend."

" 'Imprinted in London at the Three Cranes, in the Vintry, by Thomas Dawson.' Er, that's of no interest, so let me see. Ah yes. 'The witch's crimes are thus. That she did have four imps to serve her, a black dog, a gray cat, a brown rat, and a jackdaw, and that they did help her perform the Devil's work. That she did bewitch to death one Robert Cansford, his wife . . . ' " The clergyman broke off in surprise. "Well, Martha, one can only surmise that this Robert Cansford was one of your forebears."

Martha nodded. "It would seem likely, Reverend, for there have always been Cansfords in Wychavon."

He returned to the book. " '. . . that she did bewitch to death one Robert Cansford, his wife, ten of their beasts, and all his fowls. That she did lame an old woman who offended her, and that she did bring grave illness upon a small and innocent child. But her greatest crime was that she did bewitch to death Lady Montacute and her unborn babe, which she did by diabolical means, and with malice aforethought, because her ladyship's husband had at the stroke of midnight on All Hallows Eve, destroyed a circle of stones where the witch was wont to worship her mistress, the Devil's servant, Hecate, Goddess of Witchcraft and Darkness.' "

Martha exhaled slowly. Halloween, the day Judith Villiers had appeared in Wychavon. And as for Hecate's stone circle, well, the goddess could still be summoned to the grove, as she, Martha Cansford, had seen with her own eyes. . . .

The clergyman read on. " 'The witch made a pact with Hecate, that she would serve her all her days, and in return be able to spellbind, seduce, and marry Lord Montacute, before doing him unto death as she had his wife and unborn child, and thus escape her lowly existence and live in riches to the end of her days.' " He broke off a little faintly, taking out a handkerchief to mop his brow at the thought of such wicked and ungodly conduct.

Martha was shaken. Meg had intended to punish Lord Montacute for offending Hecate, by using black arts to murder his wife, then attempting to bewitch him into marriage? After that he would have been murdered too, and Meg would have become a widow of wealth?

The Reverend Crawshaw had recovered a little, and looked reluctantly at her. "Er, do you wish me to continue?"

"If you please, Reverend."

With a sigh he read on. " 'Fearful was the mischief she wrought in the service of the great Demon, and abominable was her defiance as she admitted her crimes before the court. She was condemned as the most dangerous and malicious witch that ever lived in this part of Shropshire, and was put to the flame on Halloween, that being the anniversary of the destruction of the diabolic stone circle. The witch, a young and beautiful woman of some five-and-twenty years, expired unrepentant, and with a curse upon her lips. She swore vengeance upon the name of Montacute and Villiers, and drew her last breath without calling for God's holy mercy. She was put to the flame by one Joseph Cansford, son of the unfortunate Robert Cansford. He wore a hood for fear she would cast a curse upon his name as well. As the final scream was torn from the witch's lips, it was said among the crowd gathered there that her spirit was seen to flee from her body into the remaining stone of the vanished circle. Ever after it was believed that she was trapped there, waiting to be freed to carry out her vile curse.' "

The clergyman closed the book in relief. "That is all I can tell you, Miss Cansford."

Martha looked at him. "Is it certain that one of my ancestors held the torch to the stake?"

"So it states in the book."

"Reverend, I—"

He cleared his throat to interrupt her. "Miss Cansford, I have a great deal to do this morning, and feel I have granted you enough of my time. I have read all that the book contains, and know nothing more. Nor do I wish to know more of such a shamelessly pagan and entirely reprehensible personage."

Martha got up. "I quite understand, Reverend, and I thank you for your consideration."

"Not at all." He hastened to the door and opened it pointedly.

Martha emerged into the daylight again and paused by the vicarage gate to gaze across the green at the excited gathering of villagers around the peddler's cart. Some of the children now had the wooden spoon and saucepan, and were chasing each other noisily to and fro, shrieking with laughter. Martha glanced at them and smiled briefly, but then her thoughts returned to everything she had just heard at the vicarage.

Judith Villiers *was* Meg Ashton, there was no doubt in her mind now that she had heard the full story. The wisewoman drew a long breath. Judith had already begun to carry out Meg's dying curse. She had married the admiral and then murdered him because of the long-dead Judge Villiers who had sentenced her. And now, again because of his ancestor's actions, she intended the same fate for Nicholas Montacute. Why else had she acquired something belonging to him? The seal could be used in a spell to bring him under her influence, and so it would have done if Verity hadn't found it on the green.

Martha paused by the ford. She was now more glad than ever that she had taken the precaution of giving Verity the snakestone, for her interference with the seal had cost the witch dear, a fact that Judith would not forgive lightly.

The old woman began to cross the stepping stones, her musings moving on to Nicholas. He was undoubtedly in danger, but at least there wasn't another Lady Montacute to stand in the witch's way this time, and Nicholas was himself safe enough while the seal remained in the church.

If it should fall into the witch's hands, however, his days on earth were numbered. . . .

But at that moment, Judith was taking steps to retrieve the seal. She was approaching the garden wall at the rear of Sadie's cottage.

Sadie was hoeing among the rows of vegetables, and there were tears in her eyes as she worked, because she was losing hope for Davey. She heard the noise caused on the green by the peddler's arrival, and the tears wended their way down her cheeks. Summer was almost at an end now, and Davey had been ill since spring. He seemed to be suspended somewhere between life and death, without showing any signs of either recovering or finally fading. Dr. Rogers had done all he could, and the child had now been taken back to the Lady twice, but still he just lay in his bed like a little lost soul. She had to face the awful possibility that Martha might be right, and he had been overlooked by the admiral's widow. No, she wouldn't think of such a thing, she wouldn't!

Gritting her teeth, she jabbed the hoe into the earth, but suddenly the hairs at the back of her neck stood on end, and a horrid feeling crept over her. With a gasp she whirled about to see Judith standing just beyond the garden wall. The witch was motionless, and her veil was turned back to reveal her gleaming eyes. Sadie wondered how long she had been there. Could she read thoughts? There was something in that cold, glittering gaze that suggested she could.

Sadie swiftly wiped her tears away, and looked guardedly at the menacing figure. "What—what do you want?"

"I need the seal your sister has hidden beneath the altar cross in the church," Judith replied quietly.

"I—I don't know what you mean," Sadie replied truthfully, for she knew nothing about the seal.

"You do not need to know anything, just that if you wish to save your grandson, you must bring the seal to me. I've been keeping the child from death's final clutches because I knew he might prove useful, so if you want me to give him back his health, you have to give me your help. Refuse, and he will die tomorrow."

The chilling words sank icily through Sadie, for they proved that what Martha said was true, Judith Villiers *was* a witch.

Judith held her gaze. "Well? What is your answer?"

Sadie's eyes fled toward the cottage. She could almost feel Davey's labored breathing.

"Your answer!" Judith said sharply.

Sadie flinched. "I—I will do as you ask," she whispered.

A slow smile spread on Judith's lips. "Bring it to me tonight."

"I can't!" Sadie said quickly.

"Can't?"

"That's right. The church is locked completely now. I—I've heard there's been more damage found on the roof. I don't know when I'll be allowed to go inside."

Judith's eyes flashed furiously, but she knew Sadie was telling the truth. "Very well," she breathed, "but you are to bring it to me the moment you can. Delay by even one hour, and it will be the worst for the boy. Do you understand?"

"Yes," Sadie whispered fearfully.

Without another word, Judith turned and glided silently away.

Chapter Twenty-two

In London, thanks to the tittle-tattling servants at Dover Street and Grosvenor Square, the passage of only a few days saw news of Lord Montacute's astonishing match spread throughout society.

The *beau monde* was startled to learn of the midnight marriage, and, predictably, the less kind were disposed to suspect her new ladyship of being in an "interesting condition." White's betting book soon received entries hazarding the expected date of the lying-in, the sex of the child, and even its weight, until Nicholas discovered the offending pages and tore them out, with the warning that if anyone else was so unwise as to wager on the subject, his seconds would call. It was a warning to which great heed was taken.

In the face of such a stir, it was inevitable that Verity's first public appearance as Lady Montacute would attract undue attention. When she had been insignificant Miss Verity Windsor, her arrival at the beginning of the summer hadn't caused so much as a ripple, but now, all of a sudden, she was the belle of the Season. Everyone wished to scrutinize the new bride, so, with his wife's well-being in mind, Nicholas decided the kindest introduction would be for her to accompany him for a ride in Hyde Park.

This she did, and no one could find fault with the way she handled the gray Arabian mare from his stables, or with her dainty figure and pretty blond looks. Her shyness was thought most becoming, and since it was clear that she and Nicholas adored each other, no one could doubt that whatever the bride's condition may or may not be, the marriage was most definitely a love match of the highest order.

Verity sadly accepted the absence of a personal message from her uncle when all her belongings arrived from Dover Street. She didn't give up, however, but wrote daily to him at Wychavon, although not a single word of response traveled in the other direction. The severing of relations was apparently complete. As far as Joshua Windsor was concerned, he no longer had a niece.

She did her best not to let the apparently insoluble parting of the ways spoil what was still the happiest time of her life, and during her first weeks of marriage she did everything that was expected of her new position. After that first excursion in the park with Nicholas, she went there every day, sometimes with him, sometimes with Anna, who soon became her very dear friend. The names of Lord and Lady Montacute suddenly appeared on the guest lists of numerous dinner parties, assemblies, balls, and so on, and at first each occasion was something of an ordeal for Verity, but as the days passed, she became more and more confident. That was, until the Wednesday morning at the end of September when Nicholas informed her they would be attending that night's subscription ball at Almack's.

He broke the news before they got up. The early-morning sun shone obliquely through the window, and the gardens outside were beginning to show the tints of early fall. The days were a little shorter now, and the temperature cooler, but in the cozy luxury of their velvet-hung bed, after making love again, they were very warm indeed as they lay naked in each other's arms.

Nicholas suddenly leaned up to smile into her eyes, which to him were still a strangely magical green. "I love you, Lady Montacute," he murmured, toying with the snakestone around her throat.

"The feeling is more than reciprocated, sir."

"In fact, I more than love you, I absolutely adore you, and wish to show you off properly tonight."

"Tonight?"

"At Almack's."

Her eyes widened. "Almack's? Oh, but—"

He put a finger to her lips. "At least three of the lady patronesses number among my friends, and all of them have made vouchers available in the hope that you will accompany me this week."

She sat up, pushing her unruly hair back from her face. "Nicholas, Almack's is the most superior and exclusive place in the whole of London, and I really don't think—"

He put the finger to her lips again. "Hush, my darling, for you aren't mere Miss Windsor now, you're Lady Montacute, and as such entitled to the same privilege as any other lady of rank. You'll carry Almack's off as effortlessly as everything else, and besides, I'll be at your side, and Anna and Oliver will be there too," he added.

"But what if I let you down?"

"Have you let me down yet?"

"No, but—"

"Then have done with these buts, my lady, for Almack's will be at your feet," he murmured, his gaze moving over her body. "Tell me, madam, when did I last tell you you were lovely?"

"I don't think it was very long ago, sir."

"But did I say it ardently enough?"

She smiled, her alarm about Almack's dissolving into the early stirrings of renewed desire. "I'm sure you must have done, sir," she whispered.

"And have I told you you're a very passionate and warm-blooded woman?"

"Am I?" She searched his face.

"Oh, yes, my lady, very passionate and warm-blooded indeed, in fact, I'd say you were born to make love."

Her cheeks colored a little. "You say that as if I am out of the ordinary, sir."

"You are, my darling, for you relish the delights of the marriage bed most gratifyingly," he murmured, easing one of her thighs around him so she could feel his manhood, which hadn't entirely softened after lovemaking.

She closed her eyes with new pleasure. "Perhaps it's because I have had such a skillful tutor, my lord," she whispered, holding her breath and then exhaling slowly as she felt him hardening to enter her a little.

He smiled down at her. "It seems I can never have enough

of you, Lady Montacute," he breathed, penetrating still further.

She raised her parted lips to his as her body welcomed him.

Martha was on the green at Wychavon, purchasing a new basket from the peddler. He usually would have moved on by now, but for some reason this year he had decided to stay on a little longer. His wares remained on display on the grass, the piebald horse grazed nearby beneath the autumn-tinged willows, and a bubbling pan was suspended over a crackling fire.

The nurse still had no idea what had happened in London, because contrary to his original intention, Joshua hadn't journeyed straight home, but had stopped off in Cheltenham to take the waters. More shaken by Verity's betrayal than he cared to admit, he felt that the spa regimen would be of some comfort. The nurse was a little puzzled by the arrival at Windsor House of Verity's letters to her uncle, but presumed there must be some very ordinary explanation, and so was quite unconcerned as she endeavored to argue a farthing off the price of the basket. The peddler was equally determined not to give an inch, and so the haggling was quite lively when suddenly it was interrupted by a disturbance from the direction of the vicarage.

The Reverend Crawshaw appeared on his cob and had clearly lost control, for the animal was galloping toward the ford with the unfortunate clergyman clinging to its mane. His feet were out of the stirrups, and he bounced alarmingly on the saddle, shouting for help at the top of his lungs.

The peddler acted in a moment, dashing toward the ford and leaping into the water in time to seize the runaway horse's reins. The vicar had now slumped in the saddle, with his arms tightly around the animal's neck, and his eyes were tightly closed as the horse reared and plunged. The peddler held on tightly, but hadn't reckoned on the creature's sudden panic. It tried to wrench free and almost pitched into the river, but the peddler didn't let go. A hoof struck him on the chest, but as he released his hold and fell back, his head was dashed against a stepping stone. His body went limp, and he floated facedown in the water, only the stepping stones preventing him from being swept away by the current.

The vicar could do nothing except try to regain control of the still unnerved cob, so in dismay Martha began to run toward the peddler. In a blur she saw the corpse candle again and the shadowy outline of the watcher's cart. She saw the admiral alight and gather the peddler's soul gently into his arms, then place it carefully in the cart, before climbing back and driving away. He was unseen and unheard by anyone except Martha, who therefore knew before she waded into the water, that the brave peddler was dead.

Other villagers ran to help, and as they dragged the body out of the river, the vicar at last managed to calm the cob. His face was ashen with guilt as he dismounted and hurried over to look down at the dead man. "Oh, dear! Oh, how very dreadful! This is all my fault!" he cried.

Martha put a hand on his arm. "It was an accident, Reverend."

"I should never have kept the horse once I realized I couldn't manage it," he said.

She said nothing to this, for it was the truth.

He swallowed. "Does he have family?"

"I believe he has a sister in Shrewsbury, but I do not know her name or her address," Martha replied.

He sighed. "She will have to be found regarding his estate, but in the meantime, the least I can do is provide him with a proper Christian funeral. I'll see that his belongings are collected and the horse taken care of." He took out a handkerchief to mop his brow. "Oh, what a terrible thing to have happened, and what a valiant fellow he was. I owe him my life!"

Some of the men carried the peddler to the vicarage, and the vicar turned briefly to Martha. "I—I trust you and your sister Sadie will perform your usual duties, Miss Cansford?"

"Preparing and laying out the body? We will, my lord."

"I'll notify the Ludlow authorities about the accident and mention that he's believed to have a sister. When I'm permitted to arrange an interment, I will notify you."

"Very well, Reverend," Martha said.

She remained by the ford as the chastened clergyman led the

troublesome cob after the men with the body. The other villagers dispersed, and soon all was quiet again. Martha shivered, for she alone had witnessed the admiral collecting his successor. The appearance of the watcher's cart and the corpse candle here by the ford was now explained, but that still left their appearance by the track to the grove. Someone else had yet to die in Wychavon.

Her gaze was drawn inevitably toward Sadie's cottage. It must be Davey, she thought sadly, for who else was there? Sadie feared the same, it had been written all over her this past fortnight or so. She had become very quiet and withdrawn, frightened each day that she would find the child dead in his bed.

The evening shadows were lengthening across Grosvenor Square as Lizzy put the final touches to Verity's hair for the Almack's ball. The long golden curls were twisted into a knot from which were looped a number of plaits, and the knot was encircled with jeweled flower ornaments. Verity's white silk gown was very décolleté, and had little petal sleeves that left only her upper arms bare before her long white gloves commenced. She wore dazzling flower-shaped diamond earrings Nicholas had purchased for her at a fashionable Pall Mall jeweler, and there was a delicate silver lace shawl over her arms. She carried a fan and a reticule, in which reposed the snakestone, because she didn't intend to leave it behind, even tonight.

Nicholas awaited her in the hall and came to the bottom of the staircase as she descended. He wore a tight-fitting black velvet coat and white silk breeches, and the pearl pin she had given him was fixed among the ample folds of his unstarched neckcloth.

As she reached him, he took her hand. "You look wonderful, my darling," he breathed, kissing her gloved palm.

She flushed a little. "Do you really mean that?"

He smiled. "When we return tonight, I promise to demonstrate my adoration with all due passion."

She lowered her eyes. "I would much rather do *that* now, than go to Almack's," she said truthfully.

He pulled her closer and brushed his lips to her cheek. "You have nothing to fear, my love, and I promise you that once this hurdle is over, you will be firmly established in society. The nine-days' wonder will definitely be over by tomorrow."

He drew her hand over his arm, accepted his tricorn from the butler, and then they went out into the misty September dusk, where the lamps of his town carriage shone over the cobbles.

Chapter Twenty-three

Almack's, also known as Willis's Rooms, was a dull building on the outside, the presence of six large round-arched windows on the second floor being the only indication that anything extraordinary lay inside. It stood next to the Golden Lyon Tavern in King Street, and its main entrance was a pedimented doorway to which had been added a rather ugly curved porch that projected to the pavement railings. All in all, it was nothing if not drab, and certainly didn't appear the sort of place to which the cream of high society would jealously adjourn at every opportunity.

But if the exterior of the building was unremarkable, the elegant ballroom more than made up for it. One hundred feet long and forty feet wide, it could accommodate no fewer than seventeen hundred people, and its floor and acoustics were generally agreed to be among the finest in London. It was approached up a staircase that was guarded at the bottom by a man who examined every voucher. As a consequence there was a great queue of the high and mighty in the foyer, but such was the social cachet of being accepted at the rooms that no one made even the slightest murmur of protest.

Anna and Oliver were waiting near the staircase and pushed their way to join Verity and Nicholas. Anna wore poppy gauze over cream satin, and a tall ostrich plume sprang from her cloth-of-gold turban. She shimmered with opals, and a feather boa was draped lightly around her throat and shoulders. They all four joined the queue, and once their vouchers were declared valid, they went up the staircase toward the ballroom, where a polonaise was in progress.

Their names were announced, and everyone turned to look at the new Lady Montacute. Verity steeled herself and went in on Nicholas's arm.

In Davey Cutler's bedroom at that moment, the contrast with Almack's could not have been greater. It was a humbly furnished chamber, and in the hearth was the first fire of the autumn. The child's breathing was shallow and labored. His little face was gray and thin in the candlelight, and his eyes were closed. There seemed hardly anything of him, Sadie thought as she stood sadly in the doorway. She had to do the witch's bidding and take Lord Montacute's seal from the church. What other choice did she have if she was to save her only grandchild? She would go now, for the workmen had finished that afternoon, and the church was at last open again.

She took her shawl from the hook behind the cottage door, then went out into the smoky chill of the September night, where the mist swirled and early autumn leaves hung in the still. There was no one around as she crossed the road toward the lychgate. The vicarage was in darkness because the Reverend Crawshaw had gone to Ludlow to report the peddler's death and wasn't expected back until the following day.

Sadie thought the whole village had retired for the night, but suddenly Judith's black-clad figure appeared in the road next to the churchyard. Sadie's steps faltered with fear, but then she went slowly past the silent witch, passed through the lychgate, and hurried up the churchyard path to the porch. For a moment she feared the verger, who was in charge in the vicar's absence, may have taken the precaution of locking the door after all, but to her relief it opened to her touch.

Her steps echoed in the shadowy nave as she hurried down the aisle toward the altar, just as Martha had done all those weeks before when she had brought the seal here to hide. Sadie took the seal from beneath the cross, then she glanced toward the lectern, where the great leather-bound Bible was still open at the Reverend Crawshaw's last text—"For the wages of sin is death. . . ."

She clutched the seal to her heart. Was she sinning now by helping the witch? Or was it right to do all she could to save Davey? Her anguished eyes moved to the cross. She whispered a prayer and then backed away from the altar. She felt as if all the carved faces of angels on the church corbels were gazing accusingly at her, and suddenly it became too much and she gathered her skirts to run outside to where Judith waited.

The witch smiled. "Give me the seal," she breathed, holding out an eager hand.

But Sadie still clutched it close. "First promise me that you'll save Davey."

"You have my word."

"Can I trust that word?"

Judith smiled. "That is for you to find out," she said coolly.

Sadie knew there was still no choice. She simply couldn't risk Davey's life. Slowly she held the seal out, and Judith's rapacious fingers closed over it like claws. For a moment the witch's hazel eyes burned green, and sparks of the same color danced from the seal, but then all was dark again.

Sadie backed fearfully away, but Judith gripped her wrist. "One word of any of this, and it will be the worst for the boy. Do you understand?"

"Yes," Sadie whispered.

"I refer particularly to your sister. She above all is not to know."

"I—I won't say anything," Sadie promised.

"Go then."

Without waiting for anything more, Sadie hurried away, stumbling a little as she reached the cottage gate. She didn't look back as she went up through the garden and then inside.

Judith remained by the lychgate. She glanced down at the seal, conscious of the power harnessed deep within it. To transfer that power from Verity to herself, she had to seek Hecate's aid. Without further ado, she hurried away along the Ludlow road toward the grove.

Verity knew nothing of the calamity to come as she and Nicholas danced a waltz at Almack's. His arm was about her waist, and his fingers twined lovingly with her as they circled the crowded floor. They gazed into each other's eyes, oblivious to everything else.

*　　*　　*

A few minutes later, Judith danced too, moving anticlockwise around the circle in the grove. The night air was chill, and the mist swirled eerily as Hecate's terrible face appeared on the granite of the Lady. The seal lay on the grass at the foot of the stone, and the candles swayed, their green light looming and retreating in the draft of the witch's shadowless dance.

The water had become still in the millrace, not a ripple marred the surface of the pool, and the invisible hounds bayed as Judith performed the ancient ritual. The ointment on her skin began to affect her. She drifted weightless again, her senses swimming from the potent blend of hemlock, nightshade, aconite, and opium, but her voice was clear and strong as she begged the goddess's favor.

"Hecate, restore to me the power I sought before, make the seal my strength, so that I may make Nicholas Montacute return to Wychavon again. Make him forget Verity Windsor, make him grant me everything I ask, make me all that matters to him in this world . . ."

Green lights winked and flashed in the seal, illuminating the tiger's eye quartz, and the faster Judith flew around the Lady, the more the lights darted. Other words fell from the witch's lips, dark words from the beginning of time, and the seal began to glow brilliantly, its green radiance so powerful that it lit the whole grove.

Suddenly Judith became still, her breath escaping on a triumphant sigh as the sparks from the quartz began to form into the shape of a man. The witch gazed at the glittering apparition. "Thou art fully mine now, Nicholas, no one stands in my way. Come to me . . ."

She embraced the phantasm, and it bent its shimmering lips to hers.

At Almack's, the waltz had given way to a *ländler*, and Verity and Nicholas held each other's arms as they danced. But suddenly Nicholas came to an abrupt halt. Slowly he let go of her.

Startled, she looked anxiously at him. "What is it? Is something wrong?"

He stared into her eyes, and saw their green loveliness turn to the shade of lilac he remembered from the past. Suddenly she was just Joshua Windsor's niece again, and of no interest to him whatsoever, whereas Judith . . .

"Nicholas?" She became a little concerned, for some of the other dancers were glancing curiously at them.

Still he didn't respond.

"Are you feeling unwell?" she asked, putting a worried hand on his sleeve.

He snatched his arm away. "Don't touch me, madam," he breathed.

"Nicholas?"

"I don't profess to understand why I've been such a fool these past few months but you may rest assured that I've come to my senses now." His tone was clipped.

"I—I don't understand . . ." Confused tears sprang to her eyes. What was the matter? Why did he refer to her by her maiden name?

"There is little to understand, madam. I don't wish to have anything more to do with you."

Stricken, she stared at him.

More and more people had begun to notice them as they stood in the center of the floor, and Anna and Oliver made their way swiftly over to usher them both to the side of the room. The *ländler* continued, but most eyes were upon the little scene beneath the orchestra apse.

Oliver touched Nicholas's sleeve. "What is it, Nick?"

"Nothing a good stiff drink won't cure," Nicholas replied coldly, gazing at Verity as if he despised her.

Anna was bothered. "What's happened? For heaven's sake, one simply *doesn't* cause a stir at Almack's." She glanced around and snapped open her fan to waft it busily to and fro.

Nicholas looked at Verity again. "I swear I will undo all the damage, madam, and will be free of you as soon as possible." With that he turned on his heel and walked away.

Verity would have hurried tearfully after him, but Anna made her stay. "Have a care, for everyone's watching."

"But I must go to him!"

"To what purpose? Verity, he's clearly in a fury with you right now, so it's best left until he's calmed down a little."

Oliver nodded. "Anna's right, Verity." He paused. "Do you want to tell us what happened? Maybe we can help . . ."

"I don't *know* what happened."

"Eh? But—"

"It's the truth, Oliver. One moment we were dancing and loving, the next he'd come to a standstill and was the way you saw him!" Tears wended their way down Verity's cheeks, and she tried to use her fan to hide them, but to no avail.

Anna and Oliver exchanged glances and then guided her gently from the ballroom. Behind them, the *ländler* came to an end amid a rustle of whispers.

Anna linked Verity's arm as they went down the staircase. "It must be a silly misunderstanding," she said reassuringly. "All will be well in the end, I'm sure."

"Oh, Anna, he was so cold and distant. Like a stranger . . ." Verity's steps faltered as she saw Nicholas's town carriage drawing away from the door.

Anna and Oliver saw too, and Oliver drew his wife aside. "Take Verity back to our house. I'll go to Grosvenor Square and see what this is all about."

Anna nodded. "Make him see sense, whatever you do, for what he's just done is quite unforgivable." She hurried back to Verity, and soon the two women were ensconced in Oliver's town carriage on their way to the Henderson residence in Park Lane.

Verity was so bewildered she didn't know what to say or do. She huddled on the red leather seat, her hands clasping and unclasping in her lap, while tears poured helplessly down her cheeks. In the space of a heartbeat, her wonderful dream had become a nightmare.

Oliver hailed a hackney coach to take him to Grosvenor Square, where he arrived in time to see Nicholas's carriage driving around to the mews lane. Alighting from the coach, he hastened to the door.

The butler admitted him. "Why, Mr. Henderson . . ."

"Good evening, Charles. Where is Lord Montacute?"

"In the library, sir. Shall I—?"

"Don't bother to announce me." Pushing his tricorn and gloves into the man's hands, Oliver hurried up the staircase.

Nicholas had already poured himself a large glass of cognac and was removing the black pearl pin from his neckcloth as

Oliver entered unannounced. He turned to face the newcomer. "What brings you here?" he asked lightly.

Oliver's brow darkened. "Don't play games, Nick, you know perfectly well what's brought me."

Nicholas dropped the pin into the portable escritoire on the table and then sipped his drink.

Oliver stepped closer. "What's the matter, Nick? Why are you behaving like this?"

"Like St. Paul on the way to Damascus, I've suddenly seen the light," Nicholas murmured, swirling his glass and sniffing the bouquet.

"I trust you mean to explain?"

"Is it really any of your business, Oliver?"

Oliver met his eyes. "I'm making it my business. How could you treat Verity so appallingly? And at Almack's, of *all* places!"

"I can't help it if Almack's is where my eyes were opened."

"Opened to what?"

"The fact that due to a rush of blood to the head—and other parts of my person—I've married a woman I cannot abide, whereas . . ." Nicholas broke off as Judith's beautiful face seemed to hover before him.

"Whereas what?" Oliver demanded.

"It doesn't matter."

"Damn it, it matters very much!" Oliver cried. "And what do you mean you 'cannot abide' Verity? That's rubbish, and you know it!"

"Verity Windsor is an encumbrance of which I intend to free myself with all possible haste."

"How can you possibly speak like that about her? You and she have been gazing besottedly into each other's eyes for—"

"For far too long," Nicholas interrupted coolly.

"Are you in your cups?" Oliver asked then, unable to think of any other explanation.

"Never more sober in my life."

"Then I think you shabby," Oliver replied shortly.

Nicholas didn't reply.

"What do you intend to do now?"

"Now? I'm returning to Wychavon. Alone." Nicholas glanced away, for suddenly he found himself unable to think of anyone but Judith Villiers. Beautiful, sensual Judith, whom he had rejected so foolishly in favor of Verity. Oh, Judith, Judith . . .

Oliver's temper snapped. "Damn it, Nick, you can't just leave Verity like this!"

"I can do whatever I damned well please, and right now it pleases me to be rid of my unwanted wife. Is that clear enough for you?"

Oliver stepped back. "I don't think I know you at all," he breathed, then turned on his heel to stride from the house.

Nicholas finished his cognac and then rang for the butler. "I intend to leave for Wychavon tonight, Charles."

"My lord?" The man was startled.

"Have my traveling carriage prepared as quickly as possible. Lady Montacute will be remaining here."

"Yes, my lord."

Chapter Twenty-four

Joshua at last arrived at Windsor House the morning after the Almack's ball, and the sudden sight of his travel-stained carriage at the gate caused an uproar among the servants.

Martha hurried out to greet him. His sudden return alone, together with the many letters that had now arrived for him from Verity, bothered the nurse considerably. Something was clearly very wrong. "Where is Miss Verity, sir? She's sent you a number of letters, and—"

He interrupted coldly. "My niece is never to be mentioned again in my presence, is that clear?"

Martha was shaken. "S-Sir?"

"Verity has chosen to become Lady Montacute, and so I wash my hands of her," he said, and then walked into the house.

Martha stared after him. Verity had married Nicholas? The wisewoman's gaze flew instinctively to the manor house. What would the witch's reaction be now there was another Lady Montacute to stand in her way? Verity was in the utmost danger, at least, she would be if it weren't for the snakestone. Martha smoothed her shaking hands against her skirts, praying that Verity and Nicholas stayed in London. Without the seal, there was little Judith could do to either of them, and while it was secure in the church, it was safe from the witch's reach.

With a sigh, the nurse went back into the house, not realizing that it was already too late, and only hours earlier her own sister had placed the seal in the sorceress's hands . . .

Joshua had gone into the library and closed the door quietly behind him. The air smelled of beeswax because one of the maids had just polished the furniture. He sat at his desk, where a large pile of letters awaited his attention, including those from Verity, which had been set aside on their own. He gazed at them for a long moment and then snatched them up to throw them unread into the wastepaper basket.

Then he leaned back wearily. Beyond the ticking of the clock he could hear the servants scurrying around to prepare the house for his unexpected return, and through the sunlit window he could see the gardens behind the house. Autumn flowers were in bloom now, chrysanthemums, dahlias, Michaelmas daisies, and late roses. The leaves had turned more this far north, and some had already begun to fall. Winter approached, he thought bleakly, and this time it would be very bitter indeed.

There were tears in his eyes as at last he sat forward to take a sheet of writing paper. Then he dipped a quill in the ink and began to write. The nib scratched savagely over the paper, for the letter was to Nicholas.

Judith had watched Joshua's return, and she gazed in puzzlement out of the manor house window as the empty carriage was taken around to the rear of the house. Why had Verity stayed in London?

The witch's fingers drummed thoughtfully on the sill, then she turned to pick up the seal, which lay on the table beside the commodious bed she had shared so briefly with the hapless admiral. The quartz scintillated with green lights as her fingers enclosed it, and she smiled. What did it matter why Verity hadn't returned with her uncle? The only thing of consequence was Nicholas, and he must already be on his way north again because she had willed him to.

"You'll soon be in my arms, my lord of Montacute," she whispered, raising the seal to her lips. The green lights danced, and Hecate's power surged through her.

Many miles away in a carriage traveling swiftly toward Shropshire, Nicholas' eyes opened suddenly. He had been dozing after traveling through the night, and for a moment he felt a little disoriented. Then he remembered, and glanced out at the passing countryside. His feelings hadn't changed. Verity meant nothing to him now, and the only face he saw reflected in the carriage glass was Judith's.

A smile touched his lips. What a fool he had been to choose the magistrate's dull daughter when a woman as fascinating as the admiral's widow was there for the taking. Well, mistakes could be corrected, and as soon as he reached Ladywood he would put matters right. He knew who he wanted, and it certainly wasn't Verity Windsor!

As her new husband drove out of her life, Verity was seated sadly on the window seat in Anna and Oliver's deserted drawing room. She was reflected in the painted mirror above the white marble fireplace, and the gilded wood of the crimson velvet furniture shone in the golden light of the September morning. The scene outside was busy. There was a great deal of traffic bowling to and fro along Park Lane, and in Hyde Park the parade of fashion was as vain and colorful as ever beneath the changing trees.

She had borrowed one of Anna's gowns, a blue-and-white gingham with a wide blue ribbon around the high waistline, and her hair was pinned up loosely on top of her head. Her eyes were red from crying, and she twisted a handkerchief in her hands as she tried to understand what had happened.

Her thoughts kept returning to that moment during the *ländler* when her world had disintegrated. From gazing adoringly into her eyes, Nicholas had suddenly become an ice-cold stranger. If anyone had told her such a thing could happen, she wouldn't believe it. But it had happened to her. . . .

The door opened behind her, and Anna came in, looking very graceful in a fawn muslin gown sprigged with little brown leaves. Her eyes were concerned as she came to put a gentle hand on Verity's shoulder.

"How are you now, my dear?"

"Numb."

"I'm so very sorry it's come to this, Verity."

"So am I."

Anna sat with her. "I still can't believe Nicholas has behaved so unspeakably."

Verity twisted the handkerchief still more. "I—I keep asking myself if it was something I said or did, but I can't think of anything that might have made him change so much."

"You mustn't blame yourself for his odiousness," Anna said firmly.

Verity was silent for a moment and then gave a rueful smile. "If I was the center of scandal before, I'm sure to be doubly so this morning, am I not?" she murmured, glancing out at the riders in the park, and wondering how many of them had heard of the shocking way Lord Montacute had walked out on his bride in front of everyone at Almack's last night.

Anna drew a long breath. "Society adores gossip, but never dwells long upon one thing because there's always another to take its place."

"A nine-days' wonder," Verity said quietly, remembering what Nicholas had said.

"Exactly." Anna hesitated a little awkwardly, and then spoke again. "I made Oliver go to Grosvenor Square this morning, but I'm afraid Nicholas really did leave for Shropshire last night, just as he said he would. However, at least it seems he left the house at your disposal."

"I suppose I should be grateful he hasn't thrown me out on the streets."

"Not even he would do that, for no matter what, you're his legal wife," Anna pointed out, then she looked at Verity again. "What will you do now?"

"What choice do I have except to go to Grosvenor Square? I can't return to my uncle, nor can I follow Nicholas, for neither of them want me, and I don't have any other family."

Anna put a kind hand over hers. "You can always stay here with us, you know."

"You've already been kind enough."

"But I don't like to think of you on your own . . ."

"Being on my own would appear to be something to which I must speedily become accustomed," Verity replied, getting up. "If a hackney coach could be secured, I'll leave now."

Upset, Anna rose to her feet as well. "Please don't rush off! I feel as if you think I want to be rid of you!"

Verity hugged her. "I don't think any such thing, I merely feel it's best if I get on with things. Besides, you and Oliver are

Nicholas's friends, and I wouldn't wish to jeopardize your closeness to him."

"To Hades with Nicholas!" Anna declared angrily. "I cannot believe now that I ever thought fondly of him, and one thing is certain, he will never be welcome beneath this roof again!"

Fresh tears sprang to Verity's eyes. "But whatever he's done, I still love him with all my heart," she whispered, then caught up her skirts to hurry from the room.

It was getting dark as Martha and Sadie stood by Davey's bedside. There was no mistaking the boy's fever had abated, and his breathing became less labored. Martha leaned forward to put a cool hand to his forehead.

"He begins to mend," she said incredulously, turning to look at her sister. "I cannot think how, but after all these months, suddenly he begins to mend!"

Sadie nodded, keeping her eyes lowered.

Martha searched her face curiously. "Sadie?"

The other said nothing. Judith's warnings rang in her ears, and she was terrified that as easily as the witch had lifted the curse, so it could be imposed once more.

Martha continued to study her. "What's wrong, Sadie? You've been strange for some time now, and I've been putting it down to worry over Davey, but suddenly I begin to be less sure. Have you something to tell me?"

"No!" Sadie replied quickly.

"I know you too well. Tell me what's up."

"There's nothing wrong, it's just been Davey, that's all." Somehow Sadie managed to meet her sister's shrewd gaze.

Martha looked intently at her, then at Davey, then back to her again. "I don't believe you, and I have to wonder why he has so suddenly turned the corner after all this time. I also have to wonder why you, Sadie Cutler, seem so odd about it, it's almost as if you suddenly expected him to recover."

"That's nonsense."

"Is it?" Martha's eyes were sharp and suspicious. "Have you made a pact with the witch?" she asked suddenly.

Sadie went white and backed away, but Martha caught her arm.

"Tell me the truth, Sadie!"

Sadie stared miserably at her. "She—she said that if I did something for her, she'd spare Davey."

Martha's heart began to sink. "What did you have to do?"

"Get the seal you'd hidden in the church. That's all, I swear!"

"That's *all*? Oh, Sadie, what *have* you done?" Martha whispered.

"I had to do it—for Davey's sake!"

Martha looked helplessly at her. "I know why you did it, and I understand, believe me I do, but I wish to God you hadn't."

"Why? What's so important about the seal?"

Martha told her all she knew, and ended with the news that Verity was now Lady Montacute.

Sadie's complexion was like wax. "Oh, no, please, no . . ."

"I'm afraid it's the truth, Sadie, and if I'm right in all I suspect about the witch, it means Miss Verity is now in danger, just as that other Lady Montacute was centuries ago." Martha drew a long breath. "It also means, of course, that Lord Montacute himself has almost certainly fallen into the witch's power now. The seal is his property, and I'm certain it has been enchanted to gain control over him."

Sadie's eyes widened. "But—but it may not be enchanted, it may just be a seal," she said, trying to convince herself.

"Of *course* it's enchanted! Why else would it be of such importance to the witch?" Martha snapped, and turned away with a sigh. "Oh, if *only* I could think of a way to defeat her . . ."

At that moment they both heard a carriage enter the far side of the square. They hurried to the window to look out and saw the vehicle's lamps shining in the gathering autumn dusk as it drew up outside the manor house. They recognized it as Nicholas's traveling carriage, and glanced at each other as his tall figure alighted.

Then Judith appeared. She had discarded mourning and wore instead a bright flame red gown that was vibrant even in this light. Her chestnut hair was loose, and there was a smile on her lovely face as she ran to fling herself into Nicholas's arms. Their lips met in a hungry kiss that left little to the imagination, then Judith took his hand and led him toward the manor house. Her hair caught on a low-hanging branch by the gate, and dying leaves scattered over the path, but she hardly seemed to notice as she smiled up at him.

Martha watched them as they walked through the topiary garden, but Sadie's gaze remained on that low-hanging branch by the gate. Her eyes were alight, and in spite of everything there was suddenly a smile on her lips. Everyone thought Martha was the clever sister, the one with knowledge, while Sadie was just ordinary. But sometimes ordinary sisters knew a thing or two as well, and maybe the witch had just made a grave mistake. In fact, she may have just made the mistake that would cost her everything.

Judith led Nicholas into the manor house and then turned to face him in the entrance hall, where wall candles cast a warm light over the paneled walls and stone floor. "You came to me, my lord," she whispered.

He stared into eyes that were suddenly as green as Verity's had been, but Verity was now no more than an echo on the edge of his memory. He was under the seal's influence and therefore enthralled by Judith. It was as if he were drugged with laudanum, moving in a dreamlike state where fact and fantasy were one, although somewhere in the depths of his heart he knew something was wrong. He just didn't care, though, for all he could really think of was this beautiful redheaded woman, and the sensuous invitation on her lips as she moved closer to him.

"Do you want me, my lord?" she breathed, undoing the little buttons at the front of her bodice so that the fullness of her breasts was more apparent.

"You know I do," he replied, conscious of desire washing helplessly into his veins.

She smiled and continued to undo her bodice until her breasts were completely revealed, their nipples standing out eagerly because she was excited by triumph. He was hers now, and thus her final goal was in sight.

Suddenly he could bear it no more, and he caught her close, putting his parted lips to her throat. She gave a low laugh and pressed her body to his, exulting in his arousal. He could feel all control slipping away. The need to possess her was paramount, and wild exhilarating desire thundered over him as she drew him into a room where no one could see.

He made love to her against the wall, without ceremony or

tenderness, just a white-hot passion that engulfed him completely. It was a harsh coupling that the real Nicholas Montacute would have despised. But he wasn't the real Nicholas anymore, he was finally in Judith's complete power.

In the small hours of that night, Sadie slipped silently out into the cold night air, where the smoke from cottage chimneys seemed to hang in the stillness that engulfed the village. There was no moon or stars, and moisture dripped occasionally from the trees as she hurried stealthily toward the ford. She crossed to the other side, and then made her way to the manor house gate.

A candle burned in Judith's bedroom, and two shadows moved against the curtains. Sadie gazed up at them for a while and then turned her attention to the branch on which the witch had caught her hair. All was quiet as she reached up for the red-gold strands, and more leaves fell as her fingers closed determinedly around them. Her glance flew briefly back to the lighted window. She had been forced to aid and abet evil, but there was nothing to say she could not strike back. Martha may not have thought of a way to defeat the witch, but Sadie Cutler knew what to do. . . .

She hastened back to her cottage, where, in the candlelit kitchen, she began to make Judith's effigy out of sticks, candle-wax, and bits of cloth. The hairs she tied around the head, and when it was complete she held it up in both hands.

"You'll be ready on Halloween, and so I dedicate you to that night. At midnight on All Hallows Eve, you'll come of age, my lovely, and then we'll see what you can do," she whispered, then she hid it in a corner near the fire.

When she accompanied Martha to lay out the peddler's body for burial, the witch's image would go with her.

Verity lay alone in her bed at the Grosvenor Square house. A fire burned low in the hearth, and the soft glow warmed the room, but her heart was as cold as ice. She stretched out a hand to where Nicholas should be lying beside her, but the sheets were empty.

She closed her eyes, remembering the times they had made love, and suddenly, for a few sweetly deceiving moments, it seemed he was lying with her again. She felt his lips upon hers, and his body pressing down. But then the fantasy was over, and she was on her own again. She curled up into a tight ball and hid her face in the pillows.

Chapter Twenty-five

It was cold, dull, and overcast two days later as Wychavon prepared for the peddler's funeral, but it wasn't with the burial that the village concerned itself. Instead everyone spoke in shocked whispers about Lord Montacute's scandalous liaison with Mrs. Villiers, for since his return from London, he had spent nearly every minute at the manor house, and no one was in any doubt as to what he was doing when he was there. It was considered outrageous enough that the admiral's widow should have discarded mourning so soon, but that she should have so publicly taken a lover was thought very reprehensible indeed.

In addition to that, of course, there was the equally startling fact that his lordship was now married to Verity. Wychavon positively hummed with gossip and speculation, and everyone longed to know the details, but no one knew anything at all. The only fact of any certainty was that Nicholas had deserted his new bride to be with his mistress, and didn't seem to care who knew.

Joshua was as shocked as everyone else about Nicholas's return, but he said nothing, nor did he write to Verity in an endeavor to rebuild the bridges between them. His loathing for Nicholas could not have been greater, but Verity's name was still banished from Windsor House. As far as the old man was concerned, the whole business was now closed forever, but inside he was brokenhearted.

Nicholas spent the night before the peddler's funeral at the manor house with Judith, and two hours before the burial was to take place, his carriage returned to take him back to the castle. Every curtain around the green twitched as the vehicle arrived, and countless shocked eyes watched as he and his brazen mistress emerged to walk to the gate.

Judith no longer made any attempt to appear respectable, and in spite of the September chill, was wearing nothing over her flame red gown. She still left her bright hair brushed loose, as if to emphasize the flouting of propriety, and there was a defiantly triumphant tilt to her chin as she walked, holding on his arm.

The village saw the effrontery and sinfulness of the scarlet woman, but Martha, who had halted at the manor house gate on her way to collect Sadie in order to prepare the peddler for burial, saw the witch, shadowless, conscienceless, and bent upon wickedness and revenge. What was not so clear to the nurse was what Nicholas thought or felt, for his face gave nothing away. He neither smiled nor frowned, and didn't glance to the left or right.

Martha's feelings were mixed. She felt hatred for and fear of Judith, but uncertainty regarding Nicholas. He was bewitched, and his life was in jeopardy, but telling him the truth about Judith would do no good, for sorcery clearly dominated him now. The most certain way to release him would be to place the seal in his hands, for he was its rightful owner, but Judith was hardly likely to have left it where it might be found.

The nurse thought one thing very strange, however, and that was the witch's obvious air of gloating triumph. It was as if Judith thought victory was already hers, and yet how could it be when a Lady Montacute once again stood in her way? Unless, of course, she still had no idea there *was* a Lady Montacute. Had Judith's magic so beguiled Nicholas he hadn't even mentioned the bride he had deserted in order to come to her?

The wisewoman gathered her shawl closer around her shoulders as they drew near, then she slipped her hand into her pocket to hold the holy wafers. Nicholas might not be entirely beyond redemption, and it was up to her to do what she could to make him remember that which enchantment may have made him forget. She ignored Judith and spoke only to Nicholas. "Good morning, my lord."

His eyes swung to her. "Miss Cansford?"

Judith's gaze flashed furiously, and her head jerked back as she caught the stench of church surrounding the old woman.

Martha continued to address only Nicholas. "I understand

congratulations are in order, my lord. Will the new Lady Montacute be coming from London soon?" she asked, knowing it was safe to mention Verity, who was out of reach to the witch.

Judith stared at her.

Nicholas seemed confused. "I, er . . ."

Judith's eyes were like gimlets. "What does she mean, Nicholas?" she asked levelly.

Martha smiled and answered for him. "Why, simply that Miss Verity is now his bride. Or is that not so, my lord? Maybe it's untrue, but I was told you'd married Miss Verity?"

"You, er, were told the truth, Miss Cansford," he murmured uneasily.

Judith's face drained of color, and her fingers tightened over his sleeve like talons. Disbelief lurched through her. The magistrate's cursed niece was his *wife*?

Martha watched Nicholas's face closely in those seconds, and she saw a puzzled look pass through his eyes, as if he couldn't quite understand what was happening to him. She also saw a nuance of recollection lighten them for a moment, a softening, as if a sweet memory had briefly crossed his consciousness.

Judith saw it too, and her snarl became an ugly grimace of unutterable fury. She trembled from head to toe, and was so beside herself she could have struck both him and Martha. History had repeated itself, and as had happened two hundred years ago, she had to cut down a wife in order to fully reach her objective!

Martha inclined her head and walked on. Her heart was beating swiftly, and she could feel Judith's hot gaze following her, burning into her back like a fiery dagger. The old woman's hand tightened over the wafers, crushing them into crumbs.

Judith didn't like being made to seem foolish, and that was just what had happened. More than that, she had been made to realize she still hadn't achieved what she wanted! Her furious glance flashed to Nicholas. "Why didn't you tell me you'd married Verity Windsor?" she demanded through clenched teeth.

"I—I don't know," he replied truthfully.

"If you want me, you'll have to be free of her. You realize that, don't you?"

He hesitated.

Her fingernails dug through his sleeve. "You do want me, don't you?"

"Yes, of—of course . . ."

"Then you must be rid of her."

He had no will of his own, for his will was Judith's now. His role was to obey, not to reason, so he immediately acceded to her wish. "I will instruct my lawyers . . ."

She gave no sign of her inner rage as she kissed him farewell, but as he drove away, her eyes flickered malevolently. Lawyers took too long, and she didn't intend to wait. By marrying him, Verity Windsor had signed her own death warrant. Snakestone or not, the new Lady Montacute would die!

The witch drew a long, steadying breath. She must not let this setback affect her too much, for she had immediate things to do. Before learning about Verity, she had decided to see how powerful the seal really was. Until now she had only been able to transform herself into a hare with Hecate's direct help from the grove, but now, if the seal was fully potent, she ought to be able to change wherever she was. It had to be tested.

Gathering her bold red skirts, she turned to hurry back into the house. There, in the privacy of her room, she undressed to rub ointment over her body. Then she dressed again, drew a circle on the floor, and stood inside it with the seal at her feet. She whispered a magic spell and began to turn around and around. The room soon whirled dizzily, and she felt herself diminishing in size. Suddenly she was a hare, nimble and swift, and no one saw her as she fled down through the house.

She bounded triumphantly along the valley, leaping through the damp early autumn undergrowth, where spiderwebs were draped like shrouds, and the first dead leaves scattered in the draft of her passing. She outpaced the carriage and reached the castle ahead of it.

Nicholas alighted as the team halted in the courtyard. He was thinking of how to word the promised letter he had to send to his Gray's Inn lawyers regarding divorce, but then the flutter of Judith's red gown caught his eye. He stared at her in astonishment, for in spite of his bewitchment, he knew it was impossible for her to have reached the castle first. There was only one road from the village to the castle, and no one had ridden past.

As she came down the steps, he felt enervating shackles coiling around him, and there was nothing he could do to resist. He seized her in his arms, but as he tried to kiss her passionately, she drew her head back tantalizingly.

"Do you swear to make me mistress of Wychavon?" she whispered.

"I swear I will shed Verity as soon as I can," he breathed, closing his eyes as her parted lips moved sensuously against his.

A little later, Martha and Sadie arrived at the vicarage to lay the peddler's body out. They worked silently and efficiently, for they had performed their duties countless times over the years, and the vicar remained with them, it being his custom to read prayers on such occasions.

As his voice droned solemnly around them, Martha became increasingly conscious of something odd in Sadie's manner. "What's wrong?" she whispered at last as she watched Sadie fumble with the buttons of the peddler's coat.

"Nothing," Sadie whispered back, and then she straightened suddenly to interrupt the vicar's prayers. "Reverend, do you have an old prayer book to lay in the coffin?"

Martha stared at her, and the vicar was taken aback. "I—I beg your pardon, Mrs. Cutler?" he said.

"The peddler was a very God-fearing man and should have such a book buried with him."

The vicar couldn't hide his astonishment. "Well, if that is what you think should be done . . ."

"I do, Reverend."

"Very well, I'll find one." Putting his own rather beautiful volume aside, he hurried from the room.

Martha immediately caught her sister's arm. "What are you up to, Sadie Cutler?"

"Nothing." But Sadie had her fingers crossed behind her back. She had no intention of saying anything to anyone about what she intended to do, for secrecy was the key. Suddenly she glanced past Martha at the window. "Oh, what does *he* want?"

Martha turned. "What does who want?" she asked blankly, for there wasn't anyone there.

In a trice Sadie had slipped Judith's effigy into the peddler's coat pocket. Then she straightened. "I—I thought the verger was out there trying to attract our attention," she explained.

Martha looked at her again. "You're addled this morning, Sadie," she muttered.

"Maybe so," Sadie agreed, and then they said nothing more as the vicar returned with a rather battered prayer book.

Shortly after that the pallbearers came to carry the coffin to the lychgate, and as the bell began to toll, a line of villagers filed past to pay their respects before the peddler was taken into the church itself for the brief service.

When it was over, and the coffin was taken out for the interment, Martha paused to look intently at the cross on the altar. "Remember, Lord, that it says in the Bible 'Thou shalt not suffer a witch to live.' Exodus, chapter twenty-two, verse eighteen. Bear it in mind, I beg you."

Sadie had joined the mourners at the graveside. It had begun to rain, and while the church bell continued its dismal tolling, she watched until the last spadeful of earth was heaped upon the grave. Everyone else then quickly dispersed, but she remained where she was, with her wet shawl raised over her head, and her shoulders damp with moisture.

The grave's secret must be left to come into its own now, then, at midnight on Halloween, Judith's anniversary, its existence would be made known. By then it would be too late for the witch.

Chapter Twenty-six

There was no rain in London, but it was very cloudy, and darkness had closed in as Anna and Oliver called upon Verity. She received them in the candlelit drawing room, where she had been endeavoring to distract herself by doing some embroidery. She was wearing a cheerful primrose gown that was patterned with white stars, but there were shadows under her eyes, and it was plain to both of them that she had been crying again.

Anna's coral taffeta skirts rustled as she hastened over to take her hands. "We've come to make sure you're all right, Verity. I know you'd probably prefer to be left alone, but you need friends at a time like this."

Verity managed a smile. "You're both being so kind to me," she said, glancing from Anna's gown to Oliver's evening clothes. "You're going out somewhere?"

Anna nodded. "To sample a genuine French dinner at the Clarendon, and *you* are going to come with us," she declared, squeezing Verity's fingers kindly.

Verity shook her head and drew her hands away. "Oh, I couldn't possibly, I—"

"Yes, you can," Anna interrupted determinedly. "You must face society, Verity, for the longer you leave it, the harder it will be."

"Maybe so, but I'm really not up to it."

"Oh, yes, you are, my lady. A little bit of powder and a dab of rouge, and no one will know you've cried at all."

Oliver came closer. "Anna's right, you know, Verity. Find the courage to venture forth now, and you'll begin to carve your place in London society, which is, after all, what you must do.

Be practical, my dear, you cannot return to Wychavon, and this house is your home now."

"But for how long?" she murmured.

"Nick cannot and will not throw you out, for no matter what his change of heart, he cannot deny that he married you. Right up until that last moment at Almack's he was proclaiming his love for you all over town, even to the extent of threatening pistols at dawn upon those who made unwelcome wagers upon . . . Well, we, er, know what upon. So I'm certain you're secure in this house, and Anna and I think you should begin to make your mark on London. Besides, tonight's little excursion is only a little *diner à trois*, not the full glare of Almack's."

She hesitated. "I—I'm not sure, Oliver . . ."

Anna linked her arm briskly. "I am. Come on, I'm sure your maid and I can turn you out more than adequately."

Verity gave in, but the last thing she really wished to do was go anywhere at all.

Half an hour later, wearing a blue velvet cloak over a pink silk evening gown, with the snakestone at her throat and her hair dressed up *à l'Égyptienne*, she was seated in the carriage as it drove through the lamplit Mayfair streets to the renowned Clarendon Hotel.

Albemarle Street possessed few private residences these days, being almost entirely devoted to hotels, of which the Clarendon was by far the most superior. It was kept by the renowned French chef, Jacquiers, and its frontage stood in adjacent New Bond Street, but all carriages came to the rear. There were a considerable number of private vehicles drawn up at the pavement as Oliver assisted his two ladies to alight, and Verity had to summon all her waning courage as he offered her an arm. They went into the fashionable premises, where to her dismay the hum of voices indicated a crowded evening in progress.

The following two hours were a torture she would have preferred not to endure. She could feel eyes upon her from all directions, and knew she was practically the sole topic of conversation. There didn't seem to have been a single corner of London into which her sorry story hadn't crept, nor a single soul who didn't find her of most riveting interest, but she did her best to rise above it all, and by the end of the meal she knew she had succeeded in drawing some admiration for her courage.

Driving back to Grosvenor Square, however, her brave facade began to crumble away, and there were tears on her cheeks as Anna and Oliver accompanied her into the house. They wanted to stay with her, but although she thanked them very much, she insisted that they go home. All she wanted to do was curl up into a ball in the dark, and give in to the misery that echoed through her hollow heart.

But as she stood at the foot of the staircase watching Charles close the door behind them, her glance fell upon the console table where all the recently delivered post lay on a silver platter. In his haste to depart, Nicholas had omitted to leave instructions for the sending on of any mail, and as a consequence the platter was now quite full. She had paid little attention to its contents, but one letter now caught her eye, for she recognized her uncle's handwriting.

She went closer. Although it was addressed to Nicholas, she couldn't help picking it up and hiding it in her reticule before the butler noticed what she had done. It wasn't her habit to read other people's mail, but in this instance she was filled with the sudden hope that her uncle might have relented. Gathering her skirts, she fled up to her room.

It was some time before Lizzy finished attending her, and she was alone in bed to open the letter. Her face fell as she saw the angry scrawl.

Windsor House

Sir,
Your flagrant disregard for my feelings and wishes is no more or less than I would expect of a man of such base character. You, sir, are a disgrace to your illustrious name, and it grieves me to the very core that my foolish niece has so fallen under your wicked influence as to marry you. Her action is something I cannot and will not forgive, for she turned her back upon me in favor of a man who can only be described as a dissolute blackguard, totally bereft of honor.

Verity stared at the letter in dismay, for there wasn't anything in the least conciliatory about such heated words. She knew she shouldn't read on, but just couldn't help herself.

I do not profess to know what your motives are in making Verity your bride, for it cannot be pursuit of her fortune, which in no way compares with your own. Nor can it be for love, since you are incapable of such an honest sentiment.

Verity blinked back tears, but still she couldn't put the letter aside.

My lord, it may amuse you to trifle with my unfortunate kinswoman, but at least I suppose she has the comfort of your ring upon her finger, which is more than can be said for the last hapless recipient of your vile attentions. I have to inform you that several months ago poor Amabel Sichester was brought to bed of your daughter in Geneva, although no doubt the news is of little concern to you.

Verity's heart seemed to have stopped within her, and she suddenly felt so cold it might have been midwinter. Nicholas and Amabel Sichester? A daughter? She could hardly hold the paper because her fingers were without sensation. Past phrases and glances began to be clearer, but most of all she understood why her uncle had suddenly begun to loathe Nicholas so deeply. Lady Sichester had clearly confided in her trusted old friend before protecting Amabel's reputation by taking her to Geneva for the lying-in.

Almost blinded by tears, she made herself read on, for if anyone had the right to know everything, it was Nicholas Montacute's bride.

I am sickened to the heart that any so-called gentleman could conduct himself as despicably as you have, sir. To seduce the innocent, and then desert them to face the consequence of the union is perhaps the lowest level to which any Englishman of rank can sink.

I wish now that I had had a little less regard for the proprieties, and had informed Verity of the truth about you. If she had known that I despised you because you sired an illegitimate child and deserted its helpless mother, maybe she would not have been taken in by your blandishments.

Amabel Sichester is the lady who should be your bride, my lord Montacute, and you should have had the decency and regard for your own flesh and blood to grant your daughter the dignity of legitimacy. Your failure on both counts damns you in the eyes of the world. May you rot in Hell.

Joshua Windsor

Verity's shaking fingers closed over the letter, crumpling the paper into a ball before she flung it wretchedly across the room. Then she hid her face in her hands. What a fool she had been. Nicholas's true character had been there before her all the time, first in the mill, then in her bedroom at the castle, and on every occasion after that. But why had he married her, not Amabel, who had breeding, expectations, *and* beauty? Unless, of course . . .

She lowered her hands in fresh dismay. What if the marriage ceremony had been a pretense? What if the priest hadn't been a priest at all? Had she been the victim of a cruel hoax? Was Nicholas merely biding his time to expose her as a green chit who was gullible enough to think he had made an honest woman of her?

She tried to think clearly. The wedding certificate—fake or not—identified the priest as being appointed to the Grosvenor Chapel, South Audley Street, in the parish of St. George's, Hanover Square. She would have to go there first thing in the morning to see if he really existed. Oh, please, *please* don't let there be the ultimate humiliation and disgrace of a false wedding!

It was three in the morning before it stopped raining and Judith was able to go to the grove. This time her dark arts were directed at Verity, who had to be brought back to Wychavon to be done to death. To this end something belonging to Verity had to be enchanted, just as the seal had been before, and the witch was using the length of yellow embroidery silk she had tripped over so fatefully on May Eve, but although she danced around the circle, Hecate did not come. The candles didn't burn, the invisible hounds didn't bay, and the water continued to flow through the millrace.

Judith shivered angrily as she at last stood still in the damp night air. She knew what was wrong. The magic wouldn't work because Verity was too well protected by the snakestone and couldn't be reached at all. Something else would have to be done to bring her back to Wychavon.

The witch considered for a moment, and then she began to

smile, for although the snakestone shielded Verity, it didn't shield her uncle too. What had been done to Davey Cutler could be done to Joshua Windsor, and if he lay close to death, in spite of the differences between them, his niece was bound to hurry north to be with him. Once she was here . . . Judith's smile deepened, for the snakestone couldn't protect anyone from murder by mortal means.

The witch began to gather her things, but then something caught her attention in the dying undergrowth at the edge of the grove. It was a soft golden light, steady and beautiful, and Judith's lips parted incredulously. Was it . . . ? Could it possibly be . . . ? She hurried across the wet grass and dashed the autumn leaves aside to stare down at the gleaming gold filigree fronds of druid's moss, the rarest and most magical plant of all. She had only seen it once before, and that had been during her life as Meg. It only appeared after rain, when, night or dry, it unfolded for a few hours in the damp. Once gathered, it granted its finder a single opportunity to put someone into a trance during which he or she could be instructed to do anything the finder wished. The victim wouldn't recall the instructions afterward, but would carry them out anyway.

Judith's eyes shone, for now she knew how to finally dispose of the new Lady Montacute. Once Verity had returned to Wychavon, the druid's moss could be used to make none other than Nicholas Montacute lure her to her death. And that death would take place here in the grove, as had the admiral's, and as, in due course, Nicholas's would too.

Judith's fingertips shook as she touched the moss. The temptation to snatch it up now was almost too much, but she restrained herself. Druid's moss had to be gathered ritually, with a silver blade and a white cloth, or it was of no use at all. So with a smile the witch left the golden fronds where they were and hurried back to collect her things and hide them in the mill. Then she returned to the village.

An hour or so later, Joshua's sleep became suddenly restless. He had been in a deep slumber, but now he tossed and turned as nightmares began to beset him. He felt as if a great weight were pressing down on his chest, suffocating him and making his heart feel as if it would burst.

With a cry he awoke, struggling for air. He was drenched in perspiration, and as a wave of nausea swept over him, he had no time to do anything but lean over the side of the bed to retch. Several minutes passed before he was able to lie back on the pillows again. His body now felt cold and clammy, and his head was still spinning unpleasantly.

The night breeze crept in through the open windows, rustling through the trees outside and making the curtains billow like ghosts. Dread images hovered before him, and terror began to rise. He cried out in fear and reached for the handbell beside the bed.

Martha hurried in response and found him leaning over the bed again, his whole body heaving with fresh nausea. "Oh, sir, whatever is it?" she cried, hastening to him.

"Send for Dr. Rogers," he whispered. "And be quick!"

It was dawn before the doctor drove swiftly along the Ludlow road toward Wychavon. He passed the track to the grove, where Judith was gathering the druid's moss with a silver dagger and white cloth. The witch heard the tilbury rattle along the road, and glanced up smilingly, but then returned her attention to the moss, all the time whispering the incantation that would make it serve her.

At Windsor House the doctor could do no more than prescribe laudanum and promise to return later. He suspected the shellfish Joshua had eaten for his supper, but could not be certain. As he drove away again, Sadie crept from the bushes to attract Martha's attention.

"What is it, Sadie?" the wisewoman asked quietly.

"If Mr. Windsor is ill, you may count upon it that it's the witch's work," Sadie replied, glancing uneasily around for fear that Judith might be near.

"Why do you say that?"

"Because I saw her during the night. She stood in front of this house with her arms spread out. She didn't move for a long time, then walked back to the manor house."

Martha looked away. The evil eye. But why would Judith overlook Joshua?

Completely ignorant of anything that had happened in Wychavon, at midmorning Verity walked nervously to the chapel in South Audley Street, where to her relief she learned that her marriage to Nicholas was valid. So she really was Lady Montacute, she thought as she left the chapel again afterward, but instead of returning to Grosvenor Square, she went to Park Lane to confront Anna and Oliver. Given what she had now learned about her husband's recent past, she couldn't believe they had known nothing about his affair with Amabel Sichester.

Only Anna was at home, and received her in the drawing room, hurrying warmly over to take her hands. "How are you this morning, Verity?" she asked.

"To be truthful, I'm not quite sure."

Anna looked at her. "Why? Has something happened?"

"What do you know about Nicholas and Amabel Sichester?" Verity asked quietly.

Anna let go of her hands. "Who told you?"

"So you knew all about it, and yet said nothing to me? Oh, Anna, how *could* you!" Close to tears, Verity turned away.

"Nicholas swore there was no truth in any of it."

"Amabel has had his child!" Verity cried.

Anna stared at her and then sat down on a sofa and patted the seat beside her. "I—I'll tell you what I know, which isn't a great deal."

Verity joined her reluctantly, and Anna began. "Nicholas and Amabel were very much the thing last year, in fact Oliver and I daily expected an announcement, but then suddenly it was all over. Nicholas gave no explanation at all and never mentioned her name, then Lady Sichester hurried Amabel off to Geneva, and the next thing we knew, your uncle had taken their house during their absence. Inevitably there were whispers, for daughters have been hastily whisked to Switzerland before in order to avoid scandal, but no one knew anything for certain where Amabel was concerned. When Oliver and I heard some of the whispers, Oliver asked Nicholas to his face if there was any truth in it all, but he denied being in the wrong over anything, and certainly denied being the father of any child Amabel may or may not be expecting. Oliver believed him, and, in the end, so did I. No, that's not strictly true, because I still nursed doubts, but that was all they were—doubts."

Anna glanced away a little guiltily, recalling similar, still un-expressed doubts concerning Nicholas' dealings with the admiral's widow. But now wasn't the moment to mention them, not when Verity already had so much to cope with. Anna pursed her lips a little. *Damn you, Nicholas Montacute*, she thought.

Verity considered what Anna had said and then nodded. "I believe you, Anna, and I'm sorry I came here thinking the worst of you."

"You had every right to think the worst." Anna drew a long breath. "I confess I wish now that I *had* said something to you about Amabel, but I really couldn't finally believe that Nicholas would be so monstrous as to desert a woman who expected his child. I'd come to think of him as something of a lothario, but not truly heartless."

"Well, it seems that heartless is precisely what he is," Verity replied. "If I could turn the clock back, I would. Maybe my spinster life at Wychavon was dull, but at least it was happy. Still, I'm not the one I should be feeling sorry for, when it's poor Amabel who's been treated really cruelly."

"Well, maybe . . ." was the measured reply.

Verity looked inquiringly at her. "Why do you say that?"

"Because I've never liked Amabel. She looks as if butter wouldn't melt in her mouth, but there's something about her that I simply cannot take to."

"I don't know her well, but I always found her charming."

Anna smiled. "Some say Lucretia Borgia was too, so charm hardly signifies, does it?" She put a hand over Verity's. "Try to be brave. Last night at the Clarendon you began your new life, so please continue to put Nicholas behind you. London is your oyster, you know, and somewhere in its streets and squares there lives another handsome gentleman who'll steal your heart."

Verity gave an ironic half smile. "Anna, if there's one lesson I've learned, it's never to trust a handsome gentleman."

As Verity and Anna sat together in Park Lane, in Wychavon the doctor had called again to see Joshua, whose condition hadn't improved since the night. The old man's face was gray, his eyes were dull, and he lay weakly in the bed, his body exhausted from the unremitting waves of nausea. More laudanum had been advised, and then the doctor had driven away again, watched by Judith.

The witch smiled. It wouldn't be long now. Soon Verity would be sent for.

Chapter Twenty-seven

But September ended, and the weeks passed. October drifted mellowly toward November, and the countryside was ablaze with vivid autumn colors, but Judith still waited in vain for Verity's return.

Like Davey Cutler before him, Joshua continued to slowly sink, but while the whole village waited daily to hear of his sad demise, his niece remained inexplicably in London. Judith was both puzzled and anxious. Halloween was approaching, and she wished to dispose of Verity on that all-important night. Surely word had been sent south by now? If so, why hadn't anything happened?

The truth was that even though he was so ill, Joshua was determined not to repair the rift with Verity. He extracted a promise from Martha and the other servants that no communication would be made, and there the matter seemed to rest. But in the end his wishes *were* flouted, although not by anyone at Windsor House. It was Nicholas who was destined to apprise Verity of her uncle's piteous condition, and it happened because of a chance meeting on the Ludlow road, when he was returning to the castle after a morning ride.

It was a crisp day, and leaves lay thick on the ground. There had been a frost overnight, and the scent of woodsmoke hung sweetly in the air. The valley was a glory of crimson and gold beneath a sharp blue sky, and about half a mile away the castle battlements looked almost white in the sun. The horse's breath billowed in silvery clouds, and its hooves drummed satisfyingly on the hard ground as he rode toward the gates into the park.

He was still under Judith's spell, but outwardly no longer seemed so trancelike as he had at first. He was far from being his own man, though, and had given Verity very little thought for the past weeks, except to wonder if his lawyers had obeyed his instructions about contacting her regarding a divorce. He felt no remorse, not even a moment's sorrow over the anguish such a cold legal communication was bound to cause her. She had simply ceased to matter to him, it was Judith who filled his life now. Only Judith.

The doctor's tilbury drove toward him from the direction of the village, and he reined in as he recognized it. Dr. Rogers happened to glance out and see him too, and lowered the glass to instruct his coachman to stop.

"Good afternoon, my lord," the doctor said.

Nicholas doffed his top hat. "Good afternoon, Doctor."

"I trust I find you in excellent health?"

"You do."

"You're fortunate not to be in the same sad state as your fellow magistrate," the doctor said then, measuring his words with care because he had heard all the wild rumors connecting Lord Montacute's name with those of both Verity Windsor and Judith Villiers.

Nicholas was puzzled. "My fellow magistrate? Are you referring to Joshua Windsor?"

"I am indeed. I fear he's beginning to lose the battle."

Nicholas looked blankly at him. "Battle?"

"Surely you know how very ill he is? I wish I could hold out hope for him, but since he's failed to respond to my every effort, there seems nothing more I can do, although it has to be said that when the Cutler boy suffered the same debilitating symptoms, I gave up hope with him too, but suddenly he began to recover."

Nicholas was shocked. "I—I'd heard the old man was unwell, but had no idea he was as ill as that!"

"It's very sad, especially as he will not countenance sending for his niece. They were so very close, but now it seems they have fallen out beyond redemption." The doctor cleared his throat uncomfortably, for he didn't like mentioning Verity, but the situation at Windsor House was now causing him such grave concern that he had to say something. It wasn't right that the new Lady Montacute—if that was indeed what Verity Windsor had become—should remain in London when her uncle lay at death's door here in Shropshire. If no one beneath Joshua's own roof would do anything about it, perhaps Nicholas would.

Nicholas shifted a little in the saddle. "Are you telling me no word has been sent to London?" he inquired in surprise.

"That's correct, my lord. Mr. Windsor is most obstinately set on the matter, and none of his servants will go against his wishes."

"I see." Nicholas lowered his eyes for a moment, a little taken aback that Joshua's loathing for him should extend to such a degree. Then he looked at the doctor again. "You clearly feel a message should be dispatched."

"Yes, I do."

Nicholas nodded. "Then I will do it, for no matter what you may have heard, I am not entirely without honor. My wife will be speedily informed of her uncle's condition."

"Thank you, my lord."

"Sir." Nicholas doffed his hat again, then urged his horse through the castle gates.

The doctor gazed after him for a moment before instructing his coachman to drive on.

As the road became clear again there was a rustle of dry leaves at the verge, then a hare sprang out of hiding and leapt away toward the village.

On reaching the castle, Nicholas gave instructions for a messenger to stand by to ride to London, then he adjourned to the solar to write to Verity without delay. A log fire crackled in the vast stone hearth as he sat at the table where his portable escritoire was still open after being used earlier, but as he picked up the last sheet of paper, he saw the black pearl pin Verity had given him. It had lain there since he had tossed it there after returning from Almack's.

Slowly he took it out and turned it between his fingers. A strange forgotten warmth tingled through him, and the present faded as his thoughts returned to the wedding night. Verity was beneath him on the bed, her body quivering with awakened pleasure as his lovemaking swept them both toward climax.

Nothing could compare with the emotions he had felt then, and nothing he had felt since returning to Wychavon had come even close.

This last thought shocked him, for he couldn't believe he had ever put Judith in second place to the wife he had rejected. He quickly dropped the pin back into the escritoire, but still gazed at it as all manner of memories continued to surge to the fore. Veils seemed to be lifting away from his eyes, and with each one he saw a little more clearly. Verity suddenly ceased to be an unwanted figure on the edge of his memory, but was sharp and clear before him, as if he could reach out and touch her.

A keen pang of conscience plunged confusingly through him, and he rose swiftly from the table again. He had deserted Verity to come to Judith, but it had been the right thing to do. It had! *Judith* was the woman he really loved. He closed his eyes. Why had thoughts of Verity begun to plague him like this? And why did he suddenly wish he hadn't instructed his lawyers concerning divorce? He ran his fingers through his hair and went to pour himself a glass of cognac, even though it was still well before noon.

Judith watched him from the shadows at the far end of the room. She wore a simple marigold velvet gown, and her hair was twisted up almost nonchalantly on top of her head. Her hazel eyes—so green to him—had become sharp and suspicious as she watched the expressions on his face after he had picked up the pin, which she could tell brought back pleasant memories that did her cause no good. So she remained where she was, watching, and gauging.

Nicholas sipped the drink. A little of the truth had begun to shine like a beacon through his darkness. Things were not as they should be. He was caught in a web, and the spider was the beautiful flame-haired woman whose wishes he could not deny. His thoughts broke off as the butler tapped at the door and came in.

"My lord, the messenger is ready to leave for London."

The letter to Verity! "Wait while I write it," Nicholas said, resuming his seat at the table. The quill flew over the paper, then it was sanded, sealed, and handed to the waiting servant. "See it's delivered posthaste to Grosvenor Square. The rider will be well rewarded on his return."

"My lord." The butler bowed and hurried away.

As the door closed behind him, Judith suddenly spoke. "I'm here again, Nicholas."

He started from his seat, and for a split second she was sure she saw revulsion written large in his eyes, but then it had gone. She moved to the escritoire and held up the pin. "What is this to you?" she asked, holding his gaze.

"Just a pin," he replied, suddenly determined not to discuss anything about Verity with her.

"*Just* a pin?"

"Yes."

She tossed it aside and came closer to him. "Is something wrong, Nicholas?"

"No."

She searched his face. Contrary to what he said, she knew something was *very* wrong. The change in him was almost tangible, yet how could he have changed at all now that she had the seal? She reached up to touch his cheek, knowing that physical contact was certain to affect him.

The brush of her fingers seared his skin, and he began to draw swiftly away, but as she continued to touch him, he felt her spell encircling him again. The power of the seal resumed precedence over his feelings for Verity, and Judith's bewitching bonds slid relentlessly around him once more.

The witch smiled and took his glass. "Allow me to pour you another," she murmured, going to the decanter. When he couldn't see, she took a vial of golden liquid from her pocket, and emptied it into his drink. It was made from the druid's moss, and she had brought it with her now because after hearing him promise the doctor he would write to Verity, she intended to prepare him for his role in that lady's demise. She wished she knew what had caused the fleeting change in him, but it was over now, and she was satisfied he was under her complete control again.

Still smiling, she took the glass back to him. "Drink," she urged softly.

He obeyed, and thought it tasted a little odd, but if Judith wished him to drink it, he would. He didn't feel anything as he froze into complete immobility, standing like a statue. His eyes were sightless, but he heard everything the witch said.

"Listen to me, Nicholas. Soon it will be Halloween, by which time Verity is sure to have returned to Wychavon to be with her uncle. I want you to go to Windsor House after dark on that day. She is bound not to attend the celebrations on the green because the old man is ill, so you're certain to be able to see her. When you do, you'll know you adore her with all your heart, and the last thing you will wish to do is proceed with a divorce. You'll be anxious to regain her trust, and when you have, you'll convince her that you wish to seek a reconciliation. You will tell her you believe I am a witch who has cast a spell over you, and that to be free of me, you need her help. She is to be persuaded to meet you in the oak grove at midnight, and she must give her word not to tell anyone. You will then leave Windsor House, and the moment you do, you'll forget everything you thought, said, and did while beneath its roof. You will meet Verity in the grove, I will, and I will see that soon we will be free to be together always."

He gave no sign that he had understood anything, but she knew he had, and that he would do as she instructed. She touched his cheek again. "Wake now, for it is done," she said softly, moving behind him.

He turned, but there was no one there.

Chapter Twenty-eight

Verity was destined to be out on the day Nicholas's message about her uncle arrived, although as she sat at the breakfast table, the last thing she felt like was leaving the house. Her face was pale and wan, a situation that wasn't improved by the lavender shade of her woolen gown, and she was beset by a general feeling of malaise that had rendered her quite low for over a week now.

There had been an overnight frost, and everything in the garden still glistened icily, but the sun was already up, and she knew it would be another glorious October day. This had been one of the most beautiful falls she could recall, but she could take very little pleasure in its loveliness. She wished she were back at Wychavon, still plain Verity Windsor, still Uncle Joshua's beloved niece. . . .

Her wandering thoughts were brought back to the present as a footman brought her a letter that had come for her from Nicholas's lawyers. The contents were very brief. Nicholas intended to seek an early end to their marriage. She fought back tears, for no matter how much she told herself she wished she were still Miss Windsor, what she really wished was that Nicholas would return to her. Now she knew that that would never be so.

The footman returned. "Begging your pardon, my lady, but Mrs. Henderson has called."

Verity composed herself. "Please show her in."

"My lady."

Anna wore a bottle green riding habit and top hat, and her smile and manner were brisk as she came to the table. "You, madam, are coming for a ride in the park. The roses have quite gone out of your cheeks, and I intend to put them back."

"I—I'd rather not, Anna . . ." Verity began.

But Anna held up a hand. "You have no choice in the matter. I've instructed your servants to have a horse saddled for you, and all you have to do is toddle up to change."

Verity had learned by now that it did no good to argue with Anna, so she got up from the table. "I'll be as quick as possible."

As she went out, Anna's glance fell on the letter. She moved closer and read the curt lines, then her eyes darkened. Nicholas Montacute went from sin to sin. How could he be so beastly to Verity? The poor girl had done nothing to warrant this loathsome treatment, yet he behaved as if she had committed every wifely crime under the sun.

When Verity reappeared in her royal blue riding habit, Anna smiled. "You were in that on the day you nearly fell beneath our carriage."

"At least I feel entitled to wear it," Verity murmured.

"Why do you say that?"

"Because Amabel Sichester was kind enough to select my London wardrobe."

"You shouldn't feel awkward, Verity, for you aren't at fault." Anna hesitated. "I'm afraid I've been impertinent enough to read your letter."

"Well, it will hardly be a secret once things are in motion," Verity replied quietly.

"What do you mean to do about it?"

"Do?"

"If you let this proceed without contesting, you'll lose everything, but if you fight, you stand to gain. You are Lady Montacute, and you should remain so, for you aren't in the wrong, Nicholas is."

Verity lowered her eyes. "I still love him very much, Anna, and what I really want is a reconciliation, but I now know that that is out of the question. Perhaps it's best if I simply bow out gracefully."

"Verity—"

"Let's go for that ride," Verity interrupted brightly, then turned and hurried out, and after a moment Anna followed.

There were only a few riders in Hyde Park because it was early morning. The air was cold, especially beneath the trees, and a deep carpet of fallen leaves rustled against the horses' hooves, but in spite of the late October chill, Verity felt uncomfortably hot. The sun seemed to beat down on her as relentlessly as if it were high summer, and after a while she began to feel strangely detached. Sound seemed to echo a little, and then shadows began to close in on all sides. A shrill whistle sounded in her ears, and she felt herself slipping from the saddle. She heard Anna's alarmed cry, and then knew nothing more.

Anna dismounted in dismay and knelt beside her among the leaves, then an elderly gentleman who was riding nearby urged his horse over and dismounted too. He introduced himself as Sir Henry Stowell, the fashionable physician, and Anna smiled with relief as he crouched to examine Verity.

"I'm so glad you were near, Sir Henry. I—I am Mrs. Oliver Henderson, I believe you and my husband are acquainted."

He nodded. "Why, yes, indeed. I'm pleased to meet you, Mrs. Henderson. May I inquire who your friend is?" he asked then, returning his attention to Verity, who had yet to regain consciousness.

"She is Lady Montacute," Anna explained.

"Ah," he murmured, for in common with the rest of London, he knew all about the Montacute match. Verity stirred, and he looked attentively into her eyes as she regained consciousness. "Please lie still, my lady, for I must ascertain if you've sustained any injuries."

She gazed up in puzzlement at the sky and lacework of autumn leaves beyond him, then her eyes focused on his face. "Who—who are you?"

Anna leaned over. "It's all right, Verity, he is Sir Henry Stowell."

"What happened?"

"You fainted."

Sir Henry examined her as best he could and soon concluded that she hadn't broken any bones. He assisted her into a sitting position, and then looked intently into her eyes again. "How have you been feeling lately, my lady?"

"Feeling? Well, a little unwell, actually. No, not exactly unwell, just odd. Oh, I don't really know, I just haven't been feeling quite right, that's all. Why do you ask?"

"Because I have the honor to be one of the capital's foremost *accoucheurs*, and in years of experience I have learned that a woman's eyes tell a great deal about the state of her health. There is no doubt in my mind that you are with child."

Verity stared up at him. "With child?" she repeated.

He nodded. "A hardly impossible state of affairs, given that you are married."

Anna felt close to tears. A child, and only that morning Verity had learned that Nicholas wished to divorce her!

Verity struggled to get up, and as Sir Henry helped to steady her, she looked anxiously at him. "Are you quite sure?"

"As sure as I can be without a full examination. When was your last monthly showing?"

Verity's lips parted, for she hadn't even given it thought. Now that she did, she realized she hadn't seen anything since her stay in Kent, and heaven knew how many weeks ago that had been.

Sir Henry smiled a little. "I can see by your expression that you have all the necessary confirmation."

She nodded.

"I will be delighted to attend you if you wish."

"You—you are most kind, Sir Henry."

"My advice now is that you go home and rest, for riding accidents are not to be recommended for ladies in your condition."

Anna stepped forward. "I will see she rests, Sir Henry."

He helped them both to remount and then rode away.

When Verity felt able, the two women rode slowly back to Grosvenor Square, where for a moment Anna prevented Verity from dismounting. "You realize that divorce is now quite out of the question, don't you? You have a child to think of now, and if it should be a son, the Montacute title and fortune will be his birthright. Even a girl should not have her future blighted by the stigma of divorce. At all costs you must remain Nicholas's wife."

"Anna—"

"Listen to what I'm saying, Verity. Oliver and I have been denied the joy of children, but you have not. As a mother, it is your duty to do all you can for your baby. And it is Nicholas's duty to be a proper father," she added fiercely.

Before Verity could say anything in reply, the door of the house opened and Charles the butler hurried out. "My lady, an urgent message has been delivered from his lordship!" He handed Nicholas's letter up to her.

She broke the seal and read the hastily scrawled lines. Her already pale face went still more white, and she raised stricken eyes to Anna. "It's my uncle, he's so ill he's not expected to live," she whispered.

It was several days before she was able to set off for Wychavon, because Anna wouldn't hear of her embarking upon an arduous journey so soon after her fall. To make certain Verity was sensible, Sir Henry was sent for, and he too forbade any traveling until he was content she was up to it. Anna stayed at Grosvenor Square to be sure the patient did as she was instructed.

Verity was racked with worry over her uncle. If he had been ill for so long, why hadn't she been notified before? The incongruity of it having been Nicholas who had written would have been amusing, had it not been so painful. He was the very last person she would have expected to show concern for her or her uncle, but she'd long since given up trying to understand the man she'd married. Nicholas Montacute was a mystery to her, and likely to remain so.

There were still four days to Halloween when at last Sir Henry relented and allowed her to leave London. She set off through the frosty dawn wrapped in a fur-lined cloak, with her feet resting on a warmed brick, and her hands thrust deep into a muff. Because of her condition, the swaying of the carriage soon proved very disagreeable, and by the time she reached Cheltenham, where she intended to stay overnight, she was relieved to be able to go to bed and close her eyes, but worry precluded much real sleep.

It was Sunday the following day, and when she arrived at Wychavon at dusk, the whole village seemed to be at evensong, for there wasn't a soul to be seen, and she could hear the congregation singing at the church. On the green, preparations were already in hand for Halloween. The traditional bonfire had been commenced on the site of the maypole, and several mounds of leaves and old wood were ready to be added over the following day or so.

Verity alighted with a heavy heart, for she didn't know what awaited her in the house. She wore a brown woolen spencer and a peach-and-white striped gown beneath her cloak, and her brown bonnet had a posy of artificial flowers pinned beneath the brim. She turned to collect her reticule from the carriage seat and didn't notice that the drawstring hadn't been properly closed. Nor did she notice as the snakestone slipped from the little bag into the carpet of leaves on the road.

She instructed the coachman to take the carriage around to the stables at the rear of the house, but as he urged the tired team forward again, the wheels rolled over the precious talisman, burying it still further under the leaves. From that moment on, Verity was without protection.

It was quiet in the house, with just the ticking of the clock in the shadowy hall to break the silence as she took off her cloak. She lit a candle at the fire in the library, and then glanced around at the room that was so very much part of her uncle. Tears pricked her eyes, and she shielded the candle flame to go out into the hall again, then gathered her skirts to go upstairs to her uncle's room.

She heard his labored breathing before she reached the door, and when she looked through the doorway, she was deeply dismayed to see how shrunken and frail he'd become. Martha was asleep in a chair by the fire and didn't awaken as Verity put the candlestick on the mantelpiece and then went to take Joshua's hand. His sunken eyes flickered weakly open, and he looked up at her, but she didn't know if he even recognized her. After a few seconds his eyes closed again, and tears wended down her cheeks as she knew Nicholas's message hadn't exaggerated, her uncle really was close to death.

The small sound she made disturbed Martha's sleep, and the wisewoman looked up with a start. "Miss Verity!"

"Why didn't you send for me sooner, Martha?" Verity asked accusingly.

The old nurse got up. "Mr. Windsor forbade me to, Miss Verity. He was adamant, and made me promise. I didn't want to, for I thought you should be here."

"Well, I'm here now. I came as quickly as I could."

"But how did you know?"

Verity told her about the message from Nicholas, and then added, "I don't know why he informed me, for it's clear he feels nothing for me anymore. In fact, I don't even know why he bothered to marry me at all, because I realize now that he certainly never loved me."

Martha put a sympathetic hand on her arm. "Miss Verity, there are things I have to say, painful things that will hurt you. I would have said nothing, but you must be told now you're here."

Verity's heart sank. What more could there be than had already happened?

Martha glanced at the bed and then turned toward the door. "Come downstairs, for we must talk."

Verity followed her to the kitchens, where they sat on the settle by the inglenook as Martha made a cup of tea. The copper kettle sang on the fire, and Verity's eyes reflected the flames as she listened to what the nurse had to tell.

She didn't speak until Martha at last got up to pour the boiling water into the teapot. "You—you're saying that Nicholas was spellbound by me because of the seal, and now he's spellbound by Judith Villiers for the same reason?"

"There's no doubt in my mind. As soon as Sadie took it from the church and returned it to the witch, your husband came back from London. It was no coincidence, I'd swear, and when I spoke to him that once at the manor house gate, I could tell he was bewitched. Oh, so darkly bewitched . . ."

Verity lowered her eyes. "I think you're right, Martha, for he changed toward me at Almack's, it was so sudden and complete that he was like two different men." She bit her lip sadly. "So he never loved me at all, he was only interested because he was enchanted by the seal."

"That I cannot say, my dear," Martha said gently, pressing a cup of tea into her hand, "but there's no doubt in my mind that the seal has caused him to cleave to the witch now. She's with him at the castle at this very moment."

Verity struggled against the lump that rose in her throat, then gave the nurse a wistful smile. "But maybe he still feels a little for me? After all, he did send word to London."

Martha drew a heavy breath. "I don't want to hurt you more, Miss Verity, but I fear he may not have done so of his own volition. You see, Sadie and I are almost certain that your poor uncle has been overlooked, just as little Davey was, and the only reason I can think why the witch would do that would be to bring you back here when she found you could not be bewitched. She needs you here, my dear, because you stand in her way, just as that other Lady Montacute did two hundred years ago. She must be rid of you in order to take your place, so that when she wreaks full vengeance on the last of the Montacutes, she will inherit everything. She already possesses all that belonged to the Villiers'."

"Nicholas is in great danger, isn't he?"

"Not yet, my dear, *you* are the one in danger now. You must be on your guard where he is concerned. It's clear you still love him, and that makes you vulnerable. Judith must know you're protected against her sorcery, which is why she's had to reach you through your poor uncle. I think she's almost certain to use Nicholas next, so if he should come to you for any reason at all, you must not trust what he says, for it will not be the real Nicholas Montacute speaking. He is under enchantment and will always do Judith's bidding."

Verity blinked back tears. "I'm frightened, Martha."

"Just be on your guard, my dear, and keep the snakestone close. You *do* still have it, don't you?"

"Yes, it's here in my reticule." But when Verity set her cup of tea aside and looked in the reticule, she saw no sign of the talisman or its chain. "It's gone! I swear it was there, but it's gone now! Maybe it's in the carriage. I must look!"

They both hurried outside, where dusk had darkened to night, but a quick search of the carriage revealed nothing, and Verity looked unhappily at the nurse in the shadows. "Oh, Martha, I've lost it. It must be at the Cheltenham Inn, for I *know* I had it with me when I arrived there."

Martha was deeply anxious, but tried not to show it. "Well, the witch cannot know you've returned, indeed nobody knows yet, and we can keep it that way if we wish. The whole village is at the church this evening, because the Reverend Crawshaw is to say prayers for Mr. Windsor. I'm the only one not at the service, because someone had to stay here. Now, it's a while yet until evensong ends, and if we send your carriage back to the last posting inn, no one will have seen anything suspicious. The other servants will say nothing if instructed, and if you stay in the house at all times . . ."

"But how long for?"

Martha looked helplessly at her, for she didn't know what to say. Her only thought was Verity's immediate protection, beyond that, she had no solution.

Verity was quiet for a moment. "Martha, a few minutes ago you spoke of Nicholas as the last of the Montacutes, well, he isn't, not anymore. I'm expecting his child."

Martha stared at her. "Oh, my dear . . ."

Verity gave a brave smile. "And according to the account of Meg Ashton's trial that the vicar read out to you, the other Lady Montacute was carrying a child too, wasn't she?"

"Yes, my dear, she was, but I won't let the same fate befall you as befell her. If it's the last thing on this earth that I do, I'll shield you from the witch!"

Chapter Twenty-nine

Two days later, on the frosty morning of Halloween itself, Verity was awakened in very much the same way as on May Day all those months before. There was a great deal of activity on the village green as the final touches were put to the bonfire, and she got out of bed to look out, being sure to keep out of sight because no one as yet knew she had returned.

The sun was high, the sky a cloudless blue, and the seasonal colors magnificent. The willows by the ford were a clear shining yellow, while the woods beyond the village were a riot of every autumn hue, from the richest copper brown, through crimson and gold, to the palest pink and beige. Curls of smoke rose from cottage chimneys, and rooks soared around the church, their raucous calls echoing above the noise on the green.

The men had been working on the bonfire since first light, and it was now so tall that ladders were needed to reach the top. After dark tonight all the children would dress up as ghosts, witches, or devils, and turnip lanterns cut into fiendish faces would be set at every cottage window. Then there would be a procession around the village, and torches and more turnip lanterns would be carried past every door. Everyone would sing at the tops of their voices, and when the procession returned to the green, the bonfire would be ceremonially lit.

All over England there would be similar festivities. Flaming wheels would be rolled down exposed slopes, and fires would flicker in every village and from every hilltop. Mulled ale would be drunk, potatoes would be roasted in the flames, and for the children there would be toffee apples and honey cakes.

All manner of Halloween games would be played, from bobbing apples, leaping over embers, to throwing marked stones into the flames to see what the future held. There would be dancing, and as much merry-making as on May Day, with morris bells jingling and hobby horses rushing to and fro to make the children squeal.

But all this, of course, was the respectable face of Halloween, for there was another, darker side, when all manner of mischievous pranks were played on the unsuspecting. Alarmingly dressed children would hurry around in groups trying to frighten the unwary, animals would be swapped around in barns, field gates would be removed, cottage doors would be tied together so they couldn't be opened, and sometimes sods of earth were put on chimney tops to fill the dwellings below with smoke. And all the time the leering turnip lanterns would shine like demons through the darkness, reminding everyone that this was the night when ghosts, witches, wizards, and even the Devil himself, went abroad.

A sad smile curved Verity's lips at this last thought, for a year ago she would have laughed and called it superstition, but this Halloween was very different. She couldn't laugh now, because she knew there were indeed such things as witches. And if there were witches, then probably all the other supernatural beings existed as well, and maybe they *did* come out on this special night. After all, Judith Villiers had appeared twelve months ago to the day. . . .

Some of the village children dashed past the house, kicking the autumn leaves and laughing, and she was pleased to see Davey Cutler among them. How good it was to see him well again, although his return to health had been at the expense of her poor uncle. Tears stung her eyes as she thought of Joshua, who hadn't shown any signs of even recognizing her, let alone wishing to speak to her since her return. He sometimes seemed barely alive, and her heart was squeezed with wretchedness as she thought of the recent past, when he had been so hale and hearty. Except for his dyspepsia, of course . . . Oh, if he were to recover now, she would never criticize his eating habits again, *never*!

Davey suddenly paused to look directly up at her window, and she drew quickly back. Martha was right, it was best that she kept her return secret for as long as possible. Without the snakestone she knew how much at risk she was from Judith, and even though Martha had provided her with wafers from the church, she still felt very vulnerable indeed, especially now that she was expecting Nicholas's child.

She closed her eyes for a moment as a wave of sick light-headedness came over her, as so often happened each morning now. Martha warned that this queasiness lasted for the first four months, and right now four months seemed an eternity.

Martha tapped at the door. "Are you awake, Miss Verity?"

"Yes, Martha, please come in."

The nurse looked into the room. "Come quickly, Miss Verity, Mr. Windsor wishes to speak to you."

"He does?" A wild hope lurched through Verity, and the morning sickness was pushed to the back of her mind as she quickly donned her wrap and hurried from the room.

She went quietly up to his bed, and his dull eyes swung immediately toward her. "Verity?" he whispered.

She felt the sting of salt tears as she sat on the edge of the bed and took his wizened hand. "Oh, Uncle Joshua . . ."

"Forgive me my anger," he murmured, his voice so weak it was barely audible.

"If you will forgive me too," she replied, so overcome she found it hard to speak.

"You will always be my beloved niece, my dear, no amount of foolish anger could really change that. In my heart of hearts I didn't stop cherishing you."

She kissed his fingertips and then looked at him. "I—I read the letter you wrote to Nicholas, Uncle, so I know why you despised him so."

He looked away. "I should have told you the truth, my dear, but Lady Sichester told me in confidence, and I respected her wish that nothing would go any further. You do understand, don't you?"

"Yes, of course."

He drew a shaking breath. "But because of my silence, you are now his wife . . ."

"Not for long, I fear. He wishes to set me aside."

"For the Villiers creature?"

"I—I believe so," she replied.

"You must not let it happen, my dear, for Martha tells me you have a child to consider now, and no matter what else, that child, boy or girl, will be Nicholas Montacute's legitimate heir. Bear that in mind at all costs, my dear."

"I will." Verity drew a long breath, for his words were an echo of Anna's. They were both right, she had to fight on behalf of the new life she carried within her.

His fingers relaxed a little in hers. "I—I feel so tired and helpless. I should be your strength, but instead I am . . ." He closed his eyes as his brief minutes of lucidity began to draw to an end. Moments later, he had lapsed into unconsciousness again.

Verity could taste her own tears as she bent forward to kiss his forehead.

Outside at that moment, the bustle around the green was brought to a temporary standstill by the sight of Judith's carriage returning from the castle. As it splashed through the ford and drew up at the manor house gate, everyone by the bonfire paused to watch.

Only the children failed to notice, and continued their noisy game among the leaves, squealing with laughter as they kicked and threw them in all directions. Suddenly Davey trod on something hard on the road in front of Windsor House, and with a wince of pain bent to see what it was. He picked up the snakestone on its chain, and turned it over curiously. Then he shrugged and shoved it into his pocket, meaning to show it to his grandmother later. The find was soon forgotten altogether as he rejoined the others in the fun with the leaves.

But of all the people on the green, Judith was the one who witnessed his discovery. Until that moment she had been sunk in despair because she thought Verity had ignored Nicholas's message, and that thus Halloween would pass without her revenge even properly commencing, but as soon as she saw Davey pick something up from among the leaves, she not only realized what it was, but the significance of its being here in Wychavon. The snakestone could only be in the village if Verity Windsor had returned after all!

Fixing her gaze on the house, the sorceress concentrated with all her strength, and after a moment a smile crept to her lips.

Yes, Verity was there, and without the protection of Merlin's talisman! Turning, she instructed the astonished coachman to take her back to the castle immediately. Within seconds her carriage was splashing across the ford again.

Nicholas was in the billiards room, and he straightened as he heard the rustle of the witch's scarlet gown. "Judith?" he murmured, smiling into her green eyes.

She smiled too. "I've come to tell you your wife has returned. She's at Windsor House now. Perhaps you should call on her this evening."

"I have no wish to see her."

"But you must discuss the divorce."

He put his cue down on the green baize table. "I'd rather leave it to the lawyers."

"*I* want you to see her."

He smiled then. "If it's your wish, I will do it," he murmured. "I'm always expected to put in an appearance at the Halloween celebrations on the green, so I'll go to see her then."

"Make sure you return to the village celebrations after you've seen her, and that you remain there until everything is ended," she said suddenly. "You must be one of the last to leave."

He looked quizzically at her. "What on earth for?"

"Just do it," she whispered.

Her eyes compelled him. "I'll do anything you say," he murmured.

She smiled. "There's something I forgot to tell you. I'm leaving for Ludlow now," she announced lightly.

"Ludlow? But—"

"I will return tomorrow," she interrupted.

"I'll miss you."

"I know," she murmured, moving closer to him and beginning to unbutton her bodice. "I don't have to leave just yet," she whispered.

His eyes moved to the soft breasts she revealed.

"Make love to me here on the table," she whispered.

He pulled her roughly into his arms, and as she returned his kisses, Judith was content that before this day was out her way to his marriage bed would be clear. She wasn't going to Ludlow, but to the grove to prepare for what must be done that night, and when Verity's body was found in the millpool, it was best if everyone thought her husband's mistress hadn't been anywhere near Wychavon at the time. Nicholas himself wouldn't be suspected because he would be on the green in front of countless witnesses when his wife went to her tragic demise.

The evening shadows were long as the villagers gathered for the revels. The torchlight procession was beginning to form, and all the food and drink had been brought out into the misty night. Turnip lanterns flickered softly from every cottage, and the children carried more on long sticks, ready to take them around the village. The bells of the morris men could be heard, and there were bursts of excited laughter from time to time as the hobbyhorse darted from person to person.

Only the Reverend Crawshaw and the verger couldn't approve of Halloween celebrations, and so stayed at home, but everyone else in Wychavon turned out to enjoy the fun. At last the morris men's musicians struck up, and there was a cheer as the procession set off, with everyone singing as loudly as they could. *It's Halloween tonight, it's Halloween tonight, give us a candle, give us a light, for it's Halloween tonight!*

The torches smoked, and the lanterns bobbed as the long line of villagers snaked around the cottages, but at last everyone returned to the green and formed a circle around the bonfire. Then there was another huge cheer as the lighted torches were flung onto the great pile of dry wood and leaves, and in a moment flames began to lick high into the night sky. Everyone linked hands to dance around, still singing the Halloween song. After that the business of enjoying the food, drink, and games began. There was much laughter and fun, for few believed there really were dark spirits abroad on this night.

No one noticed as Nicholas rode into the green and left his horse well away from the bonfire. The last thing he felt like was mingling with villagers who made little secret of their shocked disapproval of his liaison, but anything Judith wished was now a command to him, and later he would mingle as much as he could. First, however, he had to obey her by going to Verity.

He couldn't see her among the faces on the green, although Martha Cansford was there with her sister and the boy Davey, so he knew she had stayed in because of her uncle's illness. He crossed to Windsor House, where turnip lanterns shone on the gateposts. The only light in the house itself appeared to be another turnip lantern at Verity's bedroom window. He brushed past the lilac tree, and its dead leaves fell over him as he went up to the door to knock.

The sound echoed through the house, but no one responded. He tried again, but still there was no response. Puzzled, he stepped back to glance up at the lantern in Verity's window. She must be there, he thought, and so he tried the door handle. It turned easily to his touch, and the door swung open to reveal the shadowy hall beyond. The hall clock ticked slowly as he slipped inside and put his hat and gloves on the table.

After listening for a moment in case some of the servants had stayed behind after all, he went upstairs, not liking to call out in case Joshua was sleeping. He reached the old man's room and looked in. Dr. Rogers had said how ill he was, but Nicholas was still shocked to see how very frail and shrunken the once stout and proud old man had become.

Taking a heavy breath, Nicholas moved on toward Verity's room at the front of the house. Her door stood open too, so that she could hear her uncle, he supposed, going very softly to look in. She had fallen asleep on the bed, the coolness of her peppermint green gown warmed by the light of the Halloween lantern on the windowsill. Her hair was loose, and the delicate wool of her gown was so soft and clinging that it outlined every curve of her body.

The moment he saw her, the subconscious instructions Judith had given him under the influence of the druid's moss came to the fore. From caring nothing for the woman he had married, suddenly he adored her again. Verity became everything to him in those few precious seconds, and the knowledge that he loved her was like a welcome glass of iced champagne in an overheated ballroom. It soothed and comforted him and made him want to weep with joy. This was the woman he wanted, the woman he needed to be with until the end of his days. . . ."

He went into the room and gazed down at her as she slept. Oh, to be able to make love to her now, to be one with her again and cleansed of all that had happened since he had left her. She stirred a little so that he could see how perfectly her gown's bodice cupped her breasts and how beautifully proportioned her legs were, her thighs long and slender, her ankles small and shapely. Temptation overwhelmed him, and he reached out to touch her hand. Her fingers curled a little, and she sighed in her sleep. Lily-of-the-valley perfume drifted poignantly over him, reminding him of the nights of passion he had spent with her. "Oh, Verity, my darling," he whispered.

She awoke, her breath catching with alarm, but he stopped any cry by putting his hand over her mouth. For a moment he was shaken to see her eyes were still the same shade of lilac they had become at Almack's. But it was Judith's eyes that were green now. . . . He forced aside all thoughts of his mistress. "Please don't be frightened, Verity, for I mean you no harm."

She stared up at him, and he met her gaze intently. "Please let me talk to you," he begged. "If I take my hand away, do you promise not to scream?"

After a moment, she nodded, and he let go of her and moved a step or so back from the bed. "Forgive me for coming to you like this, but I *must* talk to you. I love you so much, Verity, and I want everything to be as it was."

He believed what he was saying, but he had come to carry out Judith's wishes. His task was to lure Verity into the ultimate danger, yet his smiles and words were those of a lover.

Chapter Thirty

Verity sat up slowly in the bed, gathering the coverlet to her chin. Her golden hair was a tangle, and there was wariness in her eyes as a thousand and one fears skimmed through her mind, for no matter how loving and sincere he might seem, he was Judith's lover now.

"What do you want of me, Nicholas?" she asked.

"I want you to trust me again."

"Trust you? How can I do that after all that's happened?"

He stepped closer. "Verity—"

She recoiled. "Don't, please!"

He halted in dismay. "I haven't willingly hurt you, I swear!"

"No?" The pain of having to mistrust him was almost unendurable, but she made herself remember all that Martha had said.

He spread his hands. "I love you, Verity."

She wanted to accuse him about Judith, but it was another name that came to her lips first. "Is that what you said to Amabel Sichester too?" she asked quietly, holding his gaze in the Halloween lantern light.

"Amabel? What has she to do with it?"

"Please don't try to deceive me, Nicholas, for I know all about it. You seduced her, and when she was expecting your child, you deserted her."

He exhaled slowly. "Did Anna tell you?"

"No, I read a letter my uncle wrote to you."

He drew a long breath. "Well, I've realized for some time that Lady Sichester must have told him, for that was the only thing that would explain the sudden depth of his dislike for me, but her ladyship has been deceived by Amabel. There's no truth whatsoever in the claim that I am the father of Amabel's child, nor did I seduce her, rather was it the other way around, for she's certainly not the demure young thing she seems. I happened to be the only bachelor in her long line of married lovers, and when Amabel fell pregnant by one of them, she tried to trick me into marriage."

Verity looked away. "It's always easy to blacken a woman's name."

"And easy to attempt to foist another man's child on an unsuspecting fool. I would have married her, but then chance took a hand, and I went unexpectedly to Dover Street one night in time to see a married fellow I know being shown in. Before the door closed, I saw Amabel run into his arms in a manner that could hardly be described as innocent. Unable to believe what was staring me in the face, I waited outside until he left at dawn, at which time they thought themselves so safe from prying eyes they kissed passionately on the doorstep. Anger being what it is, I decided it was best not to confront her there and then, and so returned later. She immediately told me she was expecting my child."

"What if the child was indeed yours?"

"I called upon the fellow I'd seen with her, and he admitted fatherhood, but apart from that, although I don't deny making love to her, I certainly do deny the ability to perform miracles. You see, Amabel overlooked the fact that Mother Nature and the relevant dates eliminated me from the proceedings because I'd been in Scotland."

She lowered her eyes at that, for Mother Nature and the relevant dates didn't eliminate him from being the father of her own child, in fact they did the very opposite.

He went on. "I left Amabel in no doubt that I wouldn't accept responsibility for another man's child, but I also gave my word not to spread the story around society and thus harm her reputation. I didn't imagine she'd blacken my name anyway, or that her mother would accuse me to your uncle." He looked imploringly into her eyes. "Please believe me, Verity."

After returning his gaze for a long moment, she knew he wasn't lying. A strange sort of relief passed through her, and she nodded. "I do believe you, Nicholas."

"Oh, Verity—" Encouraged, he took a step nearer, but she shook her head quickly.

"No, Nicholas, for believing you about that is one thing, forgiving you everything else is quite another."

"Please forget what I've done in the past, Verity, for it's the future that matters."

"But it would seem your future doesn't include me, for you've decided to end our marriage."

"You must believe me when I say there was nothing truly voluntary about that decision. Nothing I've done since leaving you has been voluntary."

"Nothing? Not even going to Judith Villiers' bed?" she asked quietly.

"Especially not that. I don't want her, Verity, I never have and I never will. You're the one I love."

Martha's warnings rang far too loud and clear in her head, and she said nothing.

He ran his hand through his hair and then looked at her again. "I know you won't believe this, but I—I suspect Judith is a witch. No, more than that, I *know* she is a witch!"

Verity stared at him, shaken that he should actually say it. Surely he wouldn't have done so if he were here under Judith's influence?

He held her gaze again. "Say something, please, for I know only too well the monstrousness of what I've just said."

"Why do you think she's a witch?" she asked at last, feeling her way carefully through the treacherous maze that seemed to be all around her.

He gave an ironic laugh. "Would you believe because she told me? She's so sure of her hold on me she no longer cares. But her hold isn't absolute anymore. The other day, when I wrote to you about your uncle, I found the pearl pin you gave me. I picked it up and began to realize that I still love you. That's why I've come to you tonight. I want to make you understand that I came to her because I was bewitched, not because I preferred her. Finding that pin made all the difference, Verity, for now I have the chance to be free. We both do." His words were a convincing blend of truth and fiction, and because of the druid's moss, he believed each and every one.

Oh, how persuasive he was, she thought, longing to stretch

out a hand and whisper forgiveness, understanding, unending devotion. . . . But the doubts wouldn't go away. She was afraid to put her faith in him, afraid for herself, and her unborn child.

"Please, Verity," he whispered.

"You ask too much," she replied, unable to keep the tears from her eyes.

"If I ask too much, I also offer the greatest of prizes. We were meant to be together, Verity, and if words will not persuade you, maybe actions will." He stepped closer, and before she knew it he had caught her hand and pulled her up into his arms.

She tried to push away from him, but he was too strong, and his lips brooked no denial. He pressed her to the contours of his body as her perfume reached out to him. She felt warm and exciting in his arms, and as he slid a hand to one of her breasts, he felt her tremble against him. He caressed her through the thin wool of her gown. He knew she didn't want to respond but couldn't help herself.

He drew his head back, his eyes dark with emotion. "I love you with all my heart and soul, Verity," he breathed.

"I love you too," she whispered, for how could she deny the truth when she was in his arms like this, and her whole body was alive to everything about him?

He lowered her gently back to the bed, and the light from the Halloween lantern fell softly over her as she knelt there looking up at him. Need pounded through his body, but suddenly he couldn't proceed. Although he wanted her more than anything in the world and was still her husband, he had hurt her so much that he no longer felt he had the right to make love to her.

But need was pounding through her veins too, and right now all she wanted in the world was to know his lovemaking again. Nothing else mattered, not Judith, not Martha's warnings, nor anything else that had happened. She untied the drawstring around the high waistline of her gown, and as the delicate peppermint wool fell away to reveal her breasts, she whispered. "Make love to me, Nicholas."

His heart seemed to turn over within him, and he slowly began to undress. When he was naked, his body hard and strong in the eerie light from the windowsill, he pulled her gown over her head so that she was naked too. The lantern light seemed to move seductively over her, making soft shadows advance and retreat over her skin as she lay back and then raised her arms toward him.

He got onto the bed and put his lips to hers. Her arms moved around him, and her mouth softened yearningly against his. A tumult of love and desire cascaded through him then, and his hand slid adoringly over her smooth thigh. His erection pressed potently between her legs, and she moved against it, her breath catching now and then in delight. Wonderful feelings warmed her entire body, and her parted lips were helpless beneath his.

He pushed deep into her warmth, and as she held him close she was conscious of so many little waves of pleasure that she felt weak. His heat and hardness filled her for a long moment, before he drew slowly out in order to plunge in once again. She was lost in a whirlpool of fulfillment. Her feelings for him hadn't diminished at all, he was still the man she adored, the man she would always adore. . . .

She moved in rhythm with him, gasping as his strokes raised her to new heights of ecstasy, and at last they shuddered together in a tide of joy. They both drifted on waves of love and pleasure, and as the ripples washed ever more gently over their bodies, they sank back against the pillows, their arms entwined adoringly around each other.

He raised his head to look down into her eyes. "Tell me that you know I love you," he whispered.

"I know it."

"Forgive me for what I did, for I wouldn't willingly have hurt you."

Tears shone in her eyes. How could Martha still be right about him? Maybe he *had* been under Judith's spell, but everything he had said and done tonight proved he was now free of the witch's dark influence. And in his freedom, it was his wife he wanted, not his mistress.

The clock chimed down in the hall, and he got up from the bed. "I—I should go now . . ."

"When will I see you again?"

He didn't answer as he quickly got into his clothes again.

Concerned by his silence, Verity sat up on the bed. "Nicholas?"

He finished dressing and then put a hand to her cheek. "Do you want to help me defeat the witch?" he asked.

She searched his eyes. "Yes, of course."

"Then met me at the mill at midnight tonight."

She stared at him. "The mill? But why? And why in the middle of the night?"

"There's no time to explain now. Just trust me."

"I—I do, but . . ."

"Together we can conquer her, my darling," he whispered, bending to brush his lips to hers again. Then he went to the door and paused to look back. "Just be at the mill at midnight, that's all you have to do."

She nodded. "I will come."

He smiled, and then was gone.

Her senses were still tingling after his lovemaking, and her heart bade her discount Martha's warnings. She trusted him because he wouldn't have said the things he had tonight if he were still under Judith's influence. Her faith in him was steady and sure, and she meant it when she said she would meet him at the mill as asked.

But as Nicholas left the house and rejoined the gathering on the green, the druid's moss had already made him forget everything that had happened in Verity's bedroom. His thoughts were all of Judith, and he had no idea at all that he had just persuaded his wife upon a course intended to lead to her death.

Chapter Thirty-one

The smell of bonfire smoke was acrid on the green, and the air was thick. The night air was cold, and mist encroached on the village from the surrounding countryside, promising another frost before morning.

Martha and Sadie were eating roasted nuts and sipping mulled damson wine, and Davey was with them, chewing on the largest toffee apple he had been able to find. Martha's expression was thoughtful as she kept glancing at the seemingly deserted manor house. Sadie's attention was on the time, and whenever the church clock struck the quarter, her breath caught with anticipation. Midnight was edging nearer and nearer. . . .

Davey's long illness seemed a thing of the past, and he had still forgotten all about the snakestone. He was dressed as a demon, his body swathed in a flowing red sheet, and his face blacked with soot. Two paper horns protruded from his head, and he carried his grandmother's toasting fork. He had enjoyed tonight more than he had ever enjoyed Halloween before and wasn't remotely tired, even though it was long past the hour he usually went to bed. He laughed from time to time as he watched the hobbyhorse chasing people around the green, and his eyes had only widened with alarm once, and that was when he saw a ghostly white-robed figure dancing on the vicarage roof, but it was only the village blacksmith trying to frighten the vicar into paying up for the cob's new shoes.

Suddenly Martha turned to Sadie. "I see the widow isn't at home tonight, I suppose she's at the castle, although why she didn't accompany his lordship I can't imagine. She's brazen enough for anything, and so is he, for that matter," she added, glancing across the green to where Nicholas was standing with Dr. Rogers.

Davey looked up at her. "Mrs. Villiers isn't at the castle, she's gone to Ludlow."

"Ludlow? How do you know that?"

"I heard one of the castle servants say so. She won't be back until tomorrow." The boy's attention returned to the bonfire.

Martha looked at the darkened manor house. "Now why has she gone to Ludlow, I wonder?" she murmured.

Sadie drew a long breath. "Does it matter?"

"Yes, everything that creature does matters," Martha replied, and then suddenly handed her wine cup to her sister. "You and Davey keep watch, I'm going to look for the seal."

Sadie was horrified. "She's probably taken it with her."

"And she may not. I have to see, and what better chance will I ever get? There's absolutely no one inside, and his lordship's right here on the green. If I can find that seal and give it back to its rightful owner, the spell will be broken."

"Please don't go," Sadie said anxiously.

"I must, Sadie."

"But there maynot be any need to—"

"No need? There's every need in the world!" Martha snapped incredulously, and before Sadie could say anything more, she hurried away toward the manor house.

Sadie gazed after her in dismay.

It was half past eleven when Verity slipped out of Windsor House. One of the maids had returned to the house with a headache, so she didn't feel bad about leaving her uncle. She was careful to keep her face hidden though and raised her cloak hood as she reached the lilac by the gate, then she hurried toward the stepping stones without even glancing toward the activity on the green.

But Davey had happened to look across at the very moment she raised her hood, and his mouth dropped a little. Miss Verity was back? Why hadn't Aunt Martha said? The boy knew that everyone in the village was talking about Verity, Lord Montacute, and the admiral's widow. He didn't know what it was all about, but he did know everyone thought Verity Windsor was still in London. It seemed she wasn't.

He tugged Sadie's sleeve, but she was too busy watching

Martha's shadowy figure moving up the manor house path, and she frowned down at him. "Not now, Davey, there's a good boy," she said.

With a sigh he watched Verity cross the stepping stones, then hurry away past the church, and disappear into the Halloween mist.

The noise from the green echoed through the silent manor house as Martha went cautiously across the entrance hall. Judith's bedroom seemed the obvious place to look for the seal, but as the nurse began to go up the staircase, suddenly she came up against an invisible barrier. Disgusting fumes seemed to fill the darkness, robbing her of air, and she was driven back down to the hall.

Overcome by nausea, she leaned weakly back against the wall and had to take huge breaths to steady herself. As the unpleasant sensations died away, she gazed up the shadowy staircase. She knew it was because of her purpose that the concealed defense had worked. If one of the manor house maids went upstairs, nothing would have happened because a servant would not have any ulterior motive. But someone with an intent that went against the witch's interests would immediately trigger the hidden safeguard. Judith had something she wanted to protect. Was it the seal?

Taking another deep breath, the wisewoman began to ascend the staircase again. The vile stench engulfed her again, seeming to draw the air from her lungs, but she held her breath and sank to all fours to claw her way through the invisible fog, and at last she managed to scramble up onto the landing, where the air was clear again.

Fighting back the waves of sickness that still washed over her, she made her way to the witch's bedroom. Over the next few minutes she searched diligently in every nook and cranny, but there seemed to be no sign at all of the precious seal. Yet she was convinced it was here.

She was just about to give up, when her glance fell on the fireplace. Of course! Why hadn't she thought of it before? Kneeling in the hearth, she felt inside the chimney. Soot fell over her hands and clothes as she groped around, but suddenly her blackened fingers closed over the seal, and with a cry she

drew it out to gaze triumphantly at the faint green lights in the
tiger's eye quartz.

She scrambled to her feet again and hurried from the room,
anxious to give it to Nicholas as quickly as possible. But in her
excitement, she forgot the protective spell on the staircase. As
she entered its confines, she breathed its foulness in, and the
cloying foulness seared her throat and lungs. It was so nauseat-
ing that she felt faint. Everything began to spin around her, and
with a cry she fainted, falling heavily down the remainder of
the staircase and lying unconscious at the bottom. The seal
rolled away across the floor, its green lights shimmering and
dancing in the darkness.

Outside, the church clock began to strike midnight, and there
was such a huge cheer on the green that even the fierce crackle
of the bonfire was drowned.

Verity was hesitant as she made her way into the grove,
which on Halloween seemed more mysterious and frightening
than ever before. She heard the chime of midnight drifting from
the village, and she paused momentarily. Dead leaves whispered in the trees overhead, and an owl called nearby. The mist
swirled unpleasantly and she couldn't see far, but she knew that
bonfires would be burning on the surrounding hills and flaming
wheels would be tumbling down exposed slopes. But here in
the grove, everything was isolated and menacing.

She shivered as she heard the mill wheel creaking, and hoped
Nicholas was here already. Holding her cloak a little closer, she
called him.

"Nicholas?"

But there was no response, so she went a little further into the
grove. "Nicholas?" she called again.

A step rustled through the fallen leaves behind her, and she
turned, but it wasn't Nicholas. Her cry of alarm was silenced as
a sickening blow caught her on the side of the head, and she
slumped senseless to the ground. She knew nothing as Judith
crouched to bind and gag her, then dragged her into the center
of the grove and left her on the ground in front of the Lady.

The stroke of midnight had left Nicholas feeling oddly disturbed. He couldn't say what it was; he just felt he no longer

wished to stay in the village. He knew Judith had instructed him to remain until the very end, but suddenly he was too restless to obey. So he took his leave of the doctor and began to walk to where he had left his horse.

The chimes of the witching hour had affected Sadie too. Her eyes shone with triumph. It was done! She, Sadie Cutler, had cast a spell! She turned impatiently toward the manor house. Oh, where was Martha? Then her lips parted as she saw her sister clinging to the doorpost, trying to attract attention.

Sadie ran to her. "Martha, what's happened?" she cried anxiously.

"Never mind that, you must give this to Lord Montacute right now!" Martha pressed the seal into her hands.

"But, I—"

"Do it now, Sadie!" Martha cried, for she was suddenly filled with an awful sense of foreboding. Something terrible was about to happen, she could feel it as surely as if it were written in fire across the night sky!

Sadie snatched the sooty seal, and turned to run back to the green. Davey was waiting at the manor house gate. "What is it, Gran?" he asked anxiously, seeing the look on her face.

"I'm to find Lord Montacute immediately. Where is he, child?"

"He's just left, Gran."

"Left? Oh, no! Run after him and give him this, Davey!"

"But he's gone on his horse!" the boy protested.

"Just be sure to get the seal to him!" Sadie cried.

Davey grabbed it and began to run. His red sheet robing flapped as he dashed across the stepping stones, then past his cottage gate. As he neared the lychgate, he could see Nicholas riding slowly away into the mist ahead. He shouted at the top of his lungs. "My lord! Stop! Please!"

But Nicholas rode on.

Green candlelight swayed in the grove, and Hecate's hellhounds bayed in the distance as Judith danced naked around the Lady, her excitement rendering her immune to the chill of the night.

Verity lay bound and gagged among the leaves in front of the stone, and on the grass beside her was the silver dagger which the witch soon intended to plunge into her heart. Knowing she only had minutes to live, she gazed fearfully at the beautiful dancing figure. Tears shone in her eyes, for it was Nicholas who had betrayed her to this dreadful fate. In the guise of the loving husband, he had overcome her defenses, and now, for being such a fool as to trust him again, she was to die.

Judith's eyes closed in ecstasy as the ointment on her skin warmed and released its intoxicating fumes. She felt weightless and liberated, and the exhilaration of victory carried her effortlessly toward her evil goal. It would be easy to just kill Verity anyway, but Hecate should be here to witness how well her handmaiden served her.

The witch whispered the ancient words, and the howling of the hounds began to draw nearer.

Davey ran as fast as he could, but as he left the village behind, he became aware of the dreadful baying of hounds somewhere in the woods. He halted uneasily, his eyes wide in his sooty face, for he had never heard a noise like that before. He didn't want to go on, but knew he must, so he began to run again, calling after Nicholas all the time.

The howling echoed eerily over the valley, and Nicholas reined in by the track to the mill, for it seemed the sound came from the direction of the grove. At last he heard Davey shouting behind him and he turned in surprise.

"What is it?" he asked, smiling a little at the child's demon costume, with its paper horns and toasting fork.

"I'm to give you this, my lord!" Davey gasped breathlessly.

Nicholas looked in puzzlement at the dusty object in the boy's hand and then recognized it. The seal Verity had told him she had found on the ground! "Where did you get it?"

"My gran gave it to me to give to you, my lord. Please take it."

Nicholas reached down, and the moment his fingers touched the quartz, there was a dazzling sunburst of little green lights. A shock darted up Nicholas's arm, and with a cry of pain he dropped the seal.

In the grove, the granite of the Lady had begun to breathe like living flesh, and the goddess's face was becoming discernible. The hounds bayed ecstatically at the moon, and the millpool was mirrorlike as the river ceased to flow. Judith's rapture was at fever pitch, but the moment the seal was placed in Nicholas's hand, the green flames of the candles leapt briefly to twice their height, and Hecate gave a terrible cry, like that of an animal in pain.

Judith went rigid with shock before falling to her knees as power drained paralyzingly from her.

Chapter Thirty-two

Nicholas clutched his arm as the green lights continued to shimmer over it. He felt the spell peeling raggedly away, like layers of skin being torn from his flesh, and the pain was so acute that beads of perspiration leapt to his forehead.

Davey was rooted to the spot with fear. He wished he were still on the green with his gran, wished he were anywhere but here right now. His frightened gaze was drawn toward the grove again as the clamor of the hounds became almost deafening. He heard a savage cry, inhuman and evil, and his knees felt so weak he could barely stand.

Nicholas inhaled deeply. All manner of truths swung back through his consciousness, forgotten images, sketches of loving nights with Verity. He tried to control the flood of memories, but then his lips parted in horror, for he was now released from all Judith's magic, including the druid's moss, and he remembered what he had done tonight. He realized too that his love for Verity transcended the spell. Maybe the enchanted seal had made him love her in the beginning, but his own heart made him love her now.

"Verity . . ." he whispered, his glance moving to the misty shadows of the track to the grove, then he snatched the reins and urged his horse toward the mill.

Davey stared after him, but then he heard the sound of hurrying footsteps approaching through the mist from the direction of the village. Already unnerved, the boy flung himself into the autumn undergrowth at the side of the road and crouched there among the leaves with his eyes tightly closed.

The footsteps passed, light, soft, and anxious, but by the time he found the courage to look out it was too late for him to have seen that it was only his own grandmother who had hurried by. He was about to emerge from hiding to run back to the village when a ball of little orange flames appeared from nowhere directly in front of him. It was silent and frightening, and Davey shrank back among the leaves again. He had heard of corpse candles and knew his Aunt Martha was one of those who could actually see them, but he hadn't realized he could too. He didn't want to see such things! His lips quivered, and he suddenly didn't look at all like a fearsome Halloween demon. "Oh, Gran . . ." he whimpered.

The rattle of a cart made his breath catch, and he turned even more fearfully toward the village. Shadowy and barely discernible through the mist, the churchyard watcher made his way to the corner and halted directly alongside Davey's hiding place. The boy stared at the indistinct figure on the seat. It was the peddler! Davey's teeth began to chatter uncontrollably, and as the watcher turned to look directly at him, nodding and touching his ribboned hat in greeting, the child fell back senseless among the cold leaves.

In the grove, Judith had begun to recover from the nausea. The seal! Someone had given it back to Nicholas, and had finally destroyed her spell! Well, his wife would die anyway!

Hecate gave a peal of unearthly laughter as the witch seized the dagger. The hounds became frenzied, the green flames fluttered, and the night air seemed to stand still as Judith raised the gleaming blade above Verity's heart.

But then came the thud of hooves along the track, and suddenly Nicholas burst into the grove. Judith recoiled instinctively as he flung his horse toward her, but then she tried to plunge the dagger into Verity in the final second. But the horse was upon her, dashing her aside like a doll. The dagger was jerked from her hand, arcing through the air to pierce the terrible face in the Lady. Hecate screamed and disappeared, and the dagger fell to the leaf-covered grass. The howling of the hounds was silenced, and the green flames of the candles began to slowly fade.

Nicholas reined in, turning his frightened horse at the very bank of the millpool and urging it back toward Judith as she tried to claw her way to Verity again. He leapt from the saddle and flung the witch aside. Then he took off his coat and tossed it contemptuously over her. "Cover yourself, madam, for you look somewhat ridiculous," he said scathingly, then knelt to untie Verity.

As Judith clutched the coat around herself, her glance fell on the dagger, which still lay in the grass, but as she reached toward it again, Sadie's voice rang out from the edge of the grove.

"It's too late, witch, you're done for! Spells aren't your sole preserve, I can cast them too! I made your effigy and put some strands of your hair on it, then I buried it with the peddler. As his corpse rotted, so your monstrous soul rotted too. The time was up at the stroke of midnight on Halloween, and there's nothing you can do to reverse the magic. It was a Cansford that put the torch to you before, and it's another Cansford that's put paid to you now. You thought you only had to watch my sister, and you discounted me. Well, breathe your evil last, Meg Ashton, for this time you will not live again, and I only wait to dance on your grave!"

Judith's face was like a sheet. Oh, fool, *fool*! Too late she remembered catching her hair on the branch. Her heart began to pound unevenly, and she felt hot. Terror suddenly loomed on all sides, and all she could think of was retrieving the image from the grave. It was her only hope. She struggled to her feet, still clutching Nicholas's coat around her nakedness, then she began to run toward the track.

Sadie stood scornfully aside. "Midnight has been and gone, witch! Your heart is already beginning to slow and your black soul shrivel!"

Judith continued to run. Her lungs felt as if they would burst, and her heart missed a beat before lurching on once again. She staggered up the track, and Sadie's contemptuous voice followed her.

"I've paid you back for what you've done, witch! You put the eye on my Davey, and on poor Mr. Windsor, you killed Admiral Villiers, and you intended to kill Lord and Lady Montacute. But you're the one who's dying now, Meg Ashton, and it's the flames of Hell that wait for you!"

A wail of fear escaped Judith's lips. The sound of her heart seemed to echo through her, and her legs felt like lead as she continued to make her unsteady way up the track. She could see the road ahead now, but Sadie's triumphant laughter seemed to be following her. She had to get to the graveyard! She *had* to!

But as she stumbled the final yards to the road, the corpse light appeared again, and as she stared at it, it turned from orange to blood red. Then she heard the jingle of harness, and a cry of abject terror was torn from her lips as she saw the watcher's cart waiting for her. Her heart missed another beat, then pumped once more before becoming still within her. The life went from her eyes, and she fell dead by the wheels of the ghostly cart.

The peddler climbed slowly down and reached down to search for what was left of her evil soul. When he found it, he dragged it from her body and threw it disdainfully into the cart, then he resumed his seat and shook the reins. He whistled softly to himself as his spectral vehicle moved slowly away, going right across the road then into the trees opposite, where it vanished in the mist.

As its passing faded away into silence, the undergrowth shook at the side of the road, and Davey crept from his hiding place. His face was white beneath the soot, and he clutched his arms around himself. Then he ducked low to run back to the village. He wanted his gran, or his Great-aunt Martha!

Martha was at that moment being helped into the kitchens at Windsor House by some of the other servants. She was still weak from the effects of Judith's invisible barrier, but in spite of the waves of sickness that continued to pass over her as she sat by the fire, she was anxious. What was happening with the seal? Had Davey given it to Nicholas yet?

There was a sudden shocked silence, and the wisewoman looked up to see what had caused it. Her eyes widened then, for Joshua had appeared in the doorway, his nightgown very white in the dim light. He clung to the doorjamb for support, and his face was still gray, but there was a new brightness in his eyes as he looked inquiringly at them all.

"I—I feel much better suddenly, and have a fancy for a slice of hot toast." He searched their faces. "Where's Verity?" he asked them.

* * *

Nicholas undid the last of Verity's bonds, then took the gag from her mouth. "Are you all right, my love?" he whispered, pulling her close.

"Yes, I—I think so . . ."

"Oh, Verity, forgive me, forgive me, I *swear* I didn't know what I was doing. It wasn't until Davey gave me the seal . . ." There were tears in his eyes as he kissed her hair. "I love you, my darling, you're everything in the world to me."

"Am I?" She looked unhappily up at him. "I was fooling myself earlier tonight, for you don't love me, except through the seal."

"I didn't need the seal to make me see how much you mean to me," he said softly. "I spoke the truth when I said I touched the pin you gave me, and knew I still loved you. Judith had the seal then, not you."

Hope lit her eyes, although she hardly dared allow it.

He smoothed her curls from her forehead. "If I'd lost you tonight, I don't think I could have borne it," he whispered.

Her lingering doubts melted away. "But you didn't lose me. And, Nicholas . . ."

"Yes?"

"There's something I didn't tell you earlier." She paused, looking up intently into his eyes. "I'm having our baby," she whispered.

He stared at her, and then his embrace tightened gladly. "Oh, my darling . . ."

As she raised her lips to his, she knew it really was all over, and now there could only be happiness ahead. They kissed, and the green flames of the candles flickered briefly, then went out forever.

It was May again, and Wychavon Castle was filled with joy as the first cries of Verity's baby boy rang out.

Life had indeed been transformed since Judith's demise, for Nicholas and Joshua were now the best of friends, although there was nothing they liked more than to argue politics after dinner. Anna and Oliver had been guests since the New Year, and seemed set to stay on for some time longer because everyone was enjoying things so much. Their happiness was particularly radiant, for, thanks to Martha's knowledge of herbs and such things, Anna was at last expecting a child of her own.

But in Wychavon village, Sadie was now held in as high respect as her sister, for everyone soon heard the full story of the secret spell in the peddler's grave. The realization that Meg Ashton had been among them alarmed the villagers, who didn't care to know that such wicked sorcery had again taken place in their small corner of Shropshire. It was decided that the facts would not travel beyond the village boundary, and there wasn't a single soul—man, woman, or child—who didn't abide by the decision.

The same agreement existed at the castle too, where everyone in the solar smiled as Martha hurried down to tell them Verity's lying-in was at an end, and as Nicholas dashed to be with his wife and son, Oliver broke open a jeroboam of champagne.

Verity was cradling the baby in her arms as Nicholas entered. Her hair was a tangle of curls about her shoulders, and her cheeks were still flushed, but her eyes sparkled happily.

Nicholas went to her, taking her hand and raising the palm to his lips. "Are you all right, my love?"

"Yes, of course."

He gazed down at the tiny new life swathed in a lacy knitted shawl, then hesitantly touched one of the little hands. The baby grasped it firmly, and Nicholas smiled delightedly. "A true Montacute," he murmured.

"But with the fair hair of the Windsors," she pointed out.

"A fitting mixture," he said, then raised his eyes to her face again. "I adore you, my lady," he said softly.

"And I you, sir."

He studied her then and gave a slight laugh. "Well, I do declare . . ."

"What is it? Do I look dreadful?" she asked, putting a concerned hand to her hair.

"Your freckles have gone."

"My what . . . ?" She broke off and stared at him. "Are—are you quite, quite sure?"

"Absolutely positive."

A pleased smile brightened her face. "It's taken a year, but the May Eve dew has worked after all! Oh, Nicholas, if you only knew how I *hated* having freckles!"

"My darling, I'd still find you adorable if every inch of you were covered in freckles," he murmured, leaning across to kiss her nose.

She drew back a little, her eyes briefly anxious again. "You—you don't think the witch will return a third time, do you?"

"No, she's gone forever now, thanks to Sadie Cutler. But I'm going to have the Lady removed from the grove. Just to be sure," he added prudently.